WHERE
BUTTERFLIES
WANDER

OTHER BOOKS
BY SUZANNE REDFEARN

Moment in Time
Hadley and Grace
In an Instant
No Ordinary Life
Hush Little Baby

WHERE BUTTERFLIES WANDER

a novel

SUZANNE REDFEARN

LAKE UNION
PUBLISHING

Text copyright © 2024 by Suzanne Redfearn
All rights reserved.

Published by Lake Union Publishing, Seattle

www.apub.com

Amazon, the Amazon logo, and Lake Union Publishing are trademarks of Amazon.com, Inc., or its affiliates.

ISBN-13: 9781662514593 (paperback)
ISBN-13: 9781662514586 (digital)

Cover design by Kathleen Lynch / Black Kat Design
Cover image: © Brendan Austin / plainpicture; © Piotr Kulas / EyeEm / Getty; © Vladimir18 / Getty

Printed in the United States of America

For
my family

A life is not important except in the impact it has on other lives.
—Jackie Robinson

Prologue

March 25, 2002

Dearest Davina,

I just received the news from Dr. Holmberg that the final grafts were a success and soon you will be well enough to come home. I have a jar of calendula ready, and the colonel will bring it to you when you get to the hospital in Manchester.

What I wouldn't give to be beside you or to trade this old worn-out body with your young one and take away your pain. Instead, pragmatist that I am, I will give you what I am able along with what you already own . . . my heart.

With the moments I have left fading, it is time I explain the truth of how we came to be a family. What you choose to do with it is up to you.

I sometimes wonder how much you remember. You were six when we met, same age as your Rose. For some, our memories go back early as two, and you were always precocious, so I imagine some of the story you know. But a child's view is also myopic, the world seen through a prismatic lens of details that make up the soft cocoon of their lives. You were especially that way. An artist like your mother, you were always so curious and observant, picking out patterns and ripples; noticing stigmas in flowers and veins in stones; recognizing a face in a cloud.

Not surprisingly, the first time I saw you, it was merely a glimpse of color. Blue. Cerulean. You always asked why that was my favorite color. You thought it was because I liked the way it rolled on the tongue like a mouthful of marbles. The real reason is because the color is how I found you, your wool coat so bright it was unnatural set against the marshy green of the bank. Your mother was there as well. Tall and slender with a curtain of black hair, also out of place in the wilderness. You were squatted at the river's edge, hidden in the grasses, looking at the wind on the surface of the water or perhaps watching the minnows darting in and out of the shadows. Your mother was filling a pail. She lifted her face, saw the boat, then grabbed your hand, and you fled, your blue coat blinking in and out of the trees.

That fleeting glance often plays in my mind, the happenstance of me turning the bend at the exact moment you and your mother were collecting water. Though when I reflect on it, I'm certain it wasn't random chance at all, but providence, God's hand on destiny. How else do you explain what followed, the intertwining of our fates?

Despite seeing you less than a second, I knew who you were. You'd have had to have been living under a rock not to have known. Your father had been on the news for months, pleading for the public's help in finding his missing wife and daughter.

Do you remember this? Your real name, Rebecca Jacqueline Dupree? Or your mother, Valentina? That you were born rich, or *that your father, Stanley Dupree, was . . . is . . . one of the wealthiest men in the country?*

If you go to the library, you will find plenty of articles on your disappearance, how you vanished outside a department store in Palm Beach and that there were shopping bags in the back seat of your mother's car with several new maternity dresses. To this day, nearly thirty years later, your story is one of the great unsolved mysteries of modern times. There are all sorts of theories about what happened, and over the years, dozens of impostors have claimed to be you or your mother.

So back to the story of our actual meeting and how you came to be my daughter.

The reason I'd been that far north that day was because I needed more cramp bark, which, as you know, is in the high brush. Though I was almost there, my first thought on seeing you was to turn around. The reward being offered by your father was substantial, and everyone was looking for you. But because I was nearly there, I decided to continue on.

I collected the bark, then started back, wondering the entire time how you'd ended up in the timberland. When I passed the spot where you and your mother had been, a thought occurred to me. As I've often said, a change in perspective often changes a point of view. And that's exactly what happened.

The thing about kids, as you well know, is that, until around the age of eight, they are incapable of true deceit. They can lie, and often do, but unless sociopathic, which most are not, complex manipulation is not within their grasp. And what I realized as

I passed the beach where I had seen you was that, in that first fleeting glimpse, was the truth. Your mother had grabbed your hand, but it was you who pulled her toward the woods, your eyes startled wide, terrified of being seen.

So I made a choice. I decided to meet you and then make up my mind. I put together a basket of bread, jam, and tea and left it at the trailhead along with a note introducing myself and explaining I lived on the property downstream. I signed it "Rosalinda, aka The River Witch because I'm a midwife and herbalist."

The following day, there was a note beneath my mat thanking me for the basket and inviting me for tea. I was stunned. But as I would find out, your mother was full of surprises.

I'll never forget the first words you said when you saw me. The door opened, and there you were, ink black hair that matched your mother's and fantastically large eyes the color of coriander (my second favorite color, as you know). Tilting your head, you sized me up and, very disappointed, said, "You don't look like a witch."

I laughed, which you did not like one bit. So I straightened the expression and said, "And how is it you think a witch should look?"

"Well, a good witch is very beautiful and has a sparkling silver gown with wings, and a bad witch is green and has monkeys."

I needed to work very hard not to laugh again, as you were obviously trying to have a serious conversation.

"Well, I'm a river witch," I said, "not a witch from Oz, so my magic is limited. No wings or monkeys and only a few small tricks that help bring babies into the world and make people feel better."

That was when your mother appeared, smiling warmly and far more beautiful than her photos. She introduced you by your real names, Valentina and Rebecca, but, after the introduction, called you Mi Cielo, which means "my sky" in Spanish.

That afternoon, we ate soup with crackers and played cards and laughed. Your mother was very funny, and she could weave a story out of anything. We avoided talk of anything serious, and I left knowing I'd done the right thing keeping your secret.

Two days later, I returned with a few games, puzzles, and books. Your mother was most grateful for the books. She was a voracious reader, which, it turned out, you inherited.

You and I did the puzzles. Do you remember that? Sitting at the table working on them?

All that fall, that was our routine, a few afternoons a week spent in each other's company. Your mother's plan was to return to her native home of Spain after she had the baby and start a new life. We never spoke of the reason you fled, but I knew by the tremble in her voice that you were running from something truly terrible.

I also figured out it was the colonel who had helped you. At that point, I didn't know him. I had seen him a few times over the years, but we'd never had a conversation beyond hello. He had served with your mother's father in Korea, and they'd been close as brothers until your grandfather was killed. The plan was for him *to return a month before the baby was due so he would be there for the birth and could then help you get to Spain.*

Of course, things went terribly wrong before that.

It was a Wednesday. I remember, because Wednesdays were the day I did my house calls. But that day, there was no visiting anyone. A blizzard had blown in, taking out the power lines and most of the roads. I was worried about you and your mom. The wood and propane were kept in the shed, and your mother was nearly seven months along and in no shape for lugging logs and tanks through the snow.

The river was too rough for boating, so I strapped on my snowshoes and set out with a pack. The snow was blowing sideways, and several times I nearly turned back, but what kept me going of course was you. Even then, you had a piece of my heart.

When I reached the clearing and saw the windows glowing, I nearly collapsed with relief. I pulled off the snowshoes, and walked through the door, and that's when I realized I had celebrated too soon. You were on the floor beside your mother, who was laid out on the couch. There was the sharp tang of blood in the air and a stain of maroon beneath her.

When you saw me, you cried, "Mama, the witch is here. She's going to fix you."

I wished with all my heart I could, but even the most powerful witch knows the limits of her magic. Your mother's lips were blue, letting me know what had happened. Possibly while she was carrying the wood or propane, the baby's placenta had ruptured, and toxins had leached into her system.

I stepped close, and her eyes slitted open. "You came," she said, the words barely a breath.

I nodded and knelt beside her.

"You'll take care of her?"

Without thought, I nodded, the moment too awful and precious for anything else. And as if that was all she had been waiting for, her eyes closed, and she was gone.

When the storm stopped, I buried her in the river and then took you home. A year later, I introduced you as my adopted daughter. I forged a birth certificate with a birth date that made you a year older and chose the name Davina, which means beloved. You'd grown a foot, lost most of your baby teeth, and bore little resemblance to the darling princess who had disappeared nearly two years before.

We never talked about your life before. I felt as if you did it purposely, so I never pressed. I hope it was the right thing to do. Those early years were full of second-guessing.

It took some time, but as the days turned into months, happy moments began to outnumber sad ones, and eventually we had a life. The day you called me Mom I thought my heart would crack wide open.

And now, at the worst possible moment, my body is failing. I wish I could will myself on, but as you know better than most, we do not choose how long we get to travel this earth. The colonel will be waiting when you get to Manchester. He's often said you were more his family than his own, and it gives me great comfort knowing he will be there for you. I can't imagine how hard this is. You've lost so much. But with time, even the worst pain fades, and you still have so much to give.

I leave you little except my knowledge of healing and my love. Hopefully that is enough.

You were my greatest blessing, and it was an honor to be your second mother.

Always,

Mom

Where Butterflies Wander

1

MARIE

June 8, 2024

The first thing I notice is that the paint on the house is chipped and peeling. Irritation flares disproportionate to the inconvenience, but it seems that's how things are these days—my already short fuse shaved to a nub and the slightest spark igniting an explosion.

I now have "tools" that are supposed to help: counting my breaths, singing to myself, or gulping water before I say or do something I will regret. And I try, but there are times it feels as if I'm trying to hold back a tsunami by sipping a bottle of Evian, the anger surging so fast and with such fury it's impossible to contain.

At the moment, I try slow inhales through my nose and exhales through my mouth.

New paint is not that big a deal. I knew there would be work to be done before we could sell the place. It's the reason we're here. Yes, it would have been nice to have known so I could have planned for it, but it's not the end of the world. *Breathe in, breathe out.*

"Is this it?" Pen asks excitedly.

I look in the rearview mirror to see her lit-up face—connect-the-dots freckles and Leo's hazel-green eyes—and almost smile before my heart slams shut like a fist. *One, not two. Half, not whole.*

I blink and look away, focusing hard through the windshield and on the task in front of me. *Park. Walk in the house. Forward, not back.*

Despite my efforts, my mind betrays me. *Pen and Bee. Bee and Pen.* Since they were born and until six weeks ago. Penelope and Phoebe—names cleverly chosen by Leo and me when we found out we were having twins. Two wisewomen from Greek mythology. Double the trouble and twice the fun. Our Honeybee and Lucky Penny, though we don't call Pen that anymore.

"Wow, it's bigger than I thought," Hannah says beside me.

I look again at the house and try to see it through their eyes. I suppose it is rather grand—classic colonial architecture, two stories tall, with round columns and a wraparound porch.

"There's a barn!" Pen says. "Are there horses?"

There used to be. When I was a girl, my grandfather had a sweet mare named Carina and a surly pony named Gus. Carina died when I was in middle school. I remember crying when my mother told me. I don't remember when Gus died. Strange the things you remember and those you don't.

Bee could recite the alphabet backward in 8.3 seconds, but for the life of me, I can't remember her favorite color. I think it was red. But that might be Pen's. Green? Was it green? *Smaragdine.* Why does that strange word come to mind?

"Mom?" Pen says, interrupting my spiraling and making me realize I haven't answered.

"No, Sweet Pea, no horses."

I pull the car beside the porch, and Pen hops out. I watch as she takes off toward the barn and realize it's because she's spotted a butterfly, her new, latest obsession. It flutters toward the trees, and she chases after it, skinny arms and legs flying, and the lump in my throat grows as I fight the waterworks in my eyes.

"Should I go after her?" Hannah asks, worry in her voice.

I start to shake my head but stop. Six weeks ago, my answer would have been certain. As a child far younger than eight, I ran in the birches all the time—my sister, cousins, and I playing tag, hide-and-seek, capture the flag, or whatever other game we could think of. It's not dangerous. The trees are spindly and the land mostly flat. She might encounter a squirrel or a rabbit, or at worst, a bit of poison ivy.

But nothing's as it was.

I stare at the back of Pen's striped shirt as she skips toward the trail and complete the shake of my head. *No.* I will not let that day take more than it already has.

"Stay on the path!" I holler after her as I climb from the car.

She lifts a thumbs-up and continues on her way.

Hannah and I carry our bags up the steps, and I unlock the door. Hannah enters first. "Whoa!" she says.

I nod and, for a moment, share her amazement, feeling like I've stepped through a time portal and traveled back to my youth, the place perfectly preserved from the last time I was here, nearly thirty years ago. I was fourteen, a year younger than Hannah is now. It's unbelievable to think how much time has passed, memory a trick able to distort minutes and years to what seems like only seconds and days.

The caretakers have done a wonderful job. The air smells of lemon polish and pine, and every surface gleams. There's a vase of wildflowers on the entry table, and the drapes have been rehung and the couch pillows put out as I requested. I inhale deeply, thinking how it used to also smell of tobacco and bacon. But my grandfather's been gone far too long for those comforting smells to remain.

Hannah wanders into the living room, a grand space with two sitting areas and a game table. The centerpiece is a massive stone fireplace flanked on either side by bookshelves filled with literary classics along with tomes on philosophy, fishing, and war.

"No television?" Hannah asks.

A smile tickles my lips as I lower my voice to the soft tenor of my grandfather and say, "Television rots the mind and turns a brain to cheese until a person cannot think but only see."

"Your grandfather said that?"

"He borrowed the sentiment from Roald Dahl, but yeah, it's what he used to say." I smile at the memory. "And if we ever had cheese for lunch or a snack, he'd point to it and say 'Television' to drive home the point."

Hannah reflects my grin. "Should I start calling Brendon cheese-head?"

"Maybe."

And I think to myself that we've all become a bit like cheese-heads lately, the six . . . *five* . . . of us constantly tethered to our electronic devices, and I wonder what my grandfather would make of this new megapixelated world.

He would hate it, and he would gloat that he'd been right. My grandfather was a man of strong opinions, some that rankled but that, more often than not, turned out to be right. Long before these things came into existence, he predicted cell phones, laptops, climate change, and conservative Christian values' decline—all of which he believed to be travesties looming on the horizon that would alter humanity for the worse.

My mother, a flower child who came of age in the sixties and marched for women and gay rights, was the first to cut ties. My uncles soon followed, and our idyllic family summers came to an end.

After that, the only contact I had with my grandfather was the cards I got on my birthday with generous checks inside. I regret now not having kept in touch. We had been close. "Duplicity personified," he used to say. He's the reason I went to Yale and the reason I studied economics. He's the one who taught me to wolf whistle, tie a dozen different knots, properly shake a hand, and ride both a horse and a bike, and he's the reason I never apologize unless I mean it.

Yes, we didn't share all the same views, but I regret not seeing past it to the common ground, which far outweighed our differences. Perhaps, had I kept in touch, I might even have been able to persuade him to see things differently, the same way my kids often enlighten me to things more progressive than I'm used to.

"Should we carry the rest in or wait for Dad?" Hannah asks.

I turn to see her squinting against the light streaming in from the tall windows. Since Hannah got her period, a little over two years ago, she's been afflicted with debilitating migraines, and brightness is a trigger.

"Why don't you go upstairs and rest," I say. "The boys can carry the rest in when they get here." I roll my eyes. "Whenever that is."

"Mom, stop. You know Dad loves his car."

"It's ridiculous."

"It's for the environment."

"He needs to recharge every seventy miles!"

"Why do you care? You're not the one who has to do it."

"Because it's ludicrous. We drove here and didn't need to stop once."

"Different strokes," Hannah says with a shrug.

She's an easygoing kid, water flowing downstream. So unlike me that if we didn't share the same gold hair and blue eyes, I'd wonder if we took the wrong child home from the hospital.

"Yeah, well, hopefully they get here before summer ends," I say, enjoying the banter that's become so rare these days.

She almost smiles but cringes instead, which makes me feel terrible. It seems a basic tenet of parenthood that you should be able to take away your child's pain. But no matter how many doctors I've taken her to, nothing has worked.

She shuffles up the stairs. I watch her go, then plop on the couch and stare out the window. I consider going to find Pen so we can explore. I could show her my favorite hiding spots, and we could pick berries or hunt for nests. We could walk to the river to see if the giant willow's still there, then climb onto the branch over the water and carve her initials next to my sister's and my own.

But I'm just so tired.

Leaning my head back, I close my eyes and breathe. *In, out, in, out.* One breath at a time. Each carrying me another inch forward until, hopefully, by the end of summer, we find ourselves somewhere new.

2
PENELOPE

The butterfly weaves in and out of the spindly white trunks as I jump from spot to spot of dancing light blinking through the leaves above.

I saw it before the car stopped, a flutter of blue beside the barn, and my heart leaped. When Mom said we were spending the summer in New Hampshire, I was worried Bee wouldn't know where we'd gone. But there she was, waiting.

She lands on the stem of a bush with large pinkish-purple poofs, and I inch closer, hoping to see her wings. If they have black lines and orange spots, she is a red-spotted purple, but if they have a white stripe with dark spots, she's a white admiral, something I've never seen.

I'm a yard away when she takes off again. I hurry after, wondering if the glimpse I caught was actually a white stripe or only my wish for it to be true. I've learned if you wish hard enough, sometimes your wishes turn real.

3

HANNAH

My migraine is really heating up, my left eye throbbing like a heart behind the lid and my insides roiling. I hate how suddenly they strike. Only moments before, I was admiring the house, excited to hear more about my great-grandfather and the summers my mom spent here as a child. I relished the smile she gave when she spoke of him, her happiness so rare these days.

But then, *bam*! The glare through the windows reflected off the floor and ricocheted into my brain like a bullet, and it was all I could do to stay standing.

I stagger into the first bedroom I come to, pull the curtains closed, and flop on the bed with my arm draped over my eyes. Tears form, and I try to push them back. I don't want to feel sorry for myself. But it is impossible. I get these stupid headaches almost every day now, and they are ruining my life, half my existence spent curled in the dark trying not to move so my brain won't rupture.

My mom's taken me to a kazillion doctors, and all of them have said the same thing: because I'm "still developing," they don't want to prescribe anything that might have long-term side effects. So each has suggested the same handful of mostly useless remedies—electrolytes,

Advil, meditation, exercise—except one who gave me pills that made me so tired I decided I'd rather put up with the headaches.

I drape my other arm over my eyes as the tears leak. I had hoped leaving Connecticut would help, that miraculously the New Hampshire air would cure me. But I'm not that sort of girl, the kind made for miracles. Plain as rain with a laugh like a donkey, and now with chronic headaches that leave me lying in bed with my arms over my face in the middle of a beautiful summer day, the exact sort of damsel in distress no prince would want.

4
LEO

Bucolic. I've always liked that word. It sounds exactly like what it means—the syllables round, smooth, and soothing. Look it up in an encyclopedia and you might find a description of a place like this, a quintessential Georgian columned house centered on a rolling green lawn beneath endless blue sky with a large red gambrel-roof barn beside it.

Marie's Highlander is out front, the hatch open, and I wonder how long they've been here. My car is not practical for long trips, and we needed to recharge three times. Marie thinks my car is ridiculous. It was one of the first EVs to hit the market, and the range is limited. But I don't mind. I like what it represents—ingenuity, change, hope for the future. A few extra minutes spent here and there when I need to go more than seventy miles seems worth it. When automobiles were first invented, they were outperformed by horses and buggies, and look how that turned out. Also, unlike Marie, I'm not always in a rush. I enjoy distraction, segues, and unexpected disruption. At our first stop, I took a turn through the Worcester Art Museum, a place I haven't visited in years. And at our second, Brendon and I were lucky enough to be parked in the same lot as a Cravin' Crab Cakes food truck, and we enjoyed some of the best crab cakes on the planet. *Nature does not hurry, yet everything is accomplished.* Lao Tzu is one of my favorite philosophers, and lately, I've found myself leaning heavily on his wisdom.

"Just what I thought," Brendon says beside me. "A whole lot of nothing."

Brendon didn't want to come here. He's a twelve-year-old boy, and his world revolves around video games, sports, and friends—things rural New Hampshire has none of.

"Give it a chance," I say, though I also have my reservations.

We've all been through so much, and I'm not sure uprooting us from everything familiar is the best choice. The books I've read on grief emphasize stability and a reliable support system. But I also understand that Marie couldn't stay in our house with memories of Bee everywhere and the pool glinting outside every window.

My throat tightens, and I force myself to swallow. A new start in a new place, or at least a gasp of breath until we figure out how to go on in this altered, distorted world.

Brendon climbs from the car with the enthusiasm of a slug, and I climb out as well.

Worried as I am about Marie, it's Brendon who keeps me up at night. He says he's fine and tells me to stop asking if he's okay, but since the accident, he hasn't been the same. Marie says he just needs time, but it's been six weeks, and if anything, I feel like it's getting worse and that we are losing our chance to reach him.

I lift the hatch as Brendon opens the door for Banjo. The dog jumps out, his tail wagging so hard his body wags with it. He offers a few happy yips, and Brendon smiles.

Thank goodness for the dog—a boy's best friend in the truest sense. While Brendon's shut the rest of us out almost completely, his devotion to Banjo is unchanged.

I carry two of the suitcases inside and stop. *Whoa!* It's like we've stepped onto a movie set, a scene from *Gone with the Wind*, and I'm Rhett Butler waiting for Scarlett O'Hara to come swooning down the steps. The home is a southern manor in the truest sense of the words—wide-plank dark wood floors, a sweeping staircase, a giant iron chandelier overhead.

"Hey," Marie says.

I turn to see her stand from a couch in the living room, or perhaps I should say *parlor*, the space the size of a hotel lobby with half a dozen couches and love seats, along with a card table surrounded by six straight-backed chairs.

Banjo bounds over, and Marie scratches him behind his ears.

"You made it," she says, her expression neutral but a taunt in her voice.

"Yep!" I say, overly bright. "Here we are!"

I've noticed, constantly now, there's a strange tinniness to everything I say, like I'm Tony the Tiger in a Frosted Flakes commercial, finger pointing in the air and shouting *They're great!* with every word. It's highly annoying, and, though aware of it, I seem unable to stop.

"Are you kidding?" Brendon says.

Marie and I both turn to see him staring at his phone.

"No internet?" he says. "What the . . . ?"

He keeps the expletive silent, which almost makes it more pronounced. Though I'm grateful he didn't say it aloud, which would have required a reprimand, which I'm not sure I could have given, considering the current state of things. Since Bee's death, I've found disciplining the kids far more difficult, seemingly unable to criticize or correct them in any way.

Brendon's face flashes to mine, then Marie's. "What am I supposed to do all summer?"

I turn as well. A summer with three electronics-addicted kids and no internet is going to be unbearable. For Brendon, his gaming is essential as oxygen. Hannah binges daily on Netflix. And Pen constantly is googling her latest curiosity and going down rabbit holes of discovery.

"A satellite dish is being installed in a few days," Marie says. "It won't be quite as fast as cable, but we'll manage."

Brendon's eyes narrow, the expression bordering on hate. "And what am I supposed to do until then?"

Marie waves her hand at the window. "Go outside. There's a whole world to explore."

Brendon looks at her like she's got three heads, and I feel bad for him. He's not accustomed to entertaining himself, and it's not like he has friends here who he can go out and adventure with.

"Maybe go with Pen," I suggest, then look at Marie. "Where are the girls?"

"Hannah's resting."

"A migraine?" I ask with concern. For over a year, her headaches have gotten progressively worse, and the recent stress certainly hasn't helped. I've done endless research to try to figure it out, but everyone's individual body chemistry is different, so it's impossible to know exactly what's causing the imbalance. Marie's taken her to a dozen specialists, and Hannah's tried everything they've recommended, but nothing has worked.

Marie nods and says, "And Pen chased a butterfly into the woods."

"Alone?" I say, hair prickling.

Marie nods like it's no big deal as blood rushes to my brain.

"It's fine," Marie says, noticing my panic. "It's not like you can get lost. Any way you go, you end up at the river or the road."

But already, I'm whirling for the door. Less than six weeks ago, we lost our eight-year-old because we were stupidly cavalier, believing it was "fine" for the twins to swim in the pool without us there. And now, Marie has let our other eight-year-old wander alone into the woods.

"Brendon," I snap, "let's go!"

Surprisingly, he doesn't protest. Perhaps it's boredom . . . or possibly guilt . . . his perception of his responsibility toward his sisters changed.

We race out the door and toward the stand of birch, my heart pounding so hard I can't see straight. *Don't let me be too late. Please, this time, let me get there in time.*

5

PENELOPE

I hear the river through the trees and know it's close. It sounds wide and lazy, not concerned in the least, as truly powerful things often are. As I walk, I collect leaves and berries to show Dad. I've also found what I think is a mushroom. It's the size of my hand and was growing from the side of one of the trees. It's not pretty like the sort of mushrooms we buy in the store with round umbrella tops and stems, but rather malformed and dark, like a chunk of burned charcoal. It smells a little like wet dirt, but I'm hoping it's actually something wonderful that Dad, Hannah, and I can cook with.

I've lost sight of the butterfly but know it's in front of me. I feel like it is leading me somewhere, or perhaps I'm wrong and she's only exploring. Bee loved adventure. She was always jumping into things and taking off one way or another. Because of that, a lot of people thought she was the leader between us, but that's not how it was. While it's true Bee was usually in front, I was most often the one deciding which way we went. It's the thing about being a twin. It's never one or the other but instead two parts of a whole, like one of those yin-yang symbols—black with white and white with black—alike and together, but the two sides not the same. Sometimes I wonder how it turned out that way, ending up so different though we were born the same—her passion for music and mine for nature; her being an athlete and me a nerd; her loud and me not. I don't remember choosing those things, but maybe we did, our way of setting ourselves apart.

The path bends right, and I follow, excited to see the river—the Merry Mack—like a jolly old character in a book. Though Dad said that's not how it got its name. He says it comes from Native American words that mean "strong place."

I stop, surprised to see a small house through the trees. It's shaped like a pointy triangle, with no actual walls but instead a roof that goes all the way to the ground. On its porch is a tattered yellow umbrella, a metal table with two chairs, and a long gray cat lying in a patch of sun.

I step closer but stop at the sound of a sharp noise like a hammer slamming into wood. I turn to see a woman with her back to me in front of a worktable. Her long black ponytail drapes almost to her waist, and in her hand is a knife, the kind with a long blade that curves to a sharp point. I follow it to the table, where a rabbit lies with its head chopped off, blood spilling from its neck.

The woman swipes the head aside with the blade, and I stumble back.

Hearing me, she turns. And when I see her face, I open my mouth to scream, but the sound sticks in my throat. Her face is only half a face, the bottom part mashed like the skin's been peeled away, and there is only one nostril and a gaping black hole for a mouth. The hole opens as if to say something, but before it can speak, I whirl and run. Legs going fast as I can make them go, tears sting my eyes as every scary fairy tale I've ever heard races through my brain—"Hansel and Gretel," "Little Red Riding Hood," "Rumpelstiltskin"—evil creatures living in the woods waiting for children to stumble upon them.

"Sweet Pea!" Dad runs toward me as if my fear made him appear.

I barrel into him and bury my face against his shirt. "A monster . . . ," I gasp. "There was a monster."

"A monster?"

"In a triangle, with a yellow umbrella, by the river."

6
BRENDON

My sister has a very active imagination. She probably saw a yellow bird in a crooked tree or a boat with a yellow-hatted fisherman. You never know with Pen. The other day she was going on about Bee hanging out as a butterfly.

Trying to distract her, Dad asks, "What's this?" He points to the brown spongy thing in her hand. Banjo sniffs at it.

"I found it," Pen says, still whimpering. "Growing on a tree."

I suck air through my nose to catch my breath, trying to conceal how winded I am. My dad is a long-distance runner, and I hate running, so he was kicking my butt as we raced through the woods.

"It looks like it might be some sort of fungus," Dad says as he bends to examine it. "Should we bring it home and see if we can google it?"

"No internet," I grumble. "Remember?"

"Right," Dad says, straightening. "Well, how about we drive into town, the three of us? I'm sure there's Wi-Fi there, and we can see what this is."

My heart lights up. *Way to go, Pen!*

"What about the monster?" Pen asks, eyes darting over her shoulder.

"Well, my understanding of monsters, especially water monsters," Dad says in his professorial, know-it-all voice, "is that they are bound to the source of their power. Which in this case would be the river. So I don't think we have anything to worry about."

Pen considers his reasoning, her wide brow furrowed as her eyes tick side to side. She's a strange kid, her great big curiosity unwieldy for her oversize brain, like she simply can't process all the input coming at her and doesn't quite know what to do with it. Bee was sort of that way as well but more tear-it-apart-to-see-what's-inside than look-it-up-on-a-computer kind of geek.

"So she can't leave the river?" Pen asks, left eye squinted, uncertain of the wonky logic but still young enough to trust adults and believe in such things.

"It was a she?" Dad asks.

Pen nods seriously. "With long black hair and only half a face."

Doesn't sound like a bird or a fisherman, and I wonder if she really did see something.

Dad takes her hand. "Half a face," he says and starts back toward the house, "that does sound scary."

I trod after them as Banjo runs ahead. And though I don't want to believe in the far-fetched tale, I, too, glance over my shoulder. Nothing but spindly trees, but still my pulse races, a bad feeling of something behind us or maybe more like something about to happen. I see a branch on the ground ahead of me, three feet long with sticks and knots along its length, and imagine seizing it and whirling at the exact moment the monster attacks, then ripping the gnarled limb across its grotesque, half-formed face.

"Bren?" Dad says, and I realize I've stopped and that he and Pen are now twenty feet ahead. Blinking away the thought, I hurry to catch up. As I pass the stick, I kick it into the bushes, which causes Dad to turn again.

I shrug as if it was an accident. *Nothing to look at. I tripped.*

Lying. Lying. Lying.

I fist my hands open and closed to force the tingle from my fingers. I don't know why I do it—lie. My whole life, without conscious thought, whenever asked a question that could land me in trouble, a fib emerges before I've even had time to consider it. A gift . . . *or a curse* . . . my mind has always been brilliant at concocting feasible alternate answers to the truth instantly, and that, along with a face that apparently looks incapable of deceit, make me a master of treachery.

"Okay?" Dad asks, brow furrowed.

I roll my eyes like the question is annoying, then fall back a step, letting him know I want to be left alone. Constantly, since Bee drowned, he asks if I'm okay or if there's anything he can do. There isn't. She is dead. D-E-A-D. Gone. As in never coming back. And if he knew the truth about what happened, he wouldn't ask if I was okay. He'd hate me and would stop caring if I was ever okay again. Everyone would.

"Do you think we can make something with the mushroom?" Pen asks.

"I hope so. Maybe a pasta."

Bee would have said pizza. She and I always agreed when it came to food.

I feel my emotions rising and work to push them down. It's always the small things that set me off—a nothing thought of me and her teaming up for pizza and winning because Bee was impossible to say no to. And as always happens when I think of her, that awful day returns, causing my blood to pump wildly until it feels like my organs are going to explode.

The morning after it happened, Dad came to my room, knocking lightly before eking open the door and sticking his head in. I was on my bed with *The Lightning Thief* open on my lap, though I wasn't reading. Closing the book, I braced myself for his anger, which made me entirely unprepared for the exhausted, concerned look on his face.

"Hey," he said, his voice a croak. "Can I come in?"

I nodded, and he stepped inside. He looked awful, his rusty hair sticking up every which way and his eyes swollen and red. He was still in the running clothes he'd had on when he came home to the chaos of the paramedics and ambulances in front of the house.

Dropping his face to the carpet, he said, "The paramedic said they found a pinprick hole in the seam of the floatie. He thinks it deflated and slipped off her arm."

Pinprick. The word stuck. *Small, tiny, infinitesimal.*

"She ended up lopsided and probably couldn't right herself."

I saw it in my head, Bee flouncing in the water, possibly twirling like she liked to do, as a silent hiss of air unknowingly streamed around with her. Caught by surprise, she toppled. No splash or scream, her face beneath the surface as her single arm waved frantically in the air for help, and as I sat a few feet away looking at my phone.

"There was no way any of us could have known. Bad luck was all there was to it. She shouldn't have gone back in without you there."

The final words floated, not making sense. I tilted my head in confusion, but he didn't see it, his eyes still on the carpet.

I was there. I was right there, sitting on the deck, playing on my phone, trying to beat my Fortnite record.

My dad had been on a run, and Hannah had a headache, so I was the one "watching" the twins that afternoon. They'd been in the pool over an hour, so I told them to get out. I was hot and bored and wanted to go inside.

Pen went into the house, and soon as she was gone, Bee stomped up and said, "My turn," then held out her hand for my phone.

I ignored her.

"My turn!" she demanded.

It was true that I owed her a turn. That morning I'd lost a bet with her over how many colors there were in a bag of M&M's. I said seven. She said six. She was right. Purple is only used in the ads. It was a total setup and typical Bee. Her prize was a game of Fortnite on my phone, which she could only play when we were alone because the twins weren't allowed to use my phone, which meant she needed to do it when Pen wasn't around.

"Not now," I said as I zeroed in on a hidden chest of weapons in a jungle.

She waved her hand over the screen, purposely blowing up my game.

"Jerk!" I yelled.

"Two-faced cheat!"

I glared at her. She stuck her tongue out at me.

"The bet was bogus," I said.

"I won, fair and square."

"Go away."

She stomped off, and I started a new game. As it was loading, I heard the splash as she jumped back in the water.

It wasn't until I finished, missing my record by half a dozen points, that I looked up to see her near the deep end, her arm dangling from the floatie and the rest of her body submerged. The other floatie, partially deflated, drifted a few feet away.

"Linguini or spaghetti?" Dad asks, swinging Pen's hand between them, breaking me from my thoughts.

"Both," Pen says. "Lin-ghetti."

I stare at the back of Pen's head, wondering if she told him I went inside because that's what I said I was going to do, and if that's how he got the story wrong. Bee was notorious for breaking rules, so it was easy to believe she'd gone back in the pool alone.

All I know for sure is, that morning, when he came to my room, I could have corrected him, set the record straight. But I didn't. Instead, when he said, "Bad luck was all there was to it. She shouldn't have gone back in without you there," without my permission, my head nodded. And there it was, the worst lie I ever told, out in the universe, where it has remained, making me nauseous and relieved each time I realize I've gotten away with it.

"Bren?" Dad says, and I realize I've stopped again.

I hurry to catch up, then glance again over my shoulder, hoping for the monster to appear so I can slash her down and destroy her.

7
DAVINA

I look at the knife in my hand and the blood on my gloves. My first instinct was to run after the girl and soothe her fear, but I understand what my appearance does to people and knew it would only make things worse.

Teddy rubs against my leg and looks up imploringly, hoping I'll drop him a morsel of fresh rabbit. The tom is always looking for a handout. Nearby, Laverne and Shirley preen, while Cleopatra watches from her perch on the balcony, the three queens also surveilling the situation but doing so more aloofly, too proud to beg but willing to take a gift if it is bestowed.

How old was she? Seven? Eight? Skinny as a beanpole but her forehead still wide. I'd guess eight.

She must have come from the colonel's house, a child of the family Rock told me was visiting for the summer.

I look down at the hare, its vacant marble eye staring back. I found the poor thing in a coon trap an hour ago. The trap is now at the bottom of the river, a leather note left in its place:

See the cruelty and the pain
That you have caused once again
Turn the tables three times three

Bring back to your actions
I will be free
When light fades and dusk comes through
The pain you've caused will come back to you
I say this spell to Karma tonight
I am witch, I stand and fight
Let cruelty, pain, and evil ways
Follow this villain through all his days
Reverse the torment he creates
To turn on him, a crueler fate

I discovered the spell online a dozen years ago and have been using it since. When I first returned home, I would find traps all the time—animals half-dead in the torture devices or fully dead by excruciating means. But over the years, my reputation has grown, and now, most hunters fear me.

Before penning the note, I rubbed the patch of leather with poison ivy, so whoever handles it will break out in hives within a day. I've found superstition to be a powerful deterrent to the miscreants too lazy and cruel to hunt for their food in a more noble way.

I learned the power of being a "witch" from my second mother, the original river witch of these parts. But she was known only as a good witch, where I've been known to cross the line on occasion. My excuse is I have been to war and she hadn't.

I blow out a breath and set down the knife. Until the girl showed up, I was having a perfectly lovely day. I enjoy my pranks and was looking forward to rabbit stew, which I rarely eat these days, having lost my own stomach for hunting years ago.

What to do about the girl?

I gave her quite a scare. Her eyes went wide as saucers, and her mouth dropped open in a silent scream. My appearance tends to do that, my face quite gruesome.

I pick up the knife again and return to skinning the hare.

Think on a problem long enough, and you might not find the answer, but at least you'll know the question. It's something my second mother used to say.

Perhaps I should introduce myself to the family and explain what happened? The idea causes my pulse to race; meeting new people is difficult and not something I enjoy.

I wrench the pelt from the carcass and set it in the pickle bath. When it's finished curing, I'll give it to Rock to give to his mother. Linda makes all sorts of things from the skins she buys off local hunters—blankets, hats, mittens. For my fiftieth birthday, she gave me a rabbit-pelt blanket. It's one of my most prized possessions, and for eight years, I've gone to sleep thinking of her kindness. It's the beautiful thing about gifts, the feelings they carry within them.

I set about butchering the meat, my mind still on the girl. I can't just ignore it. She could end up with nightmares. And if the family is here for the summer, they will need to know I'm here. Maybe I'll leave a note, explain what happened and about my deformity. Then they can go back to their lives, and I can go back to mine.

8
HANNAH

My head still pounds, but there's something I need to do that cannot wait. My dad came back from the woods with Pen and Brendon and said they were going into town so they can use the internet. They're leaving in a few minutes, and I need to go with them.

Walking gingerly so my brain won't rupture, I make my way to a picnic table beside the barn that is in the shade. Each step causes a painful aftershock in my skull, but I only need to focus a few minutes. The email is written except the final line, which I came up with on the drive to get here.

My obsession with letters to Juliet began on the vacation we took last year to Italy. While my mom was fixated on the art and clothes, and my sisters and dad were infatuated with the history and minutia, and my brother remained preoccupied with his phone and games, I fell in love with the idea of people sending letters of heartache and unrequited love to the home of a dead heroine from Shakespeare. Each year, tens of thousands of letters are sent to and left at Juliet's tomb in Verona, each seeking counsel on questions of the heart. And amazingly, each letter is answered by a legion of volunteers called the Juliet Club.

Fascinated, I went online and read some of the letters and became completely enthralled. The letters come from all over the world and are from all sorts of people. Some are long, nearly the length of a book, others brief as a few lines. Many are looking for advice, but most seem only to be seeking witness, and I found that reading them was like peeking through a looking glass into someone else's heart.

The more I read, the less alone I felt with my own feelings, and I decided I wanted to be a part of it. So I applied to be a secretary, claiming to be a twenty-six-year-old graduate student and offering to reply to letters written in English sent by email. I was stunned when the Juliet Club accepted my offer. And for nearly six months, I've received two or three letters a week to which I've written replies. I'm very careful with my responses, feeling like I've been entrusted with a great responsibility. My goal is to make each reply personal and to convey how much the letter meant and that I understand what the writer is feeling.

Which I do. Oh, how I understand.

Though I've never been in love, since I was four, I've been head over heels in love with the idea of it. I've read all the classic romances, from *Wuthering Heights* to *Gone with the Wind*, and am embarrassingly addicted to *The Bachelor*, *Love Island*, and *Love Is Blind*.

The letter I'm responding to at the moment is from a college student in California. She claims to have found her one true love, a man named Devyn, who is "the very air she breathes." They've been dating two months, and he has asked her to drop out of school to move with him to Texas. She doesn't know what to do and "awaits my thoughtful reply."

My letter back basically says that true love knows no bounds, and if Devyn's love is true as her own, he will wait for her while she finishes college. I ended by saying how much better their life will be if she doesn't give up one dream for another and then, down the road, wind up wondering what might have been.

Often when I write my responses, I find myself channeling my parents, mostly my dad, thinking what he would say, then rephrasing it in a nicer, less blunt manner. My dad would not approve of anyone dropping out of college for any reason, but least of all for a boyfriend or girlfriend.

I type in the final line that I came up with on the drive from home:

Happy wife, happy life—it's what my father always says, and it seems to work for my parents.

All my love,
Juliet

All replies to letters to Juliet are signed "All my love, Juliet."

I hit save as my mom walks onto the front porch with Banjo. She has showered, and her hair is loose and wet around her shoulders. She wears oversize gray sweats and a Nirvana T-shirt, and seeing her so casual makes me smile. At home, she's always so buttoned up, even around the house, worried what people might think if they happen to see her.

She sips a cup of tea as she surveys the lawn. The reason we came here is so she can get this place ready to sell. At the end of summer, we're moving to Farmington, a posh town twenty minutes from our current home in Hartford and hopefully far enough away for no one to know our tragic story or Brendon's role in it.

I feel terrible for my brother. The only reason he was watching the twins that day was because I had a migraine and my dad was on a run. It sucks for him. It could have been any one of us—Bee being Bee and always doing things she wasn't supposed to. But he drew the short straw that day and happened to be the one responsible.

What makes it worse is everyone knows. It was even in the newspaper: "Eight-Year-Old Girl Drowns in Pool." The article didn't mention

Brendon by name but said, "Her older brother was the one to pull her from the water," and Brendon's the only brother Bee had. He acts like it doesn't bother him, but it's pretty obvious it does. He never sees his friends anymore, hardly ever leaves the house, and it's like his smile's been permanently lost and guilt and anger are the only emotions he's allowed.

It's one of the main reasons we're moving: to give all of us, but especially Brendon, a fresh start. And while I understand my mom's logic, I'm not entirely convinced it will work. It's not like trading in a car. You can't simply replace your old life with a new one and think that's going to fix things. It seems to me, wherever we go, the dents and scratches are going to go with us and that it's going to take more than a new house in a new town in order to set things right.

9
DAVINA

The note is simple and to the point:

Hello Neighbor,

My name is Davina Lister, and I live down by the river. Your little girl happened upon me this morning, and I'm afraid I gave her quite a fright. I am a war veteran, and part of my face was burned while I was serving. It can be scary to some, especially children. I wanted to let you know what she saw so you can soothe her fears.

Best,
Davina

I didn't have any stationery, so I wrote it on a sheet of notebook paper. I also didn't have an envelope. Hopefully they won't judge me for that.

I stop at the edge of the woods and squat behind a yarrow shrub, not wanting to be seen, especially by the little girl. My intent is to leave the note wedged in the door. The problem is, once I leave the trees, there's nowhere to hide.

Standing on the porch is a woman with gold hair, the little girl, a black Labrador, and a man who looks a lot like the little girl, thin and spry with ginger coloring. I'm about to retreat, thinking I'll come back later, when I spot another figure at the picnic table beside the barn. Though she's in the shadows, I'm able to make out shoulder-length gold hair that matches the woman's. I watch as she closes her computer and stands, wavering slightly as she tucks the computer beneath her arm. She walks toward the others, and I see the determination in her face and the painful squint of her eyes.

Migraine.

She's of the age when hormones can play havoc on a system. They can throw the body's chemistry out of whack and cause all sorts of problems, including chronic debilitating headaches. I feel how much she's hurting, and watching her gives me an idea.

I'm about to turn when a boy, blond and sturdy, runs from the house. The man, little girl, and boy get into a strange-looking car, and half a minute later, the teenager climbs in after them.

They drive away, leaving the woman alone. She watches as the tail-lights fade, then turns and pans the property. And as her eyes pass, a chill—premonition or forewarning—runs through me.

10
MARIE

I forgot how beautiful this place is, and how peaceful. The afternoon is waning along with the heat, and it's so quiet it feels like I'm in a trance.

The kids and Leo have gone to town. They made it less than an hour without Wi-Fi. That's okay. We will find our rhythm. I asked Leo to pick up some board games and puzzles. My cousin Izzy and I could puzzle for hours. Others would join in here and there, but she and I were the puzzle queens. We did sixteen puzzles one summer. I still remember our favorite, a bulldog surrounded by a pile of frosted doughnuts. His expression was priceless, and we both declared someday we wanted to find that kind of happiness.

Izzy was a romantic, and her dream was to fall madly in love with a poet or writer and travel the world looking for new places where he could write, and everywhere they went, she would be his muse. She married a podiatrist, and they live in Syracuse. My dream was more practical: to be the mom of a houseful of kids who my husband took care of so I could make a bazillion dollars and change the world.

Children, of course, turned out to be more work than I thought. We had Hannah, then Brendon, and, overwhelmed with our careers and two preschoolers, decided to wait before having more, a nearly disastrous mistake. The twins required two rounds of IVF and a surrogate.

It nearly bankrupted us, but as Leo said, we could always make more money, but our children were a rare and precious commodity. I told him I loved when he talked economics. It's our private little joke, both of us with PhDs in economics from Yale.

Last year, we'd rebuilt our cushion enough to take a family vacation to Italy. And this year, we planned on going to Hawaii. I canceled our flight and hotel reservations two weeks ago. I can't imagine any of us being in the mood to take a vacation anytime soon. Plus, between the loss of income from the leave I've taken from my job, the money it's costing to fix this place, and the deposit we put on the home in Farmington, we're back down to the dregs. It's fine. The sale of this place will put us solidly back in the black, and when summer ends, I'll go back to my job, and we'll return to a positive cash flow. We just need to get there. *Forward. Forward. Forward.*

I sigh as I look at the lawn and make a mental note to add reseeding to the growing list of things to be done. Twenty years of neglect has left the yard brown and weedy.

It's hard to believe it's been that long, my grandfather's passing still so fresh I feel the same weight of regret and longing I did when my mother called and gave me the news. I wish I'd realized how little time I had to make amends. Larger than life, he always seemed immortal. But now I know no one is. Not even the most indomitable. Bee was only eight. My grandfather lived nearly ten times that. Both fearless and brazen. He'd have loved our honeybee.

I never thought we would sell this place. For years, I've harbored secret thoughts of recreating the magical summers of my youth with the next generation. But everyone's so busy these days with sports and activities and commitments, I doubt I could get anyone to come for a weekend, let alone weeks or months, like my family did when I was young.

The end of an era. This property's been in my family as far back as anyone can trace, handed down generation to generation on my grandmother's side. Though it was my grandfather who decided to build the house to make it a place for the family to gather, a dream that lasted less than a decade.

I wish I could tell him how much those summers meant, my fondest memories and the close relationships I have with my sister and cousins forged in those fleeting, wondrous weeks.

But time marches on, and nostalgia doesn't pay the bills. I try not to think how disappointed he would be if he knew we are selling it. If he were here, I'd tell him there's no choice; the plan sprung from necessity.

It was Mother's Day, a particularly brutal day, when I came up with the idea.

Leo was getting ready for bed, and, his back to me, he said, "Marie."

It was odd for him to use my proper name. From the day we met, he's called me Jags, short for Jaguar, which was the parked car I'd crashed into while chasing an errant Frisbee on the quad the first week of our freshman year. I took off the grille emblem and dented the hood while still managing to keep hold of the disk. Leo was on the sidewalk. He handed me the emblem with the fierce chrome wildcat face and the word *Jaguar* etched above it and said, "Nice catch, Jags." The emblem is in a frame on our mantel, a gift from Leo on our first anniversary. The plaque below it reads, "Wild beast that overcomes its prey at a bound," which is the etymological translation of the word.

With a sigh, he set his watch on the dresser, then, for a long time, was silent. Finally, he turned, and, his normally bright eyes so tired it hurt to look at them, he said, "Let's promise to get through this."

How? I wanted to scream but stopped myself, dropping my face to look at my hands twined together on the quilt, the nails chipped and bloody from how much I had picked at them.

"We have to," he went on. "For the kids."

Kids. Four minus one. Two plus half of two.

"It's either find a way forward or let it kill us slowly the rest of our lives."

I looked up, feeling as if it already had, that I'd drowned with her and only my body continued to live on.

But he was looking at me with such desperation that I nodded. I didn't really mean it. I simply wanted the conversation to end. But when relief flooded his face, something cracked open inside me, the thing that happens when you love someone and they are affected and you can't help but be affected as well.

He climbed into bed, and that night, we made love. Strange and stilted, as if consummating the promise. My mind felt separate from my body, as if I were watching two strangers from above, the whole time wondering how you move forward when an essential part of you is gone.

After, as I lay staring at the ceiling, I made the decision for us to move, realizing it was the only way. Leo was right; we needed to get through it, and the only way I could think of to do that was by leaving the past behind. Farmington had always been a dream, a community of rolling hills with large houses on sprawling lawns surrounded by meandering horse trails, forests, and streams—a place with plenty of wide-open space for us to heal and breathe. It was a stretch financially, but if we sold the timberland, we could swing it.

The thought almost made me happy, the first glimmer of lightness I'd felt since the moment I got the call about Bee. And I clung to it, closing my eyes and imagining the house we would buy, the furniture I would choose, the colors we would paint the walls. All night I thought about it, and it was like rubbing ice on a burn, the distraction numbing and soothing.

The next day, I got to work. I started with the real estate listings and discovered we were in luck. A new development was nearing completion, and there was one unclaimed home that would be finished at the end of summer. I sent the deposit that morning.

Banjo plops beside me, worn out from the day of running through the woods. I've always felt bad for how constrained his life is at home. He's always fenced or leashed and rarely allowed to simply be a dog. My grandfather always had dogs, five or six of them. They ran unfettered and were wildly happy.

"Hey, old boy." I kneel and scruff his chin. He moons up at me. "We're doing this."

He sets his head down and closes his eyes, and I lower myself so his warmth is snuggled against my thigh and continue to stroke his fur. *Forward, forward, forward* . . . it takes enormous effort, each breath, each step. But I will do it, an inch or a millimeter at a time. For Pen and Hannah and Brendon and Leo—for those of us who remain.

11
HANNAH

I woke up this morning with Pen curled beside me and my head only pounding half as bad as last night. It is always better in the morning.

When I went downstairs, my dad was leaving for his run, and my mom and Brendon had already gone to town—my mom to talk to the real estate agent and Brendon to play his video games.

The house is wonderfully peaceful with no one around, and for an hour, I've been puttering around the kitchen, making blueberry muffins and checking out the wonderful assortment of appliances my great-grandfather left behind, both in the kitchen and in the enormous basement below. He must have liked to cook because he owned every culinary gadget known to man, and there are enough bowls, pots, and pans to cook for an army. My dad, the twins, and I . . . I mean, my dad, *Pen*, and I . . . love to cook. I especially love baking, while Pen and my dad are big on inventing recipes for meals.

The buzzer rings, and I pull the muffins from the oven and take a deep inhale of the delicious steam rising from the pan. Banjo sits erect, watching my every move and whimpering. I call him my diet buddy. He will eat half a muffin, and I will eat half. It's easier than setting half aside.

"They need to cool," I say, which of course only causes him to whimper more.

I break off a bit of muffin top, juggle it hand to hand, then blow on it and drop it at his feet. He laps it up and returns to his beseeching pose. I'm about to break off another piece when movement through the window catches my eye. I look out to see a boy unloading wood from the back of a pickup into the barn. He looks around my age but must be older, since he can drive. He wears a dark-blue baseball cap, worn-out Wranglers, and a gray T-shirt straining its seams. His legs are thick as tree trunks, and he has no apparent neck, his sandy hair stopping just above his wide shoulders. *Strapping,* I think, then giggle at the word. It reminds me of one of the letters to Juliet I received, a widow who wrote of her dead husband and how much she missed him. *Big lug, I spent my whole life maneuvering around him and complaining about it, and now that he's gone, there's just so much dang space. It's like I'm rattling around in a great empty hole. How do I get used to that? Not having this huge thing in my life?*

Though I wouldn't call the boy outside a lug. There's a jaunty spring in his step that almost makes him bouncy.

Squinting into the light hurts my head, so I turn away, then look with dismay at my hand, which is empty, the muffin inhaled while I was watching the boy. *Ugh!* Sweets are my weakness and, when combined with my already large bones, are conspiring to turn me into a cow. A cow with migraines! My whole life, people have always commented on how much I look like my mom, a compliment I've always loved. Then, two months ago, my biology teacher, after meeting my mom at the science fair, commented, "You're like an exact replica, only bigger." *Ugh!*

I hear the truck start and peek through the window to see it driving away.

With the boy gone and needing to get away from the muffins, I grab my laptop and return to the picnic table. Yesterday, when I was in town, I checked my emails and discovered two new letters.

The day is incredibly warm, and just walking to the table causes me to work up a sweat, which, in turn, causes a new wave of migraine—heat a trigger, along with stress, bright light, loud noises, strong smells, and physical exertion—in other words, anything that might be the least bit exciting or fun.

I sit on the bench and lay my head on my arms, hoping it will pass. I pull deep, slow breaths through my nose and blow them out through my mouth, a technique I've been told by several doctors should help. It works a little, the intense, heavy throbbing dulling to a blunter thumping pulse.

When the worst is over, I turn my head sideways, and that's when I see the string. White and thin, the kind you use to wrap a roast. One end is tied in a bow to the middle plank of the table. The other drapes into the woods.

I think of the boy and wonder if he's the one who left it. Curiosity trumping the pain, I push to my feet to see where it leads. I follow it into the trees, feeling like I'm on a treasure hunt. It winds between several trunks, then under some bushes, and finishes behind a fallen log. Tied to the end is a plastic shopping bag with a folded sheet of notebook paper taped to it.

I unfold the sheet. In tight precise handwriting, written on every other line, it reads:

If you feel a migraine coming on, put half a teaspoon of the tincture under your tongue.

If you already have a migraine, drink a cup of the tea.

For immediate relief, ice the head and heat the feet.

For a really bad headache, add the mustard powder to the footbath.

I hope this helps.

Best,
Davina
(Known in these parts as the river witch.)

P.S. Please tell your sister I'm sorry for scaring her. I am only frightening on the outside.

I stare at the words for a long time, trying to make sense of them. Pen was acting odd last night, even odder than usual. She insisted on sleeping in my room, which I figured was because of being in a new place and missing Bee. But now, I wonder if maybe it had to do with coming across this woman who scared her.

From the bag, I pull out a small mason jar of clear liquid, a baggie of tea, and a tin of mustard powder. I twist the lid off the jar and lift it to my nose. It smells like alcohol, lemons, and a scent I don't recognize. I open the baggie. The tea smells like dirt and turmeric.

A witch offering potions because somehow, magically, she knows about my migraines. It's straight out of a fairy tale, the idea so wonderful, I giggle, which sends a sharp rupture through my brain.

Closing the jar, I return the offerings to the bag and carry them to the house.

I start by making the tea. As it steeps, I fill the largest pot I can find with hot water, add a tablespoon of the mustard powder, and set it beside my chair. Then I wrap ice in a towel and set it on the table.

When everything is set, I put my feet in the water, take a sip of the tea, and place the ice pack on my head. All the effort makes me certain I'm going to be sick, and I need to focus very hard on not hurling.

I count my breaths as I pray for a miracle, and when my system has settled enough that I'm no longer in danger of throwing up, I reach again for the tea. It's cooler now, so I gulp it down and return to my breathing and praying. I feel the dueling sensations of hot and cold, the heat and mustard powder pulling the pain downward as the cold helps by sending it away. The opposing forces work in bizarre synchronicity, until amazingly, the daggers behind my eyes dull to pulses barely noticeable at all.

"What ya doing?"

The ice pack drops from my head as I blink my eyes open to see Pen in her PJs in front of me, her head tilted and her curls wild on one side and smooshed flat on the other.

"Getting rid of my headache," I say, astonished as I say it.

"It smells."

I smile. It does. The kitchen smells like mustard and turmeric and dirt, a unique smell I already associate with relief and that might quickly become my favorite smell in the world.

"Is it working?" Pen asks.

"It is."

Pen does what she calls her happy dance, her skinny arms pumping the air and her butt wiggling all over the place.

"Will you play with me?" she asks.

I think of the note.

"What do you say we go for a walk? Maybe see the river?"

Her eyes grow wide, and her head shakes.

I'm about to ask what happened when the doorbell stops me.

12
PENELOPE

I leap after Banjo, who is barking wildly, as excited as I am to see who it is. I think the sound of an unexpected doorbell is one of the greatest in the world, the signal of a surprise arriving.

Hannah takes Banjo by the collar, and I swing the door open to find a boy . . . or kind of a boy . . . in front of me. His face is young, but he's taller than Dad and built like a box.

"Uh, hello," he says, looking from me to Hannah and fixing on her blue eyes before looking away.

Hannah's eyes do that to people. She inherited Mom's eyes, which Dad says are like pools of Caribbean Sea. I've always been jealous of that, my eyes a boring mush of brown and green.

"Hi," I say with a wave. "I'm Pen."

"Hi, Pen," the boy says with a sweeping wave back. "I'm Rock."

"Like a boulder?"

"Yup, and just as dumb, dense, and immovable."

He grins wide, and I giggle.

He looks back at Hannah, whose skin has pinked to the color of cotton candy, and I nearly giggle again because, though she and Rock have only just met, it's pretty obvious they *like* each other.

"Uh," Rock says, "I help take care of the place, and your ma called and said she wants it painted. Is she here?"

Ma. I smile.

"She went to town," Hannah says.

"Is your name really Rock?" I ask, thinking the name odd and wonderful.

He squats to let Banjo sniff his hand.

"It is," he says. "The first thing the midwife said when I was born was that I was solid as a rock, so that's what my ma named me."

"Midwife?" The word makes me think of a wife caught in the middle, like she's between a first wife and the last.

"It's sort of like a doctor," Rock says, "but they only help deliver babies. Though Davina does more than that because—"

"Davina?" Hannah interrupts.

"Yeah. Have you met her? She lives in the cabin down by the river."

I sidle closer to Hannah, and Hannah, seeming to sense my fear, reaches back and wraps her hand around my shoulder.

"We just got here yesterday," Hannah says. "So we haven't had much chance to meet anyone."

"She stays near the river, right?" I ask, thinking of what Dad said.

"Davina?" Rock says, then rubs his chin as if considering it. "Not really. That's where she lives, but Davina's definitely a wanderer, always traipsing off to somewhere or another, foraging in the woods for things or visiting the people she looks after. Never really known her to stay put."

Davina. The monster has a name. And Dad was wrong. She can leave the river. It sounds like she leaves all the time.

13
MARIE

The real estate appointment went splendid, far better than expected. It's a seller's market, and the property's value has exponentially increased since the last time it was appraised, which was nine years ago, when we refinanced to pay for the last round of in vitro, which gave us the twins. The sale will be more than enough to buy the Farmington house, furnish it, and recover the loss from my leave from work.

As I walk through the door, I'm the happiest I've been since . . . since *it* happened . . . a flicker of light at the end of a dark, dark tunnel. To add to my good mood, the house smells delicious, the scent of roasted mushrooms and garlic drifting past my nose and causing my stomach to rumble. Brendon, eyes fixed on his phone, continues into the living room, while I turn in to the kitchen, where I find Pen standing on a chair, stirring something in a skillet, and Leo at the counter, chopping vegetables.

"Hello, family!" I say brightly.

"Hello, wife!" Leo says, reflecting my smile back. He wears an apron that says **NIXON'S THE ONE!**—obviously my grandfather's. And seeing my liberal, tree-hugging husband wearing it makes me smile. In the background, Ella Fitzgerald croons.

"Nice apron."

He sets down the knife and holds up his hands to give the Nixon double peace sign along with a smarmy grin.

I laugh. "What you making?"

"Chaga mushroom lin-ghetti," Pen announces. "I found the mushroom on a tree in the woods."

I look at Leo. "Are you sure it's edible?"

"Almost sure," he says. "I fed a piece to Banjo, and he's still kicking, so I figure it's okay."

I look at Banjo, who, on hearing his name, thumps his tail three times.

"Where's Hannah?"

"Not sure," Leo says and returns to chopping tomatoes.

I drop my briefcase beside the table and head upstairs, hoping Hannah's not suffering another migraine.

I walk into the girls' room and bristle at the unmade bed and clothes strewed on the floor. I've talked to Leo about getting the kids to be more responsible, but obviously it hasn't done much good. We decided a long time ago that it wouldn't be right for me to have to be the hammer in the limited time I get to spend with them. The problem is confrontation is not Leo's strong suit, and I imagine him saying things like, "Hey, kids, do you think you could pitch in a little around the house?" or "How about we clean up so things look nice when Mom gets home?" to which they nod but don't actually do anything to change.

I pull up the flat sheet, then reach for the quilt, and that's when I notice a small mason jar on the bedside table and, beside it, a baggie of what looks like . . . *weed*?

I straighten, stunned. *Hannah? Really?* She's so uptight.

I bring the baggie to my nose and realize I'm mistaken. The dried leaves are more brown than green, and the smell is earthy and pungent, like an Indian spice. I twist the lid off the mason jar, surprised when my nose fills with the distinct scent of vodka. That's when I see the folded sheet of paper.

As I read it, my momma-bear hackles rise. *Who the hell is this person? A river witch? Who ever heard of such a thing? And why is she giving a fifteen-year-old alcohol? And what did she do to scare Pen?*

Ping, ping, ping—a five-alarm siren goes off in my head as I smell the liquid again, wondering if Hannah drank it, and if so, what it might have done to her, and where she is now. The jar is almost full, so she couldn't have had much of it, but still, what if it's poisonous or a hallucinogen? What if she's tripping at this very moment and has no idea what's happening?

I hurry downstairs.

"Leo, have you seen this?" I thrust the jar and baggie toward him.

It's Pen who answers. "It's the stuff that helps Hannah's headaches."

"She took it?" My ears are ringing now.

Pen looks at the floor, not wanting to rat out her sister but the truth obvious on her face.

I work to level my voice, though it still comes out tight. "Sweet Pea, no one's in trouble. I just want to know if Hannah's okay. Do you know where she is?"

Pen shakes her head, eyes still downcast.

Leo takes the note and reads it. Then he takes the jar, opens it, and sniffs.

"I think it's okay. Smells like vodka and grass."

"It's not okay!" I nearly screech. "We have no idea what that is or who the woman is who gave it to her."

He blinks rapidly, frozen by my outburst, and I watch his eyes flick side to side as he tries to decide the best way to respond.

Turning to Pen, he says, "Pea, the note says it's from a woman named Davina and that she scared you."

Pen's face snaps up to look at Leo, her eyes wide. "You were wrong!" she blurts. "You said she can't leave the river, but she can! Rock says she leaves all the time!"

"Rock?" I say, the conversation taking a bizarre Pen twist that sets my jacked-up nerves on fire. "A rock was talking to you about a witch?"

She shakes her head. "Rock is the boy who is painting the house."

"Oh," I say and realize I think I knew that.

"When did I say a witch can't leave the river?" Leo asks, sounding equally confused.

"Not the witch, the monster," Pen says.

"Monster?" I repeat, a headache forming between my eyes.

"The monster was real?" Leo says as if her answer makes sense.

"I told you; she lives in a triangle by the river and only has half a face."

Two of the dots connect.

"The woman who gave these things to Hannah lives in a house by the river?" I ask.

Pen nods.

I turn to Leo. "Near the river, there's an A-frame where the timber crews used to stay during the harvests." I have no idea what Pen means by "half a face" but let it go, the conversation already too bizarre to add to the strangeness. "And she scared you?" I ask.

Pen nods again. "She had a knife and had killed a rabbit."

Knife. Killed. Witch. Monster. Hannah!

I whirl for the door at the exact moment it opens and Hannah steps through.

14
LEO

Marie freezes in her tracks as Hannah bursts into the house, her hair wet and her cheeks flushed as if she just raced in from an unexpected summer storm. I look out the window to see cloudless dusk sky.

"Where have you been?" Marie snaps, her panic of the moment before transformed to anger.

Hannah looks from Marie to me, a question on her face. I hold up the jar, and Hannah's skin deepens from rose to crimson. Of all our kids, Hannah is the one least capable of lying, her high morals causing her Irish complexion to go ruddy each time she even considers it.

"I . . . I . . ."

"Tell me you didn't drink that," Marie says with a nod at the jar.

I pray the answer is no, and though Hannah doesn't answer, her guilt radiates. Dropping her eyes, she says, "It's for my headaches."

"Some stranger, who calls herself a witch, gives you a concoction, made from who knows what, and you drink it? Just like that? Without even considering what might be in it or how dangerous it could be?"

"Jags—" I start.

She shoots a glare, stopping me, clearly as displeased with me as she is with Hannah. She's right, of course. I was the one in charge of the kids today, and I had no idea any of this was happening. Since Bee died, I often find myself out of step, like I'm going through the motions of doing what I'm supposed to without actually focusing on it.

Marie marches to the sink and opens the baggie.

"No!" Hannah yelps. "Mom, don't!"

Marie doesn't stop. Unceremoniously, she dumps the tea down the disposal. Then she holds out her hand, and obediently, I give her the jar, and she pours it out as well.

When it's gone, she turns back and says, "Tomorrow, I'll talk to her and tell her she needs to leave."

"Leave?" Hannah says, her voice pitching high.

"Well, she can't continue to live there."

"Why not?"

"Because the cabin's not hers, and we're selling the property."

"But your grandfather said she could live there," Hannah says.

Marie and I both startle. I never met Marie's grandfather, but from what Marie's told me, he was a larger-than-life character who did things his own way and didn't care much what others thought about it.

"You talked to her?" Marie says as my hair prickles. Again, I'm wondering how I could have been so oblivious. Already, one of our children died on my watch because I wasn't paying close enough attention, and now, only moments ago, another was talking to a stranger living in an abandoned cabin in the woods, and I had absolutely no idea.

"You saw her?" Pen says, climbing down from the chair.

Hannah steps close and sets her hand on Pen's shoulder. "She's really sorry she scared you. She only looks that way because she was burned in a fire."

"But what about the rabbit?" Pen asks, chin trembling, her fear from yesterday returning.

"It was dead when she found it," Hannah says. "She was skinning it so it wouldn't go to waste. Rock's mom makes things with the fur."

Pen cocks her head, her face serious. "How'd it die?"

"In a trap. One Davina didn't set. It was bad timing, you walking up when you did."

"So she's not a monster?" Pen asks, still unsure.

I feel terrible for not believing her. I really thought she'd seen a shadow or a craggy tree.

"No," Hannah says, "just a really nice lady who was hurt in the war."

"She served?" I say as the pieces come together, "half a face" finally making sense.

Hannah lifts her eyes to mine. "She was a nurse in the army," she says, a plea in her voice, clearly already caring about the woman.

She knows the admiration I have for the men and women who protect our country. Both my father and grandfather were marines, and I carry a heavy burden of guilt knowing I didn't follow that hallowed path.

"And she knows about herbal cures from her mom," Hannah goes on. "The women in her family have been practicing folk medicine for generations."

Marie guffaws. "And you think that makes her more qualified than the best doctors in Connecticut?"

Marie and I differ when it comes to alternative methods and approaches to things. While she is entirely modern, I have a deep appreciation for the past and the notion that steeped in history and legend is often unconventional wisdom that not only often makes sense but also allows for the unknown and inexplicable. I look at the sink and wonder what was in the cures she poured out, knowing now that it was probably a folk remedy that had been handed down generation to generation and proved time and again to work.

Wisely, Hannah doesn't answer. Instead, turning back to Pen, she says, "You'd like her. She has cats and chickens, and she knows a lot about lots of things, sort of like you."

Marie shoots me a concerned look, the situation growing worse with each word Hannah utters. The woman is obviously not a drifter.

From the sounds of it, she's been living in the cabin for some time and believes she has the right to be there.

"She needs to leave," Marie says, knowing my tendency toward sympathy.

I nod, though my heart's not fully on board, struggling with the idea of telling a wounded veteran with cats and chickens who is "a really nice lady" that she needs to leave the home where she's probably lived for longer than Marie and I have been married.

"I'll talk to her in the morning," I say.

Though dreading it, I volunteer for several reasons. First, there's no way I'm letting Marie go alone to tell a knife-wielding ex-soldier living alone in the woods that she is being evicted. Second, I want to make up for today's dereliction. And last, I'm the better person for the job. While Marie's heart is large as a lion's when it comes to the people she loves, her business manner can verge on that of a stampeding rhino. She is efficient and straightforward, sometimes to the point of being blunt. I imagine her marching up to the woman and, with barely a hello, telling her she has three days to pack her things and go.

Marie's lips tighten, unsure. "You'll make sure she understands that she needs to be gone by the time the house goes on the market?"

I nod.

"Which is in less than a month?"

I nod again.

"And you'll tell her to stay away from the kids?" She holds up the empty jar.

Like a bobblehead, my head continues to nod as my heart twists tighter with the thought of it.

15
DAVINA

Hannah is great—smart, funny, and very sweet. As I wash the dishes from my rabbit-stew dinner, I think about our conversation, a smile in my heart. I was planting the fall garlic when she showed up with a basket of blueberry muffins to thank me for the migraine remedies I'd left.

I invited her to join me for some iced tea, and we spent the better part of an hour debating the greatest love story ever written. She's a fan of the nineteenth-century classics—the Brontës, Alcott, Austen—while I prefer the revolutionary writers who came after and took liberties and pushed boundaries—Tolstoy, Pasternak, Márquez.

"Read *Love in the Time of Cholera*, then tell me it's not one of the greatest love stories of all time," I said. "Your stories, while good, are so predictable. You know it's going to work out."

"Exactly," she said. "Which is the reason I love them." She giggled, making me smile, her laugh infectious, starting as a chuckle and ending with a guffaw, like an exclamation point on the end of her amusement.

Teddy, who is a very good judge of character, also took a liking and sat on the swing nuzzled against her leg, his tail swishing as Hannah rocked back and forth. Meanwhile, the three queens lounged in the late afternoon shade beside the cooler, less quick to make friends.

Hannah looked better than she did yesterday, her movements less gingerly and her face unstrained. I grabbed another muffin, though I'd already had two—I'm a sucker for sweets, and they were delicious—and held the basket toward her, but she shook her head.

"Why?" I asked, sensing the forced restraint.

"A moment on the lips, forever on the hips," she answered.

I tilted my head, not understanding.

"I'm fat," she said plainly.

I reared back. "You are? Says who?"

"The scale. The mirror."

"And the scale and mirror spoke to you and said, 'You're fat'?" I shook my head. "I think it's time to get a new scale and mirror."

The girl was tall and solidly built, her shoulders broad and her legs strong. Her body sagged as if gravity was weighing it down, but rather than seeing a girl overweight, I saw a body out of whack—her posture slumped and her vivacity, which at fifteen should be at its peak, low, like she was running on fumes. Chronic pain will do that.

"A body knows what it needs," I said. "If it's hungry, it needs food, simple as that, regardless of what some misguided mirror tells you."

She didn't answer, instead stroked Teddy under the chin as he mooned up at her.

"How's your head?" I asked, changing the subject.

"Better," she said. "Much better than it was."

"But not perfect?"

"It's never perfect."

"What you need is a reboot."

She smirked. "Sounds like a fine idea. Show me the switch, and I'll turn myself off, then back on."

"Well, that's one option. We could kill you, then resurrect you. Or . . . possibly a better idea . . . you can go for a swim." I nodded in the direction of the river.

"A swim?" she said, looking at me like I'd lost my marbles and proposed something truly outrageous, like strapping on fairy wings and launching herself off a cliff.

"You do know how to swim, don't you?"

"Yes."

"Never known a salmon to complain of a headache."

"And you've talked to a lot of salmon?"

I grinned. The kid was great. A wiseass and sharp as a tack.

"As a matter of fact, salmon and I go way back. And I'm telling you, they're onto something with the whole swimming-upstream thing."

"I've only ever swam in a pool," she said.

It was my turn to look stunned. "Really?" I said, thinking what a shame that was. Going in circles, surrounded by chemicals and walls. Where's the joy in that?

"Where we live, that's all there is," she said.

"Well, you're here now, and what you need is to go for a real swim, one that takes your breath away. Literally. What you do is swim hard as you can, long as you can, and when you're completely exhausted, you turn around and let the current carry you back." I tossed my head again in the direction of the water.

"Now?"

"Now's what we've got, and none of us knows about tomorrow."

She froze, the words touching a chord.

"I don't have a swimsuit."

"Only me and God watching, and we've both seen more naked bodies than either of us can count. Plus, you interrupted my planting. You swim. I'll garden. And we'll see how you feel when you're done."

I brushed the muffin crumbs from my pants as I stood, then walked toward the garden. I pretended not to care but, when I heard her footsteps heading toward the river, gave a silent cheer, knowing how hard it is for some people to believe in alternative approaches to healing. Though the notion of swimming in cold water to fix a headache is hardly revolutionary. In the same way an ice pack works to bring down swelling, submersion in cold water causes the vascular system to contract. And since excessive blood flow to the brain is a major contributor to migraines, lowering your body temperature just makes sense. And the exertion of swimming upstream opens the adrenal glands and creates endorphins, which in turn reduces the perception of pain. If taken to the point of exhaustion, a chemical reset can occur. And just like with a computer, sometimes a reboot is all a body needs.

I planted the remainder of the garlic, then went into the cabin and grabbed a jar of migraine tincture. When I got to the shore, I was surprised to see Hannah still swimming, her head a small dark dot in the distance. Her strength was impressive. I've been swimming the river for decades, and she had nearly reached the spot I swim to each day.

I sat in the lawn chair on the beach and looked at the water. It was my favorite time of the day, the sweet in-between moment when the light is soft and the air still warm. I lifted my face to the fading rays and let the warmth wash over me.

When I looked again, Hannah had stopped. I felt her breathlessness, then watched as she turned onto her back and then as the current took hold and carried her back. Not aware how quickly she was moving, she nearly drifted past but, at the last second, flailed from the river's hold and paddled her way to shore. She walked from the water, bashful and elated, her arms crossed over her bra and an enormous smile on her face.

I held out a towel, and she wrapped it around herself.

"Wow," she said, her smile so wide I thought her cheeks must hurt. "That's the craziest thing I've ever done." She looked over her shoulder at the water. "That was . . . it was . . . just wow."

I laughed at her astonishment, unable to help it. Normally, I do my best not to laugh in the company of people I've just met, knowing how particularly gruesome it is, my mouth turning into a gaping hole. But either Hannah didn't notice or didn't care because she laughed right along with me, a giggle of pure delight with her signature guffaw at the end.

I can tell a lot about a person by how they react to my scars. Some can't take the sight, either from too much empathy or too little. The former wince or tear up, and the latter sneer or shy away as if the wounds might be contagious. Then there are those who work too hard to pretend they're unaffected, as if not reacting proves what a good person they are. They laugh too loud at everything I say and constantly compliment me on things like my hair or eyes. Then there are the rare few like Hannah, people who notice but then, within a few minutes, move past it. Their eyes connect easily, and it's as if they've filled in the blanks and no longer see the wounded parts, just me.

I opened the tincture, extracted a dropperful, and held it toward her. "Now's when you should take the tincture. It's best if you hold it under your tongue and let it dissolve."

Hannah squirted the liquid into her mouth, wrinkled her nose, and grimaced; then she squeezed her eyes tight and stamped her feet, determined not to spit it out or swallow.

After several seconds, she opened her eyes, shook her head, and whinnied like a horse. "Yuck."

I chuckled. "Feverfew. Has a bit of a bitter kick."

"Feverfew?"

"Looks like a daisy and works wonders on headaches."

She asked how I knew about such things, and I told her about being a nurse in the army and about my second mother passing her knowledge of herbs and remedies down to me.

When we reached the cabin, I asked, "How's the noggin?"

She tilted her head one way, then the other, then shook it back and forth rapidly, as if testing it. When she stopped, she looked at me, amazed, her blue eyes wide. "It's gone! Oh my God! My brain! I don't feel it!"

I chuckled again.

"Thank you!" she said and flung the arm not holding the towel around me in an unexpected hug. I jolted with the shock of it, and she leaped away. "I'm sorry. Did I hurt you?"

I blinked rapidly and shook my head, then looked away to hide the welling in my eyes. And I realized it had been a long time since I'd been touched.

"Best if you take the tincture in the morning," I said to hide my embarrassment. "After you swim."

"Wait. So I'm not cured?"

"If you take the tincture every day, gradually it will build up in your system and become preventive, but at the moment, it's only a remedy, not a cure. Swim, then tincture: the more regularly you do it, the quicker your system will adjust."

Her mouth set into a line of determination. "Got it," she said, then leveled her eyes on mine and solemnly added, "Thank you. You're amazing."

No, I think as I put my plate in the cupboard, my heart still aglow from the brightness of her visit. *Feverfew is amazing. I'm just the lucky lady who learned about it from her mother.*

16
PENELOPE

I stare at the morning sunlight peeking through the slit in the curtains and think about the lady I believed was a monster, her scary face not what I thought. It hurts my heart to think about, knowing how even a small burn stings.

"Hannah?" I say to Hannah's back.

She grumbles. "I'm sleeping."

"Do you think I can meet her?"

"Who?"

"Davina."

"Why?"

"I don't know."

It's not true. I know the reasons. First, despite what Hannah said, I'm still scared, like the fear of that first sight is still part of me. And second, because of the butterfly. Bee led me there, and I know it was for a reason.

"Mom doesn't want us to talk to her," Hannah mumbles and shifts away, hoping I'll leave her alone so she can go back to sleep.

"Mom only told Dad to tell her to stay away from us. She didn't say anything about us going to her."

Hannah's quiet, which means she's considering it. Which is surprising since Hannah's a rule follower. She is always on time, never looks at the answers to a crossword puzzle in the back of the book, and always counts in full *Mississippi*s when she's it in hide-and-seek. Which means something's up.

"Hannah?"

She turns to face me, her eyes sleepy. "It worked," she says.

"What worked?"

"The stuff Mom poured down the sink. I took some of it yesterday when I went to see Davina, and my headache went away."

There are tears in her eyes, which makes me feel terrible for her. I can't imagine what it must be like to have headaches so bad it's hard to open your eyes. And she gets them so often now, almost every day.

A single tear escapes to run down her cheek to the pillow.

"Already, I feel it coming back," she says, her voice cracking. "Like I'm lying here just waiting for a slow-moving train to slam into my head."

And I feel myself get angry. I hate her stupid headaches. And I double hate the idea that there's something that can fix them, and Mom's too worried about the monster . . . I mean, Davina . . . to let Hannah take it.

"So we need to get more of it," I say.

"We can't."

"We can," I huff. Unlike Hannah, I have no trouble bending the rules.

"Pen—"

"No! We'll just go and tell Davina what happened, that Mom poured it down the sink, and that you need more."

"I don't know," Hannah says, but I can tell she's wavering.

"How about we just go there so I can meet her?" I say, then push up to my knees so I'm looking down at her. *"Please?"*

Hannah's mouth skews to the side. "I suppose it would be nice to see her again before she has to move."

I leap from the bed. "Exactly! Let's go."

"Now?"

"Yes. We need to go before Mom and Dad wake up." I'm a master at being sneaky.

We dress quickly and, carrying our shoes, tiptoe from the house.

"Morning!"

I nearly jump out of my skin at the voice, and both of us turn to see Rock on a ladder, a scraper in his hand.

"Where you off to so early?" he asks.

"To see Davina," I say.

"So you met her?"

He climbs down.

"Hannah did. And I want to meet her before she leaves."

His head cocks to the side. "Leaves? Where's she going?"

"She can't live in the cabin anymore," I say.

"She can't? Why not?"

Hannah answers, her eyes flicking to his before dropping to the ground, "Because we're selling the property, and we can't sell it with her in the cabin."

"You're kicking her out of her home?" Rock says, the friendliness of the moment before gone.

"Technically, the cabin is ours," Hannah mutters, her bare foot toeing the dirt.

"She's been here a hell of a lot longer than you have!" Rock roars, sending Hannah back a step and me darting behind her.

"Sorry," he mutters, but Hannah shakes her head, grabs my hand, and pulls me toward the woods.

The sticks and pebbles bruise my bare feet, but Hannah doesn't stop until we're well in the trees and out of sight of Rock.

Angrily, Hannah tugs on her sneakers, and I'm not sure if it's Rock or Mom she's mad at.

"Let's go," she says irritably as she stands.

We follow the trail, and though I was the one who said I wanted to do this, each step makes me want to turn around and race back to the house. And when I see the tip of the roof through the trees, I lose my courage altogether and stop, my heart pounding so hard it thumps in my brain.

Hannah turns. "Pen?"

I shake my head.

She returns to where I am. "It's okay. I promise." She takes my hand. "Trust me."

I close my fingers around hers and allow her to lead me forward, but when we make the turn and I see the woman on the porch, her feet on the railing and a mug in her hand, I stop again, my breath stuck in my throat. Her face is exactly as I remember—red and raw with half a nose and a hole where her mouth should be. I try to pull away, but Hannah holds tight.

"Morning, Davina!" she says brightly.

"Morning!" Davina answers, then stands and sets the mug on the table.

"This is my sister, Pen. She wanted to meet you."

She walks toward us, then, seeming to realize my fear, stops. "I was about to make some breakfast. Perhaps you girls would like to join me?"

"That would be great," Hannah says as I shake my head.

Hannah looks at me. "Pen—"

Then she says something I don't hear because, as she's saying it, a butterfly flutters past, blue with a blink of white on its wings. Heart thumping wildly, I watch as it flies to a garden beside the house, where it joins dozens, maybe hundreds, of others.

"Pen, perhaps you can help me gather the eggs while Hannah goes for a swim?" Davina says, pulling my attention back.

"That's a great idea," Hannah says and pries her hand from mine.

"This way," Davina says and turns for the house as Hannah walks toward a trail that must lead to the water.

From beside the steps, Davina picks up a basket, then continues to a fenced yard with at least a dozen chickens. I look again at the butterflies, take a deep breath, and force myself to follow.

The chickens scatter as we walk into the yard toward a tower of colorful stacked crates lined with hay.

"Lucky day," Davina says as she bends down and reaches into a blue crate on the bottom. "Hens must have known we were expecting company."

She pulls out two brown eggs, sets them in the basket, then hands the basket to me.

"Chickens have a way of knowing things before they happen," she says.

I look at the eggs resting on top of a kitchen towel, amazed. The only eggs I've ever seen or touched have come from a cardboard box from the grocery store.

She moves crate to crate and adds eight more eggs to the first two; then we walk back to the house.

"Leave them there," she says, pointing to the steps.

I set the basket down, and she picks up another, then leads me toward the garden.

"How come you have so many butterflies?" I ask.

"They like my plants. You like butterflies?"

I hesitate before saying, "It's how my sister visits."

I wait for her to give me the look everyone gives when I talk about Bee still being here, like I'm making it up because I'm sad that she's dead. But Davina doesn't do that. As a matter of fact, she doesn't respond at all, and I wonder if she didn't hear me.

When we reach the edge of the garden, she points to a row of spindly sticks with scrawny vines tied to them and says, "We need ten of those cherry tomatoes."

I search for the reddest ones, counting as I go.

As I pull off the last one, I say, "Once she was a bird."

The back of her head bobs, and she continues on.

"Spicy or mild?" she asks, stopping in front of some pepper plants.

I don't like peppers, but I don't want to be rude, so I say, "Probably not too spicy."

She points to some long yellow peppers. "Two of those."

I pick off the peppers and add them to the basket.

"My sister would have liked this. She loved cooking and making up recipes."

"Sounds like she has a great spirit," she says.

I stop. *Has*, not *had*? I'm not sure if she did it on purpose.

My heart thumps strangely, and I look again at the butterflies.

"She does," I say as I hurry to catch up. "Though she's dead now, so she can't do things like cook anymore."

She nods as if that makes perfect sense. "Then I suppose you need to do the cooking for the both of you. Tell me something she made."

I smile as the answer pops into my head. "Last year, for my mom's birthday, we made green eggs and ham because it's our mom's favorite Dr. Seuss book."

She chuckles. "Personally, I'm a *Horton Hears a Who!* fan. Always had a thing for elephants. But I like that one as well."

"That's my favorite also!" I say, unable to believe it. Everyone always picks *Cat in the Hat* or *Green Eggs and Ham* or *How the Grinch Stole Christmas!* But Whoville is awesome, and Horton's like the best hero ever.

"How were the green eggs?" she asks.

"Very green," I say with a giggle. "Green food coloring is powerful stuff. We ended up with green eggs, green potatoes, green Spam, green counters, and green us."

We thought Mom was going to kill us. Dad cleaned up most of it before she saw, but there are still a few light-green spots on the cabinets, and we needed to throw out the spatula, the plate, and our T-shirts.

"Sounds like a wonderful surprise," she says.

I nod because it was, and only after she smiles do I realize I'm looking at her, and though her mouth is still a hole, I'm no longer scared.

"Now, all we need is an onion," she says.

We walk to the far end of the garden, where a patch of thin green blades stick out in clumps from the soil.

"The way you know an onion's ready," she says, "is if it's crowning and the tops are yellow and falling over."

I point to one that looks like she described, and she nods. I dig it out and it's perfect, almost the size of my hand, golden skinned and smudged with dirt. Bee really would have loved this.

"Something wrong?" she asks.

"Bee didn't like onions," I say, still staring at it. "But I do. Which is weird because we are . . . were . . . twins."

"Still your twin," she says matter of factly and takes the onion from me, then brings it to her nose and inhales deeply. "Just 'cause someone's gone doesn't mean they're not still a part of us."

Then, not realizing I was going to say it aloud until the words are leaving my mouth, I mutter, "I'm afraid I'm going to forget."

As if she didn't hear me, she puts the onion in the basket and starts back for the cabin, and I think I probably shouldn't have said anything. People, especially adults, don't know how to deal with the weird things I feel about Bee now that she's gone.

I trudge behind her, still thinking about peppers and onions and how Bee liked one and not the other, and how I like the other but not the first, when she says, "Best way I've found for remembering someone is to keep them around." She sets the basket beside the eggs. "Come with me." She holds out her hand.

I'm surprised how comfortable I am taking it, the skin warm and the palm rough.

She leads me back to the garden to where the butterflies are. At least a hundred white admirals and monarchs flutter and perch on plants bursting with purple, pink, and blue flowers.

Nodding to a bush with cotton candy–pink flowers that look like fireworks, she says, "This is bee balm." She gives an eyebrow lift. "Butterflies are crazy for it."

Bee balm, I think, the name wonderful. *Bee's balm.* Or *Bee's bomb,* which Bee would like better, the blossoms like little explosions.

From a leather holder on her belt, she takes out a folding knife and opens it. The blade glints in the sun and makes me think of the first time I saw her, though this knife isn't as scary, the blade barely the length of her finger. Taking hold of one of the flowers by its stem, she pulls it toward her.

"When you're taking a cutting, you want to cut below a set of leaves and no more than six inches from the top."

The knife must be very sharp because it slices clean through the stalk.

"Then you remove the lower leaves."

She slashes them off.

"When we get to the cabin, I'll dip it in honey and put it in water. And when you get to the house, you'll need to put it in a sunny place and change the water every few days."

She waits for me to nod, then goes on. "When the roots are a few inches long, you plant it."

She folds the knife and returns it to its holder, then holds the flower out to me.

As I take it, she says, "When my second mom died, I felt a lot like you do."

"Second mom?" I ask, bringing the flower to my nose, surprised to find it smells like mint.

"My first mom died when I was six, and my second mom adopted me."

"Oh," I say, feeling bad for her, unable to imagine how awful my life would be without my mom.

"When my second mom died, it was really hard, and like you, I was worried I'd forget. So I decided instead I'd keep her around."

"How?" I say, feeling myself get angry. *How are you supposed to keep someone around when they drowned in a stupid pool?* "She's gone."

"Yes and no. No one loved is ever truly gone. And if we keep them in our heart"—she touches her fist to her chest—"we are able to keep them with us. My way of doing that is to collect things I know my second mom would like." She nods to the bee balm, and as if the words are a spell, I feel it. Looking at the flower makes me think of Bee like she is here.

"I collect all sorts of things," she goes on. "Pine cones, heart stones, quotes from books I want to share."

"You still do it?" I say, thinking by the way she's talking that her mom's been gone a long time.

"Yep. Just yesterday, I saved one of the rabbit's feet from that hare I found. My mom was a big believer that you could never have too much luck."

I think of the rabbit. He had four rabbit's feet, and it didn't work out so well for him. Bee would have cracked up over that.

"I keep the things in a satchel she used to carry," she goes on. "I need to clear it out now and then. Can't fit a lifetime into a bag the size of a bucket. But I enjoy taking the things out as much as I enjoyed putting them in."

I think about all the things I want to share with Bee, especially about this morning—the chickens, the garden, Davina, the bee balm. We start back for the cabin, and it's all I can do not to race back to the house with the flower and get started. Already, I know where I will keep our new memories. When we turned six, our grandmother gave Bee a wooden pirate chest with a lock that opens with a key. I got an ant farm. The chest is under her bed, and the key is taped to the bottom of our top dresser drawer. It's perfect. Until we go home, I'll keep our treasures in my backpack.

Hannah appears, wet and smiling.

"Good swim?" Davina asks.

"Amazing!" Hannah says, lit up in a way I haven't seen in a really long time.

Remembering the other reason we came here, I say, "We need more of the headache medicine."

Davina looks at Hannah. "What happened to the jar I gave you?"

Hannah looks at the ground and doesn't answer, so I say, "Our mom poured it down the sink."

"Oh," Davina says; then she's quiet a moment before she says exactly what I knew she was going to say. "I'm sorry, but I'm afraid if your mom doesn't want you to have it, I can't give it to you."

Hannah's brow furrows, and I can almost feel her headache returning.

"Maybe some breakfast will help," Davina says, but I hear the doubt in her voice.

She picks up the two baskets and walks into the cabin.

Hannah and I sit at the table, and the cat I saw the first day strolls up and rubs against my leg. He's the biggest cat I've ever seen, nearly the size of Banjo, his fur every color of gray imaginable and his face like a lion's.

"Hey, Teddy," Hannah says, and he moves from me to her.

I hear Davina humming through the open window as the delicious smell of onions and eggs drifts past, and I look from the window to Teddy to Hannah. "We can't tell her to leave," I say. "This is her home."

17
BRENDON

I'm in the woods walking toward the cabin everyone's been talking about. In my backpack is my laptop and some snacks. Banjo lopes along beside me, his tail wagging as his head darts this way and that, excited by all the sounds around us.

At least one of us is happy, this place perfect for dogs but not for anyone interested in more than chasing squirrels and running after butterflies. We've only been here two days, and already I feel like I'm going to lose my mind. Mom is reading. Dad is on a run. The girls are doing a puzzle. Mom said I should take up a hobby like guitar or painting. I'd rather watch cheese melt.

But then, a few minutes ago, a glimmer of hope. Pen and Hannah were talking as they did their puzzle, and Pen asked Hannah how the woman squatting in the cabin by the river knew about the latest *Dancing with the Stars*, and Hannah said it's because she has satellite internet.

Which means . . . if I get close enough . . . and if the network isn't password protected . . . I can log in. Boredom problem solved!

The pointed tip of the roof appears through the trees, along with two satellite dishes tacked to the left side. *Yes!* I give a fist pump, then scan for a place to sit. I step toward a fallen log to my left at the exact moment a loud hiss causes me to jump and whirl. On the trail, a dozen feet away, the largest cat I've ever seen crouches low as it faces off against Banjo, its back arched and its long gray fur bristled. Banjo bares his teeth and growls.

I open my mouth to call him, but before I can get the words out, the cat leaps, flying at him with its razor-sharp claws extended. The left paw swipes Banjo's nose, and he yowls. Spinning, he snaps, but the cat dodges the bite and swipes him again, ripping his back leg and causing another painful cry.

I step toward them, thinking I'll get between them, but when the cat turns its yellow glare on me, I stop.

Coward!

The cat returns to the fight and lashes Banjo again.

One of those moments, I think, tears in my eyes, followed by, *Another of those moments!* The kind that lives inside you and you never forget.

"Scat!"

A woman runs toward us, a broom wielded over her head. Her face is exactly as Pen described, scarred from the nose down. She swings the broom down, and I nearly cry out with relief until I realize she's aiming it at Banjo.

"Stop!" I scream as she swipes him sideways, brushing him backward as if trying to sweep him into the woods.

Dropping the broom, she scoops the cat into her arms. It writhes against her, but she holds it tight. "Settle down," she says into its fur. "The dog is leaving."

Banjo simpers as he limps, wounded, into the trees.

The woman juts her chin at me, signaling for me to follow.

I shoot a hateful glare, then hurry to Banjo, who stands quivering on the path, part of his right ear dangling and his back left paw suspended off the ground. I lift him into my arms and stumble toward the house as rage and shame consume me.

"You're okay," I wheeze. "I'll get you home, and Mom will take you to the vet. You'll be okay. I promise. I'm sorry. I'm so, so sorry."

We break from the trees, and Mom, who is on the porch, sees us and hurries our way.

"What happened?" she says as she takes Banjo.

"The witch," I gasp, my breath coming in gulps.

"The witch?"

"The woman in the cabin."

"The woman in the cabin did this?" She looks at Banjo, who is squirming to get down.

I bend over and brace my hands on my knees as I suck oxygen into my lungs, my side cramping. "Her cat. It attacked him."

"Oh, Banjo," she says and kisses Banjo on his head.

"I tried to stop it!" I cry.

"Are you hurt?"

Banjo's blood is on my shirt and hands. I look at it and grow woozy at the sight, my vision blurring in and out of focus. I stumble back and catch myself.

"Bren, did the cat scratch you?"

My head sways, and I feel like I might be sick.

"She . . . she had a broom . . ." I stagger back again. "And she hit Banjo."

"She what?" Mom's voice pitches high.

"She hit him."

Mom sets Banjo on the ground, examines his face, then his leg. "Your dad will be back soon. When he gets here, have him take Banjo to the animal hospital."

"Why can't you take us?" I ask, my wind returning, though my head still spins.

"Because I need to tell that woman to get the hell off our property."

18
MARIE

Enough! If Leo's not going to handle this, I will. I stomp into the woods, almost happy to have somewhere to focus my rage. This morning, he said he wanted to go for a run before talking to her. Now it's nearly ten, and he's still not back, and Banjo is hurt, and Brendon's distraught. As if the kid hasn't already been through enough.

Leo and his stupid runs.

It's what he had been doing when Bee drowned.

I huff angrily through my nose, trying to check the thought, knowing it's not fair.

Not his fault. Not Hannah's fault. Not Brendon's fault.

No one to blame.

Over and over, I tell myself this, rationally knowing it to be true. Leo needs to be able to exercise. Hannah's headaches are real. Brendon had been watching the twins like he was supposed to. Bee went back in the pool without permission, but she had no way of knowing the floatie had a leak.

Bad luck. A confluence of unfortunate circumstance. Not anyone's fault. Just the way things happened. Awful. Horrible. Regrettable. But guiltless. Ugh!

As much as I try to convince myself, it is impossible, feeling that something so terrible must have a reason, a genesis, a source. Pain this deep cannot simply be chalked up to random happenstance, some arbitrary fluke without intention or error.

Tears sting my eyes as I wonder for the millionth time, *Why? Why us?* If no one is to blame, then what did we do to deserve this?

The day it happened I was entirely unaware. The morning started like any other day. The twins were at the table eating cereal. Pen was reading one of the Harry Potter books. Bee was reading the back of the Cap'n Crunch box. She was slumped with her chin on her forearm as she chewed.

"Off to fight the battle of budgets," I said merrily, punching my fist in the air as if signaling a charge; then I dropped a kiss on each of their heads and continued out the door.

Those were the last words I said to her: *Off to fight the battle of budgets.* I think about it constantly, wishing I had said something better. A single tear leaks, and I swipe it away.

Forward, forward, forward . . .

Six hours later, my cell phone rang with the Super Mario Bros. theme song—Leo's ringtone, a nod to our college pastime of playing the vintage game endlessly in his dorm room. I remember being irritated because I don't like being interrupted at work.

"Hospital" and "Bee" were the only words I heard, though I know Leo said more.

I raced to the emergency room, still convinced it was going to be okay, having blocked out the impossible words "drowned" and "*tried* to resuscitate her." It took several more retellings before the words would finally stick.

Brendon was watching them. It's the piece I stumble over again and again. *If he was watching, how did she drown?*

I shake my head to clear it away, but the treacherous thought remains. *Watching* means keeping an eye on someone for the sole purpose of keeping them safe. It means being vigilant and aware. I understand Bee went back in the pool after she'd gotten out. I also know there have been plenty of times when I've lost track of one or another of my kids. Especially Bee, who had a penchant for getting into trouble, skirting the rules, and dodging authority. But regardless of all that, the niggle remains. Because at the end of the day, my honeybee is gone. And each time I think of it, my heart seizes and my brain spirals to the horrible moment of her death, and I can't get a breath, like I am drowning with her, my heart swelling with pain until I think it will burst.

I'm terrified Brendon knows, that he hears my thoughts despite how hard I work to conceal them. It's a big part of the reason we need to move. It was so much worse when we were home, the pool just outside the door and reminders of Bee everywhere. My thoughts ricocheting from her to him and back again each time I caught sight of it.

Brain on fire, I reach the clearing, the A-frame in front of me, mostly how I remember it but also transformed—a ramshackle porch now tacked to the front with a tattered yellow umbrella and a table with two chairs. A woman sits in one with her feet crossed on the railing, a book in one hand and a steaming mug in the other. So content I feel like I might explode.

Noticing me, she stands. She's taller than I thought, at least my height, and her posture is ramrod straight. In my mind, she was small and hermit-like—bent and crooked—witchlike. Her hair is long, straight, and black except for a few silver strands. And her scars are exactly as Hannah described, the bottom half of her face ravaged by burns.

She reaches me and extends her hand. "Hello, I'm Davina."

She says it as if we are meant to be friends, and I think she must be crazy. Only moments before, I was holding my bleeding dog and consoling my child from trauma she caused. I ignore the outstretched palm, and she drops it to her side.

Then, seeming to realize the situation, she says, "Sorry about your dog. Unfortunately, the cat he ran into is rather protective of his territory."

My eyes narrow, and my anger grows. *His* territory? *Our* territory. This is *our* property. *Our* cabin.

"If you'd like, I have a poultice you can put on the wounds."

"Keep your snake oils to yourself," I hiss. "You had no business giving that hocus-pocus hogwash to my daughter."

She doesn't react, not even a blink. Instead, after a beat, she says, "You're Marie?" It's more statement than question. "Your grandfather spoke of you."

"Funny," I say, "he never spoke of you."

The top of her left cheek, unmarred, twitches.

"I first came here before the house was built and returned after your family stopped visiting."

I don't know if I imagine it, but I believe there's a note of contempt in the words.

"We weren't aware anyone was living here," I say.

Her brow lifts. "Been here going on twenty-two years."

I try not to react, but know I did, because again the cheek tics. *Twenty-two years!*

When my grandfather passed, we considered visiting to deal with the estate, but Leo and I were in our final semester of college and taking time off to come to New Hampshire as well as to attend his funeral in Maine at the veterans' cemetery seemed impossible. We decided paying our respects was more important. I planned to come that summer, but after graduation, we both got jobs in DC, and by the time we moved back to Connecticut, we had kids and simply never got around to it.

"Had I realized you were here," I say, measuring my tone, "I would have addressed this sooner."

Her brow lifts again in question.

"We're selling the property," I say, "which means you need to leave."

I've never seen the point in beating around the bush when it comes to business matters. It was my grandfather who taught me: *Pulling a Band-Aid off slowly only prolongs the pain and still hurts just as much.*

Her eyes tighten on mine. "Leave?"

"The cabin was never meant to be a home."

"That's not what your grandfather thought."

"Well, unfortunately he's not here to say what he thought."

Her eyes tick side to side as if considering something.

Finally she says, "Is that all you came to say?"

"That, and that I'd appreciate you staying away from my kids."

Her nostril opens and closes once. "They came here."

"I'll make it clear to them to leave you be." Then, perhaps out of sympathy or perhaps out of regard for my grandfather, I add, "You're welcome to use our driveway to move your things."

"That won't be necessary."

I nod to the A-frame and the clutter around it. "You need to take your stuff. You can't just leave it."

"It won't be necessary," she says, "because I have no intention of leaving."

"Perhaps I didn't make myself clear—"

"Oh no. You were perfectly clear. But as I said, I've been here a long time, and this is my home, and your grandfather gave me permission to live here."

"You have proof of that?"

"I have his word."

"My grandfather is dead."

"A man's word doesn't die with him."

"Actually, it does."

Again there is a pause.

"Tell me, Marie, why, after all these years, are you selling it?"

"None of your business," I spit, regretting the flare of temper and that I've let her get the better of me.

"But it is. You come here telling me I need to leave my home, the place where I've built my life. I'd say I deserve an explanation."

"We have no use for it."

"But it's not costing you anything. The harvests pay for the upkeep."

"We're buying a new house."

"A more expensive house?"

"Again, none of your business." I hold her stare, determined to remain calm, though inside, my blood is pumping. This conversation is not going at all how I planned.

"He was right about you," she says.

"You know nothing about me."

"Aah, but I do. As I said, your grandfather spoke of you. He said you were his favorite, though you left him like the rest."

I flinch, and the cheek twitches.

"I don't need to explain myself to you. The property was left to my family, and unlike you, I have a will to prove it."

"Your grandfather had a will?" she says with another eyebrow lift, showing how well she in fact knew my grandfather, a man who never saw the need for contracts or lawyers. It was my grandmother who left the property in a trust to the grandchildren, and I'm quite certain my grandfather knew nothing about it. My sister and cousins didn't want anything to do with it, so years ago, Leo and I bought them out.

"Out of respect for him, I'll give you two weeks," I say.

Ignoring me, she goes on. "He said you had a great mind and believed someday you'd do great things." Her eyes sparkle, almost as if enjoying this. "Your problem, he said, was that you were never quite satisfied. As he put it, you always had your eye on the prize instead of the good fortune at your feet."

"Two weeks," I spit, anger sizzling. The woman knows how to wound, her words bringing a painful echo of my grandfather into my head. *Marie, happiness shouldn't need to be chased. It's with you all the time, wherever you choose to look.*

"Two weeks, a year," she says with a shrug. "As I said, I have no intention of leaving."

Calmly she turns, leaving me glaring at her ramrod-straight back. She walks to the porch, pauses to pick up her book and mug, then continues inside and closes the door behind her.

Our door. *Our* cabin. On property left to *us*.

19

DAVINA

Despite the calm I showed Marie, my heart pounds. It took all my military training and years of experience as a trauma nurse to conceal my true emotions, the conversation deeply upsetting.

Leave? Impossible. Where would I go?

I close my eyes and pull oxygen deep into my lungs, resisting the urge to claw at the edges of my scars, which have started to itch. It happens when I'm stressed, the severed nerves trying to connect with what's been lost.

She showed up looking for a fight, stomping toward me with her chin thrust out and fists balled. She scanned my wounds, then ignored them, which I appreciated.

I assume she was upset about the dog, which I do feel bad about, though there's not much I could have done. Teddy's a coon, more wild than domestic, and like me, this is his home. I stepped in as soon as I saw what was happening, swatted the dog back and scooped Teddy into my arms. But Teddy had already gotten in a few good swipes, and the dog was a bit tattered.

I don't understand why the boy didn't break it up. You see two animals going at it, you get between them. Of course, I've seen everything in war, and I know it's never clear how anyone will react in a fight. I've seen the biggest, baddest men freeze at the first sign of combat and the meekest mice turn into superheroes. A few kicks at Teddy or a swat with a stick, and he'd have run off. Most cats know better than to tussle with humans.

Marie was definitely upset, coming at me the way she did, telling me I had two weeks to pack my things and go, then offering her driveway as a consolation as if tossing me a bone.

I probably shouldn't have antagonized her the way I did with that stuff about the colonel. But I've never been good at letting go of grudges, especially when it comes to those who have hurt people I love. Her abandonment did a real number on him. The others he could get over, but his relationship with Marie was special, and when she cut him out of her life so completely the way she did, it left a tender, lasting scar.

The colonel saved me. Twice. The first time I don't remember well. I was only six and saw him less than a day. But the second is clear as light. When I made it stateside, he was waiting. I still couldn't speak, the grafts on my face too tender, and I was heavily sedated. But I was aware enough for tears to form when I saw him—the first familiar face I'd seen since I'd woken over three months before.

He looked old, much older than the two years that had passed since my last visit. I was thirty-six. He was seventy-four. My whole life, he'd seemed immortal, like King Neptune or Zeus—larger than life and indomitable. But that day, he was smaller, his posture stooped, and his once-blond hair white.

He took my hand, and his ice-blue eyes, ageless, locked on mine as he said, "I've come to take you home."

The tears leaked, not from the pain, which was constant those days, but from relief. Since I'd regained consciousness and discovered my husband had abandoned me and taken our daughter with him, I didn't know what would come of me. My mother was gone, and I had no other family. My disfigurement, along with the deeper wounds I carried inside, would make being a nurse again or living a normal life impossible. But there he was, just as my mother promised, waiting with an open heart and the promise of a new beginning.

It took several months before I was well enough to be released, and those first weeks at the cabin were nearly unbearable. The pain was constant and so intense I was sure I would lose my mind, and the nightmares that haunted me each time I closed my eyes were worse.

The colonel never left my side. He slept on an inflatable mattress beside the ladder to the loft, tended to my wounds, fed me, and kept me from going mad. Most of that time I don't remember, the days a blur of terror and pain, along with a few stunning shocks of euphoria—a sunrise that made me cry, the first time my damaged tongue recognized the sweet taste of a raspberry.

I'd like to say I thought of my daughter, Rose, and sometimes I did, but mostly I thought of my second mother, desperate for her comfort because I was hurting so bad.

Almost two years to the day after he brought me home, he died. He left the cabin one night after a dinner of fire-roasted trout and potatoes and never returned. By then, the pain was manageable, and I'd started to make a life. I had taken up my second mother's work of providing tinctures and teas along with delivering babies to the folks in the area who couldn't afford doctors and hospitals.

It was lonely without the colonel, and constantly I ached for Rose, but I managed. Then a few years after his passing, Rock came along, and suddenly, I was part of something new. And now, here I am, years later, with a life full of purpose, beauty, and love. An existence that, until a few minutes ago, I believed would continue until the end of my days.

I blow out a breath and open my eyes, relieved when I look through the window to see Marie gone. My burns still itching, I hurry to the river, strip off my clothes, and wade into the icy current. Diving beneath the surface, I swim until I feel like my lungs are going to explode, then burst upward and start to stroke. The current is strong, and I welcome the struggle, images of the colonel and my mothers and the past spiraling through my mind like a photo reel.

When I'm exhausted to the point where I can't take another stroke, I turn on my back, look up at the crystal-blue sky, and let the current carry me back. *What will be will be, and there's not a damn thing you can do about it.* I smile at how clear the colonel's voice is in my head.

I pass the willow and break from the current to swim to shore. I'm halfway there when I look up to see Rock in the lawn chair, his thick body straining the aluminum frame.

"Well, turn around," I say as I worm my way along the riverbed.

He smirks the goofy grin I've known all his sixteen years, then pushes to his feet and turns to face the trees.

I grab a towel from the chest in my boat and wrap it around myself.

"I'm going to the house to get dressed," I say. "You want a Coke?"

He nods, then plops back into the chair.

I hurry to the cabin, pull on my clothes, grab a Coke for him and a Fanta for me, then return. I sit on the rail of my boat, and we clink bottles.

"How was your swim?" he asks.

"Cold."

He smirks, then looks down at his Coke.

"Something on your mind?"

Rock has the worst poker face on the planet. His emotions float across his wide-open face like reflections on a pond, and the tips of his ears turn crimson whenever he's upset.

"Have you met the people living in the house?" he asks.

"All of them but the dad."

He looks surprised. "You even met the mom?"

"She paid a visit right before I went for my swim."

He must notice the small tremor in my voice because he says, "So you know she's aiming to sell the timberland?"

"That's what she said."

"And that they want you to leave?"

I nod, and his ears go from pink to Christmas red.

"So what are you going to do?" he asks.

"I don't reckon anything."

His sandy brows furrow, and he turns the Coke between his hands.

"Stop fretting, you'll give yourself a permanent divot in that thick skull of yours. Just because someone tells you to do something doesn't mean you do it."

Though his chin is still hairless, in the past few months, his features have grown more chiseled, revealing the strong man he will someday soon become. But at the moment, he's still a boy, sweet and naive, full of the innocent belief that the world is just and people mostly kind.

"So you're not leaving?" he asks, the tone a cross between relief and uncertainty.

"Everyone leaves at some point, but I'm not planning on going anywhere until this old body is ready to be carried out feet first to Arlington." Not wanting to talk about it anymore, I move on to something new. "I found a hare in a trap a couple days ago—"

"I heard."

"You did?"

"Danny Canton's not too happy."

"Figured it was him."

Danny Canton's been a thorn in my side since his family took over the bait shack in Franklin six years ago. The family has five kids, all of them rotten, but Danny, the oldest, is odd on top of being nasty, his brain not firing on all cylinders, and ever since he moved here, he's made a habit of setting traps in the timberland no matter how many of them I sink or curses I cast.

I smirk. "Is he itching?"

"It's not funny," Rock says. He rubs the palm not holding his Coke on his jeans. "Something's not right with that guy, and he's pretty worked up."

I wave my hand. "He'll get over it."

"I don't know." Rock shakes his head with worry. "He's been going on to anyone who will listen about you being a witch and that you got your scars because you escaped being burned at the stake."

Some might laugh at such a far-fetched tale, but I got my scars serving my country, and eight brave men died on the same mission, so for me, there's nothing the least bit funny about someone diminishing it.

My voice low and rumbly, I say, "Tell Danny to stay out of the timberland, or next time, he'll find himself cursed with worse than a case of poison ivy."

Rock looks at the dirt between his big feet and rubs his palm harder on his jeans as if trying to wear a hole through the denim. "D, you need to be careful."

I brush it off as though I'm not concerned, but my heart kicks up a notch, and I make a mental note to tuck the colonel's Glock beneath the pillow beside me tonight. I'm a terrible shot and haven't fired a gun in decades, but hopefully it won't come to that.

"On a brighter note," I say and nod toward the cooler beside the boat. "Caught a catfish yesterday. You think your ma might want it?"

Rock's face lights up, his worry erased at the thought of his mother's catfish fritters, one of his favorite meals.

"You want to join us?" he asks.

Normally, I'd say yes, but despite the Oscar-worthy performance I'm giving, I'm not in the right frame of mind for company. "Arleta's been complaining of cramps," I say. "So I need to stay near the boat."

I don't deliver too many babies these days, most young people choosing to give birth in a hospital. But there's a fair-size population of Shakers and Mennonites in these parts, along with a few folks who still prefer to have their babies at home, so every once in a while, I'm called into service as a midwife. Arleta was one of the first babies I delivered when I started practicing again, and now she's having a child of her own. She's not due for a few more weeks, but she's a tiny thing, and I'm certain she won't make it to her due date.

"Why don't you ask the girl?" I say innocently, though there's nothing innocent about the comment at all.

"What girl?" Rock says, but I know he knows who I'm talking about, his ears pulsing red.

This morning, Hannah asked about Rock. She said they'd run into him on their way to see me. Her deep blush, a match to Rock's crimson lobes, told me the rest.

"I hardly know her," he says.

"Only way to get to know someone is to spend a bit of time with them."

"It would be weird," he says, but his mouth skews to the side, letting me know he's considering it. So I nod my head as if letting it go, the seed planted and all that's left to wait and see if it grows.

20
HANNAH

I'm sitting at the picnic table trying to figure out what to say to a writer to Juliet, a woman named Anna who is asking advice about whether she could truly be in love if she doesn't feel physically attracted to the man.

I have no idea. I've never even been kissed. I've dreamed of it. Imagined it. Acted it out a hundred different ways. I've read about it—butterflies in the stomach, tingling limbs, light-headedness, sometimes even nausea. It sounds awful and wonderful, like the moment a roller coaster reaches the top, just before it plunges.

I stare at the words on the screen, considering her plight: a woman laughing with a man, their humor and interests the same, but when he leans in to kiss her, she stiffens . . . or worse . . . recoils. Can that still be love?

A few feet away, Pen lies on her stomach in the grass, her chin on her crossed arms as she looks at the jar with the bee balm cutting Davina gave her and recounts the morning, talking to the flower as if it is listening. She's a strange kid but also so beautiful, like her heart is made of fairy dust. The twins came out that way, two odd ducks with large foreheads and shocks of bright-orange hair. Whip smart, like my dad, their brains worked faster than most, and they have . . . *had* . . .

this way of going this direction and that, and because they were always tethered together, it created a slingshot effect that propelled them dizzily all over the place. Now there's only Pen, still marvelous but only half as wondrous without there being two such creatures spinning like tops around each other.

"Hey, Pen."

I look up from my laptop to see Rock walking from the woods, a white trash bag in his hand.

"What ya doing?"

"Telling my sister about the day," she says. "Not Hannah. My other sister."

"Oh," he says. "What's her name?"

"Bee. Actually Phoebe. But everyone calls her Bee."

He squats beside the jar. "Hello, Bee. It's nice to meet you. I'm Rock."

Pen giggles. "She can't hear you."

"She can't?"

Pen shakes her head. "She only hears me because we're twins."

"Oh," he says again. "Then will you tell her hi for me?"

"I will," Pen says, and Rock pushes to his feet.

He continues toward me, and I try to get my blush to behave but know it only makes it worse, my skin flaming.

"Hey," he says with a wave.

I wave back, then close my laptop and try to get myself to look at him but can't quite manage it.

"Sorry about this morning," he says. "I didn't mean to snap at you the way I did. It was just surprising, is all."

"I hate that she has to leave," I say. The truth is, I more than hate it. Since seeing Davina this morning, the idea has grown deeply upsetting. I get my parents' side of things, that in order to move to Farmington, we need to sell this place, and we can't do that with Davina living in the cabin. But it seems so unfair.

"Actually, she's not leaving," Rock says.

"She's not?" My heart leaps with hope, thinking she and my mom worked something out. Which is surprising, considering how unhappy my mom looked when she returned from talking to her.

"At least not voluntarily," he says with a smirk.

My eyes widen, and I shake my head but also smile, thinking my mom might finally have met her match. Most people are pretty intimidated by my mom. She's smart and confident, and almost always right. But I also don't imagine Davina being intimidated by anyone.

Rock's smile matches my own, and I realize I'm looking at him and that he is looking at me. He realizes it as well, and his eyes drop, his shyness sweet and making me less self-conscious about my own.

"What's that?" I ask, nodding to the bag in his hand.

He hoists it in the air. "Catfish. Davina caught it." He tilts his head. "Hey, you ever had catfish fritters?"

"I've never even had catfish."

"Really?" Again we are looking at each other, but this time, neither of us looks away. "Well then, how about joining us for dinner? My ma makes the best catfish fritters in the world."

The words hang suspended, and everything stops. *Did he just ask me to dinner? Like a date? No. Just a neighborly invite. But just me?*

"You don't have to," he stammers, his eyes dropping again.

"No!" I yelp very uncoolly. "I'd love to. I mean that would be great. I'd love to try catfish fritters. Thank you." I slam my mouth shut to stop the blathering.

"Wow. Okay. Good."

A few feet away, Pen titters, and I look over to see her watching us, amused.

Ignoring her, I turn back to Rock. "Can I bring something? Dessert? I can make cookies . . . or pie . . . or does your mom like cake?"

He smiles wide, sending a tingly current I've never felt buzzing down my spine. And I wonder if that's how quickly it happens, if an invitation to try catfish fritters is capable of altering one's chemistry and short-circuiting a brain.

"Pie," he says. "My ma loves pie." He rubs his belly. "Apple didn't fall far from the tree . . . or the blueberry bush . . . or the boysenberry shrub . . . or the cherry, peach, pecan, banana, pumpkin . . ."

"I get it," I say, laughing my goofy laugh.

He smiles impossibly wider, seemingly a fan of the odd and unusual. "Any sort of pie will do. I'm going to take this home so my ma can put it on ice, then I'll be back to paint." With an imaginary tip of his baseball cap, like a twentieth-century gentleman saying good day to a lady, he continues to his truck.

When he reaches it, he hollers, "Six. We usually eat at six." He sounds almost as excited as I feel and looks as surprised, though he was the one who suggested it.

I snap open my computer.

Dear Anna,

Thank you for your letter. While I'm sure love can exist without physical attraction, there's nothing like the spine-tingling jolt you feel when you meet someone with whom you have instant, electrifying chemistry.

Perhaps it's not a deal breaker, but it should be a consideration, mostly because I'm not entirely certain the crazy, buzzy feeling of magnetism is as based on appearance as we might lead ourselves to believe, but instead could be our reaction to the personality within—the shy smile that reveals a man's humility and courage when he builds up the nerve to ask you to dinner; the considerate pause he takes to listen to a little girl's fanciful story that shows his infinite patience and tenderness; the earnestness in his eyes as he offers an apology when he knows he was wrong.

Perhaps consider what it is you're not attracted to, and if it is truly only physical, then perhaps eventually you will be able to see past it, or maybe, over time, the attraction will grow. But if your lack of connection is deeper, something fundamentally flawed in his character that is at the root, then it's important to recognize it and move on.

Even a crooked smile can melt a heart if it's aimed in the right direction. If the spark of his soul isn't able to reach yours regardless of the packaging, then he might not be your one true love. I wish you well.

All my love,
Juliet

21
LEO

As we drive toward the house, I see the boy, Rock, on a ladder scraping paint, white chips falling like snow around him. I admire the boy. When I went for my run this morning, he was already hard at work, and now, nearly eight hours later, he's still at it.

I glance sidelong at Brendon, only four years younger, and wonder if he will grow into as hardworking a young man, then get angry for the instant *Not a chance* that pops uninvited into my head.

"Hey," I say in my annoying overly bright way, "what do you say we get changed and lend a hand scraping paint?" I nod through the windshield. "It's an awful tall order for one person to paint a house this big."

Brendon gives me a cockeyed look. "The guy's getting paid."

"Yeah. But that doesn't mean we can't help. After all, it's our house, and it's not like we have something better to do."

"Anything other than scraping paint in thousand-degree heat."

And that's the end of that.

I pull to a stop, feeling lost as a parent, as I often do, filled with the distinct sense I'm doing it wrong and screwing up the most important job in the world, a feeling I've had intermittently and frequently since Hannah was born. My whole life, all I ever wanted was to be a dad, to have a beautiful wife and a nice house filled with young laughter. But when I dreamed of it, I had no idea how little control I'd have over things, how prewired my kids would be and how little say I'd have over their personalities and dispositions. With Brendon, especially, I'm often at a loss. We have so little in common. He is obsessed with sports and gaming and has no interest in books or the small curiosities I find endlessly fascinating.

Two years ago, when I realized how distant we were becoming, I tried learning to game as a way for us to connect. I hated it, thinking it a mindless waste of time, but I was determined to stick it out. A few days after I started, I tried talking to him about it, thinking we could discuss strategy, the characters, and possibly the deeper meaning of the storylines. He got annoyed and suggested I stop playing.

I climb from the car as Brendon lifts Banjo from the back seat and sets him carefully on the ground.

"Good boy. That's it. You can do it," he encourages as Banjo limps up the steps.

Fortunately, the injuries weren't too serious—a torn ear and a couple of gashes on his nose and hind leg that required stitches. The leg is bandaged, and he needs to wear a cone to protect the sutures on his face, but the vet assured us he'll be fine.

I stop just outside the door, dreading crossing the threshold and facing Marie. I was supposed to deal with the woman in the cabin first thing this morning but decided to go for my run first; then this happened.

With a deep breath, I paint on a smile and step inside, relieved when I look into the living room and Marie isn't there.

"Hey, Dad," Hannah says.

I turn to see her in the kitchen with Pen, and my smile turns real, my heart lighting up as it always does when I see my kids.

"Hey, Banana Rama. Hey, Sweet Pea. What you making?"

"Blackberry pie," Pen announces, her mouth blue, making me wonder about the ratio of berries that made it into the filling as opposed to her mouth.

"Yum."

"It's not for you," Pen says. "It's for Rock and his family. Hannah's going there for dinner." There's a tease in her voice, and I look at Hannah to see her skin pinked to the color of bubble gum.

"Really?" I say, trying to sound happy at the idea of my daughter going to a boy's house for dinner, though there's a distinct smack of the opposite.

"His mom's making catfish fritters," Hannah says, "and he says they're the best in the world."

"Really?" I say again, seemingly incapable of saying anything else. It's then that I notice, despite her blush and excitement, her brow is furrowed. "Your head hurting?"

"It's fine," she lies as if willing it to be true, revealing how much she really wants to go to the dinner.

"What time are you supposed to be there?" I ask.

"Six."

I glance at the clock. It's a little past four.

"Tell you what, why don't you take a couple Advil and lie down. Pen and I will finish the pie, and I'll wake you in an hour to get ready."

Her chin trembles.

"It's okay, baby. Rest. And hopefully, when you wake, it will be better."

It's a futile wish. The sundowner hours between three and eight are the worst. I hate these headaches. They are turning Hannah into someone she isn't. She used to be so bright and full of energy, involved in everything and always up for an adventure. Now, the migraines make it so she can't do much of anything at all.

She sets down the rolling pin and shuffles away, her feet barely lifting off the floor, revealing how truly bad it is.

When the door to her bedroom clicks closed above, Pen says, "You need to tell Mom to let Davina give her the medicine."

It takes a minute for me to remember who Davina is—the woman in the cabin.

"Hannah said it worked," Pen goes on. "She took it, and her headache went away."

Pen looks serious, her arms crossed over her chest and a deep frown on her blackberry-stained face, the expression making her look a lot like Marie.

"But now Davina won't give it to her because she knows Mom poured it down the sink."

"Wait," I say. "You saw the woman in the cabin?"

Guilt flashes across her face, so I add quickly, "It's okay. I'm glad you met her and found out she wasn't scary."

"She's not!" Pen says. "Not even a little."

Her eyes are wide, and she shakes her head excitedly.

"She made us an omelet with eggs from her chickens and vegetables from her garden, and it was so good I didn't even care that it had peppers in it."

It's then that I notice the jar beside her with a bright-pink flower and a glob of honey on the bottom of the stem, the same technique my grandmother used when she took cuttings.

"Did Davina give you that?" I ask.

"It's bee balm," Pen says, positively lit up. "It's so I can make a butterfly garden, and Bee can visit whenever she wants."

My heart cracks open—happy and sad at her joy. Pen still has an intense, lingering connection to her sister, and real or imagined, I'm okay with it if it helps her with her grief.

"Bee balm," I say as my regard of the woman in the cabin grows. And I wonder how it's possible that the same woman who hit Banjo with a broom can also be so wonderful and kind.

"So you'll talk to Mom about the medicine?" Pen says.

I give a noncommittal nod, and Pen frowns, making it clear that she means I need to talk to Marie now, again reminding me so much of Marie I need to check my grin.

With a mock salute, I head upstairs, where I find Marie on the bed with furniture catalogs around her. She looks up from the one she's browsing and perches her reading glasses on her head. "How's Banjo?"

"Okay. I think his pride is wounded more than anything."

She gives a small smile, which I reflect back before moving to the closet to hang up my dress shirt. I was taught by my father to dress nice for appointments, and despite the world changing to habitual sloth attire for just about everything, I still follow the etiquette.

I pull on my favorite Yale T-shirt and, keeping my back turned, say, "Sorry I didn't talk to the woman in the cabin first thing."

"Probably better that I did it. She's a real piece of work."

"Yeah?" I take my time removing my watch so she doesn't see my expression, certain it would betray my torn feelings.

"She says she's not leaving," Marie says.

I turn. "Really? That's what she said?"

"Yep. Stood there, cool as a cucumber, and basically told me to go to hell."

Without meaning to, I nod.

"Leo," Marie says sharply.

"Right. She needs to go."

"Yes, she does."

"So now what?"

"So I called the real estate agent. I thought maybe there was another way we could deal with this. The cabin obviously has running water and electricity, so I was thinking we could call it a rental unit and that it might actually add value to the property."

"That's a great idea!" I say, my heart leaping with hope until her next words dash it.

"The news wasn't good." She sighs out heavily. "Not only is the land not zoned for residential, it turns out the cabin's in violation of at least a dozen environmental regulations and fire codes because it's so inaccessible and close to the river."

"Oh," I say. "That's not good."

"Nope. And it gets worse. If something were to happen—a fire or septic leak—we would be liable."

I sigh and shake my head, the day going further downhill by the minute. "So what's that mean?"

"It means we need to demo the cabin and pay to have the septic tank removed." She looks at her hands on top of the catalog on her lap. "Which is going to cost thousands."

My stomach clenches in pain, the ulcers I've developed since Bee's death releasing "angry enzymes," as my doctor calls them, a thing that happens when I'm stressed. I grew up in a family that didn't have a lot and with parents who believed in paying cash for everything and not buying things we couldn't afford. I had reservations about using our savings to put the deposit on the Farmington house, but Marie assured me not to worry, that the sale of this place would make up for it and then some. And maybe that's true, but with all the unforeseen expenses we've encountered, our bank account is running dangerously low. I'm a part-time professor at a community college with an income that barely covers our food bill, and Marie hasn't worked since the accident. Unlike me, Marie grew up never worrying about money, and she often takes it for granted that we can buy what we want and it will somehow all work out.

"So what are we going to do about the woman?" I ask.

Marie blows out a hard breath. "Right. The cause of all this misery. So after I got off the phone with the real estate agent, I called the attorney who helped us settle the estate, and he got us an emergency hearing for the day after tomorrow."

"You're taking her to court?" I yelp.

"*We're* taking her to court," she corrects with a frown. "I don't see what other choice there is. The cabin needs to be removed, which means she needs to leave, whether she likes it or not."

"Right," I say, but only halfheartedly, thinking of the pink blossom in the jar.

"Leo, we're not the bad guys here. That woman's been living on our land rent-free for over twenty years."

When I don't respond, she says, "You were the one who said we needed to find a way through this."

I nod. I did. It's just, when I said it, I didn't think that meant abandoning our old life entirely, starting over somewhere new, and booting a woman from her home in the process.

22
MARIE

I am waiting in my car for Brendon so we can drive to town—Brendon to play his games and me to talk to the attorney about the hearing tomorrow. Through the windshield, I watch Leo, Pen, and Hannah as they help the boy, Rock, scrape the house so it can be painted.

I feel as if, overnight, battle lines have been drawn. Brendon and I on one side, Pen and Hannah on the other, and Leo futilely trying to straddle the middle—those of us who want to sell the property and move to Farmington; those who want to go back to the life we had and let Davina return to hers; and my husband, who just wants everyone to be happy.

Of course, none of it is that simple. In life, you can never truly go back. The life we had included Bee. And the cabin where Davina's made her home can no longer exist in the highly regulated modern world. I understand Pen and Hannah feel bad for her, but their compassion doesn't change the facts.

I watch them bopping to music that blasts from the open doors of Rock's truck as they work. Hannah and Pen have made up a dance and work in unison—scrape, scrape, scrape, hip bump, spin, do it again. They look happy, and it causes an ache of envy and grief, wanting to be a part of it and knowing I'm not there yet, my heart twisted tight because Bee should be there with them.

A few feet away, Leo scrapes contentedly, a dazed grin on his face. He loves repetitive tasks, which is why he enjoys long-distance running. His eyes are glazed, and I know his mind is either entirely blank or working out some complex problem.

"Can we get a pool table at the new house?" Brendon asks as he climbs in.

I pull my attention from the others and start the car. "A pool table? Huh? Maybe."

For Brendon, the single bright spot of coming here has been the billiards room. My grandfather loved pool, and when I came here as a girl, we would have all sorts of tournaments. My mother was good and the only one able to challenge my grandfather. It was the only time they set aside their differences and simply enjoyed the other's company. I remember them laughing and how sad I'd be whenever a game would end.

Brendon and Leo have been playing, and Leo says Brendon's a natural. I'm glad to see them doing something together. They've always been so different.

"I'll need to see if the game room is big enough," I say, my mood brightening with the thought.

As we drive toward the road, I consider the type of pool table we might get—modern or traditional? And the color of the felt—red, blue, green? The thought is comfortingly distracting and carries me away from my thoughts of Bee.

"Mom?" Brendon says sharply.

I blink and look where he's looking. At the end of the drive, a dozen people stand across the street. At first, I'm uncertain what I'm looking at. Some sort of gathering . . . no, a protest.

"They're here for us?" Brendon says at the exact moment I realize it.

Some hold signs. Others glare. A stout older woman with tight blonde curls is directly in front of us. The white poster she holds has silver glittered edges and bloodred lettering that reads **DAVINA STAYS! YOU GO!** A young woman beside her holds a toddler in one arm and a picket sign in the other: **LEAVE THE GOOD WITCH ALONE!!!** A slender man in a suit has a neon-yellow poster with the painting of a pig's face and the words **CAPITALIST PIGS** around it. Their chant, "Davina stays!" ricochets through the windows.

"Mom!" Brendon yelps, and my face snaps sideways to see a delivery truck swerve to avoid us. The horn blares as I slam on the brakes and realize with a spike of panic that I made the turn with my eyes still on the pig.

In the rearview mirror, I see the protesters running at us, their signs raised like weapons, and I jam my foot back on the gas. The tires kick up gravel as we squeal away, my heart hammering and Brendon frozen beside me.

"They were there because of the witch?" Brendon asks.

I nod. They were. Somehow our small private dispute has turned into something more. I look at the clock, then at the temperature gauge. It's a little after nine, and the temperature is near ninety. I think of the devotion it takes for people to stand in the sweltering heat waiting just so they can let us know how angry they are and to show their support for Davina.

"She put them up to it," Brendon seethes, his left leg jiggling and his hands fisted on his thighs.

"I don't think so," I say, thinking of Davina and unable to imagine her asking anyone to fight her battles for her.

"She did," he says, rage I've never seen in him pulsing.

I stay quiet. He's upset. This thing with Davina is personal. Banjo's wounds have settled, and the poor dog is moping around, clearly in pain.

"She deserves to lose her home," he seethes. "She deserves worse."

23
DAVINA

The day started out so lovely. Rock brought my groceries at dawn and told me Hannah had in fact joined them for dinner last night. He acted like it was no big deal but mentioned her blackberry pie three times. The old proverb "The way to a man's heart is through his stomach" is probably no truer than it is with Rock. The boy likes to eat.

The conversation made me smile all the way to my toes. There's nothing quite as wondrous as first love, and I can't think of two people I like more for the prospect of it than Hannah and Rock.

I was putting away the groceries when Arleta's husband, Lloyd, called. Arleta was having contractions. I hurried to my boat and made it to their home just as the baby was crowning. She was a jewel, tiny and puckered pink, with ten fingers, ten toes, and all her other body parts in all the right places.

It was an uneventful birth, exactly as nature intended, and lasted a little more than four hours. As I was leaving, Lloyd held out a fistful of bills—tens, fives, and a whole lot of ones. I shook my head and told him bearing witness to the birth was payment enough. He looked relieved. They're young, just starting out, and now have a new mouth to feed. Lloyd promised to visit soon to help put a new roof on my woodshed.

I left with my soul full, thinking that's how all exchanges should go: you need this, and I need that, so let's work together to make it happen. A fine trade.

By the time I got home, it was a little after one, and I was starving. I was thinking of the leftover trout I had in the fridge that I would make into a sandwich with the loaf of bread Rock brought that morning. A little mayo, a little lemon pepper, a few chips. My mouth watered as I pulled the boat onto the shore.

"Afternoon."

I lifted my head to see Cory Hester standing in the shade of the birch. He was in his sheriff's uniform and wore a serious look on his normally jovial face, and a bad feeling replaced my hunger. Teddy sidled up, and Cory bent and scratched the old cat behind his ear.

"Where you coming back from?" he asked as he stepped closer.

"Arleta and Lloyd's. They had their baby. A girl."

"Wonderful." His eyes went a little misty. Despite being a sheriff and the size of a linebacker, Cory's sentimental as they come. "Got a name?"

"Not yet. I think Lloyd was pretty set on the idea he was having a boy, so it might take a bit for him to get used to the idea of a daughter."

Cory gave a small smile, then shifted his weight, and the bad feeling grew.

"You here on business?" I asked, noticing the envelope in his hand.

"I hate to be the one to do this," he said, holding it toward me. "Jeremy asked me to deliver this."

Jeremy is Judge Gaikwad to those who didn't grow up with him. Cory and I were a few years younger, but we ran in the same crowd.

I took the envelope but didn't open it, my eyes still on Cory's.

"The owners of the property filed an emergency injunction to have you evicted. The hearing's tomorrow."

Though outwardly I didn't react, my chest tightened. I knew Marie was serious about me leaving; I just didn't think she would act so quickly, and a small part of me hoped she might reconsider and drop the matter altogether.

"No one's happy about this," Cory said, looking at the ground and toeing the dirt. "As a matter of fact, it's got people pretty riled up."

I nodded. Franklin's a small, tight-knit community, and we watch out for one another.

"The hearing's at nine," Cory said, a deep frown on his face. "Need a lift?"

"I'll take the boat," I said, knowing I would need the time on the river to still my nerves. Already my scars were prickling, public appearances and crowds still difficult.

"I'll have Jim wait at the back door to let you in," Cory said. Jim is the court's bailiff and another old friend.

"Thank you," I managed, brain fuzzy and fingers tingling.

I barely heard him when he went on to say, "One more thing. Danny Canton's been going on about you again, telling anyone who will listen that you're a witch."

I bobbed my head, not really listening, Danny Canton the least of my concerns, my brain stuck on the thought of walking through town, then sitting in a courtroom with people, gavels, and other unexpected noise.

Cory left, and I sat in the lawn chair, which is where I've been since. Watching the water has a way of calming me, and for hours, my thoughts have drifted this way and that. And while I know I should be thinking about the future and where I'm going to live, mostly what I find myself thinking about is the past—my mothers, the colonel, and Rose.

The fading afternoon light flickers on the water as it puts on its final performance of the day, and I wonder for the millionth time what my life might have been like had I not been in that truck on that day or had the first truck hit the detonator instead of ours or had I never volunteered to return oversees in the first place.

My life would have taken a different course altogether. I imagine I would have stayed married, out of loyalty and for the sake of Rose and perhaps the other children Moz and I might have had. We'd have had a regular life, living in Brooklyn, where I would likely have worked as a nurse at the VA hospital. Or perhaps I'd have gone back to school and become a doctor, as I'd once dreamed. Our weekends would have been spent with friends or going to the kids' activities. Perhaps I'd have a cooking hobby or maybe something more interesting, like pottery.

Different possibilities run through my head, the thoughts fleeting as glances through the window of a passing train—endless could-haves and would-haves, fanciful at first but which leave me hollow, gutted by the possibilities of the road untraveled and with intense longing for my daughter and the life we might have shared. *Loss.* It comes in different forms—financial, physical, emotional. I've experienced them all. But none so lasting or painful as the lingering echo my daughter has left in my soul.

"Afternoon!" an overly bright voice says, and I crane my head to see Hannah and Pen's dad walking from the woods, his hand raised in a wave.

I don't feel like waving, so instead offer a wan grin as I push to my feet.

Pen takes after him. Both are thin boned, fair, with freckles, and have a bounce in their step like there are springs in their legs.

"I'm Leo."

"Davina," I say, holding out my hand.

His handshake is solid, warm, and gentle, and I sense he's a good man.

The chipper-ness settles as he says, "I was hoping we could talk."

"Why don't we go up to the house."

I lead him up the trail and, when we reach the cabin, ask, "Would you like something to drink? A beer?"

He looks surprised. People often are when they visit and discover I'm not a hermit existing off the land. Because I live alone in the woods and off the beaten path, it's often assumed I'm some sort of eccentric recluse who drinks river water and munches on moss, which couldn't be further from the truth. I have running water, electricity, and internet. A stove, an oven, and a refrigerator. And I enjoy a cold beer and bag of Oreos as much as the next person.

"Yes. A beer would be great," he says.

I gesture to the table on the porch, then head inside and return a moment later with two Michelobs along with a bowl of Ruffles.

He grabs a chip, then nods to the rain collection system I built a few years back for the garden. "Nice setup."

"It's home," I say, causing the Ruffle to pause midway to his lips.

24
LEO

While I expected the woman's scars, I was not prepared for her beauty. Sophia Loren meets Audrey Hepburn with the eyes of Hedy Lamarr—golden-era-movie-queen good looking. And it's impossible not to think how stunning she must have been when she was young and before she was wounded.

Judging by the setup around me, she might just be as smart as the brilliant Hedy Lamarr as well. The home she's made is nothing short of remarkable. Not the structure itself—a simple A-frame of log walls and a shingled roof that looks like it's been here forever—but the world she's created around it. The cabin is a mile from the nearest road and completely off the grid, yet she doesn't appear to lack for anything. There are solar panels and satellite dishes on the roof. A rainwater irrigation system for her garden. A chicken yard with at least a dozen cackling hens. And based on the buzzing I hear coming from behind the cabin, I'd guess a honey hive. While most of us wouldn't last a day without Target or a grocery store, this woman has created a self-sustained world with all the comforts of modern life. I'm drinking a cold beer while munching on Ruffles in the middle of a birch forest, and I'm sure if she invited me to stay for dinner, I'd be chowing down on trout she caught in the river and potatoes she pulled from the earth. She's like a new age Renaissance mountain woman, and it's impossible not to be impressed.

Setting down the chip I was about to eat, I lift my face to hers, determined to look her in the eyes and not be drawn to her scars. Though I find it difficult, the morbid pull undeniable.

"I'm afraid this situation's gotten a bit out of hand," I say.

She squints and tilts her head, and I wonder if it's possible she's unaware what's happened. Marie and Brendon arrived home an hour ago, Marie distraught and Brendon in a rage. They left this morning to find a dozen protesters waiting at the end of our driveway, a small, angry mob holding signs and taunting them as they drove past. And this afternoon, they returned to a crowd five times that.

"I'm hoping, together, we can figure out a solution," I say.

"A solution?" She takes a sip of beer, tipping her head back, and I realize it's because she has no lips, and my fascination and sympathy grow. This woman has been through so much.

Aware I'm staring, I look at the table between us. "We're selling the property."

"So Marie said."

"Which means you can't live here."

Ignoring the statement, she nods to the cabin and says, "Did you know I lived here twice?"

I blow out a breath and shake my head, this conversation already far more difficult than I had imagined.

"The first time when I was six."

Judging by her eyes, I'd guess her to be in her fifties, which means she's talking about nearly half a century ago.

"My first mother died here," she says.

I jolt slightly, and my eyes snap to hers as my chest tightens. The statement makes me think of Bee and the reaction I had when Marie said she wanted to move. *No!* I thought, unable to fathom the idea of leaving the memories of her behind, knowing it was all that remained.

Her left cheek twitches above her scars. "You understand," she says, and I wonder if her witch abilities extend beyond potions and herbs.

"I do," I say. "But unfortunately that doesn't change things. It's not a choice. The cabin's not to code."

"There's always a choice," she says, her eyes steady on mine.

She's right, of course. If we don't sell the property, no one's going to care if she continues in the same manner she has for the past twenty-some years.

"Did you ever meet the colonel?" she asks.

"I'm afraid I never got the chance."

When Marie and I first started dating, she told me about her grand-father, speaking of him with reverence and regret. She was deeply torn between reaching out to reconnect with him or leaving things as they were. She was worried how her family would react. When he passed, it hit her hard, and I know she was sorry she hadn't made amends.

"He loved this place," Davina says, looking off at the trees. "Called it his heartland." She looks back at me. "And if he could, he'd climb from his grave to stop you from selling it."

I drop my eyes again as my guilt pulses. I believe she's telling the truth. In the office upstairs is a painting of the colonel. Red and gold bands adorn his shoulders, and a slew of ribbons and medals decorate his chest. His vivid blue eyes stare, unapologetic, from the canvas, and his sardonic smile, immortalized by the talented artist's brush, smirks. He looks like the sort of man who lived by his own rules, the exact sort of man who would give a wounded army nurse a cabin and who would never renege on his word.

I find myself nodding even as I say, "But if the colonel were here, he'd be stuck with the same dilemma. The cabin is in violation of the building codes, and if something were to happen—"

"What's going to happen?"

"I don't know. A fire or someone gets hurt."

She takes another sip of beer, sets down the bottle, and her eyes lock on mine as she says, "If something happens, I'll take full responsibility."

"It doesn't work like that. It's our name on the deed."

"So change it," she says. "Give the cabin to me. It's what the colonel would have wanted."

I bristle and wonder if it's possible this was her ploy all along.

"We're not going to do that."

For more than twenty years, Marie and I have been paying the mortgage we took to buy out her sister and cousins. We're not simply going to give part of that away.

"But," I say, "how about instead, we offer compensation to help you relocate?"

Marie and I didn't discuss this, and she won't be happy, but I feel like an opportunity for compromise has eked open, and I don't want to lose it.

"Money doesn't interest me," she says plainly, slamming the imagined door shut.

I run my hand through my hair in frustration. "I'm trying to help! Tomorrow is the hearing, and if you go to court, you're going to lose."

She lifts her bottle in a mock toast. "True. But some battles are so worthy, it's glorious even to fail."

I blink in surprise. A few years back, the quote was a $2,000 Double Jeopardy! question in the category "Eternal Heroic Words." The correct response was *Who is Pandey?* At the time, I had no idea who that was, so I looked him up. Captain Manoj Kumar Pandey was the most decorated captain in the Indian military. He died in battle at the tender age of twenty-four, and the quote is part of his enduring legacy. I wonder if Davina knows of his early death, and if she discovered it, if it would change her opinion.

Not waiting for a response, she says, "How's Hannah's head?"

My mind struggles to switch course, my thoughts still whirling to come up with a solution that stops us from spiraling like two tornadoes toward calamitous destruction. But every argument I come up with leads to the same end—she has no intention of leaving, which means the only thing left to do is take her to court, which will add fuel to the already brewing firestorm and will end with her still being evicted.

"Not good," I say, completely deflated. "Pen said the medicine you gave her helped. Thank you for that."

"No great secret. Feverfew's been helping aching heads for centuries."

Feverfew. I've heard of the plant. I think my grandmother might have had a few bushes on her farm in Pennsylvania. White-petaled, daisylike flowers come to mind.

"That's all it was?" I ask. "Feverfew flowers?"

"Steeped in vodka to extract the essence. But yep, that's it."

I feel silly for our drama of pouring it down the drain.

Reading my expression, she says, "I wouldn't have given her something dangerous."

I nod. "It's just that recently we've been through—"

"No explanation needed," she says. "If you'd like, I can give you another jar."

"I'll pay you," I say, instantly regretting it when her eyes narrow.

She stands and disappears into the cabin. And I rub my eyes with my knuckles, thinking the conversation couldn't have gone worse.

"Remind her it's best if she takes it in the morning after her swim," she says, and I look up to see her holding a jar exactly like the first one toward me.

"Swim?" I say with surprise as I take it.

I think of Hannah walking into the house breathless, with her hair wet, but the idea of her going in the river never occurred to me. Hannah's never been into exercise or one for taking risks, and the Merrimack's no joke, the current strong and the water frigid.

Without answering, Davina pivots away and back inside, leaving me alone.

With a sigh, I drop the jar in my shorts pocket, then, realizing there's a bulge, pull it out and stick it in the waistband in the small of my back and pull my T-shirt over it.

In our whole marriage, I can't remember a time when I willfully deceived Marie, and there's a distinct feeling of vertigo knowing I'm doing it now. But I also know Marie would not approve, and I can't stand the idea of Hannah continuing to suffer needlessly.

I walk back to the house, and when Banjo sees me, he limp-runs my way, cone bouncing and tail wagging. And for not the first time, I find myself envying him, wishing I could live more like a dog, carefree and in the moment. Life as a human can feel so heavy.

While the rest of us have struggled to find our rhythm since Bee died, Banjo has continued much as he was. It's not that he hasn't noticed her absence. When we were home, he took to sleeping beside her bed and sniffing at her things. But even then, he wasn't sad, his tail thumping as if thoughts of her only brought happiness. Without pause, his life moved on seamlessly, and I wish I could figure out a way to do the same.

I pat him on his side, and together, we continue to the house. Rock is still at it, high on a ladder, scraping beneath the eaves. He waves, and I wave back. He's an impressive young man, and while I can't get used to the idea of Hannah dating, if she's going to start, he's not a bad place to begin.

I shuffle inside, my thoughts on grabbing another beer.

"Well?" Marie says, surprising me.

I swivel my head to see her looking at me from the couch.

Ignoring my thirst, I join her. I sit in the armchair across from her and rest my elbows on my knees, acutely aware of the jar straining the waistband of my shorts.

"So is she leaving?" she asks.

I sigh. "Jags, we need to talk about this. She's not. And maybe we shouldn't ask her to."

"You're kidding, right? I knew this was going to happen. You were going to go there, see her scars, and feel sorry for her."

"I do feel sorry for her. But I also feel like this isn't going to end well. For any of us."

"So what do you suggest? She can't continue to live there. We've been over this."

"She said we could give her the cabin."

"Give it to her?"

I lower my eyes. "I know it's a lot, but—"

"A lot! You want to give a stranger a piece of land worth more than your children's college funds? To jeopardize our future and everything we've worked for so as not to inconvenience her from moving?"

I don't know what swayed my thinking. Perhaps it was the gift of the tincture, or maybe I'm just so done in I don't want to deal with this anymore. Or . . . a blush creeps into my cheeks as I realize with shame the third possibility . . . I want to assuage my guilt by suggesting it, knowing there's no way Marie will go along with it.

"This is not our problem," Marie says. "There are millions . . . no, billions . . . of people in the world who are struggling, some who have suffered great tragedies. And while sad, even heartbreaking at times, we cannot be responsible for them, and we cannot be responsible for her. We're not asking her to give up a limb; all we're asking is that she move off land that isn't hers and from a cabin that, by law, needs to be demolished."

I nod, though my heart's not in it. "Well, then maybe we should at least consider putting it off for a bit. Perhaps until things cool down." I reach for her hand, but she pulls it away, her eyes hard.

"Leo, tomorrow is the hearing. Between now and then, you need to decide whose side you're on."

"Our side," I say quickly, realizing too late my head is shaking as I say it.

Angrily, she pushes to her feet and marches away. The front door slams, and I wish I could take it back . . . the moment . . . the day . . . the year. But no matter how much you wish it, time marches on, minute by minute, day by day, leaving you stumbling on with it, along with every regret and mistake you've ever made.

25
HANNAH

The front door slams downstairs, and I think it's my dad leaving. Moments before, I heard him and my mom bickering, angry words I couldn't quite make out. Before Bee died, my parents never fought, mostly because my dad reveres my mom and always backed down from her. But the stress of things has created small fissures in their once-perfect relationship.

A rap on my door causes me to blink my eyes open and squint into the dim afternoon light.

"Hey, Banana Rama," my dad says through the wood, surprising me. "Can I come in?"

I push myself up gingerly so as not to rupture my brain. "Sure."

The migraine reached its peak a few hours ago, midway through one of the most wonderful days of my life. The dinner last night with Rock and his family couldn't have gone better. His mother, Linda, is a yapper like Rock, and between the two of them talking over and around each other, their hands flying with their words, there wasn't time to be nervous. Rock's stepdad, Al, and I grinned and laughed as they told story after story, all while eating one of the best meals of my life—catfish fritters, creamed collard greens, and cornbread with honey from Davina's hives.

After dinner, we played Scrabble while eating my blackberry pie. We teamed up, me and Rock against his parents. Rock was so excited when we won, he knocked over his chair as he leaped to his feet and fist-pumped the air. It turned out he had never won at Scrabble in his life.

This morning, I woke to the sound of him scraping the house outside. And as I lay listening, I found myself thinking about him and grinning. Then after breakfast, my dad, Pen, and I offered to help, which might sound boring but wasn't. Rock blasted country music from his truck, and we bopped along as we worked. And I was incredibly happy, until . . .

The migraine came on so suddenly I barely managed a goodbye, and I staggered away feeling like a loser and certain whatever attraction Rock thought he had for me had been annihilated instantly by my pathetic-ness.

That was three hours ago, and I've been lying in bed feeling sorry for myself since.

"I've got something for you," my dad says quietly, almost whispering, though we're alone. He reaches into the back of his shorts and pulls out a jar of Davina's tincture.

"Really?" I say, looking from the jar to him. "Is that why you and Mom were fighting?"

His face drops, and he shakes his head. "No. But just the same, might be best if we keep this just between us."

I swallow as I realize how much things really have changed. My whole life, my parents have presented an impenetrable, unified front, never allowing even a smidgeon of chance for us to go around one to go to the other.

He holds the jar toward me, and as I take it, he says, "Davina said you've been swimming?"

"It helps with my head." I offer as much of a smile as my throbbing brain will allow. "I know now why you run."

His head tilts, which makes him look a little like a curious dog. "You do?"

"It's because when you do it, it's like time stands still. You stop thinking, and you're just there, in the moment, going and going and going, like nothing else exists but your breath and your body and the desire to keep moving."

His Adam's apple bobs, and his jaw tightens. It makes me think of the letters to Juliet. It's a huge thing to be understood.

26
BRENDON

The courtroom is full, dozens of people here in support of the witch. I keep my eyes on the rays of light on the table where Mom sits with our lawyer, a weaselly, twitchy man who doesn't seem to want to be here.

It was a horrible morning, the second worst of my life. Not only was the mob of protesters waiting as we drove from the house, but it had grown even larger and now included news vans parked along the street, reporters with microphones, and camera crews pointing giant cameras at us as we drove past.

A caravan followed us to the courthouse, and we walked from the parking structure to another mob waiting on the steps. If not for the sheriff, who ordered them to make room and then helped us inside, we wouldn't have made it past. Mom gripped my hand so tight her nails left marks on my palm, and when we finally got to the room where we needed to wait for our lawyer, she hissed, "I'm sorry. I never should have brought you."

"I wanted to come," I said. And I meant it. Despite how awful it was, I was glad I was there. Otherwise, she would have been alone.

I'm incredibly mad at my dad. He said he didn't want to leave the girls because of the protesters, but yesterday, I heard him and Mom talking, and I know he's on the witch's side. He said we should give her the cabin. Which is stupid. The property is ours, and she doesn't belong there.

"Oink!" someone hoots from somewhere behind us, causing me to jolt.

There's a snort, probably from the same person who oinked, and several people snort in response. Others laugh. *Pigs* is what they're calling us. Short for *capitalist pigs*, which I have no idea what that means. Also *hogs*, *swine*, and *porkers*. I feel the heat of their hate, hot as summer sun, on my neck. Mom looks back with worry, and I give as brave a smile as I can muster. The lawyer fidgets, clearly uncomfortable, and watching him, I'm pretty sure he, too, isn't entirely on our side.

I look sidelong at the table where the witch is supposed to be and wonder if she isn't coming. I hope that's the case, that this whole thing ends quickly so we can go.

"All rise!" a man in uniform who's been keeping watch from the side of the room says.

We stand, and the door on his left opens.

The judge walks through and takes his seat behind the bench.

The uniformed man says, "Be seated."

I glance again at the empty table, hope rising, the witch still not here. In the next second, it is dashed. The man in uniform pivots to a second door on his right, and the crowd goes quiet. Like a queen arriving, she appears, and there's a united holding of breath, eyes riveted on the opening.

I'm shocked how different she looks from the day I saw her in the woods. Her body stiff and straight, she stands perfectly still as she peers out from the darkness, only her eyes moving, flickering around the room. Her hair is tied back tightly, and her feet are pinned together with the toes pointed out. Her skirt and jacket are dark blue, the shirt beneath it is white, and the overall effect is that of a soldier waiting to salute.

I practically hear her heart pounding, as she continues to survey the room as if scanning for danger, which makes no sense. The room is not the least bit scary, and everyone here, except me and my mom, is on her side. Finally, her nostril opens as she takes a deep breath, and hands fisted, stiltedly she walks to the table and takes her seat.

The woman who yesterday held a glittering sign that read **DAVINA STAYS! YOU GO!** reaches over the railing and touches her shoulder. The witch looks back, and a small nod passes between them.

It's strange to watch. In the woods, she wasn't like this at all. In fact, she was the opposite—running at us with the broom, fearless as she swatted Banjo away and snatched up the cat.

"Now that everyone's here," the judge says, "we can begin."

He's about to say something more when something drops—a phone or a camera—something hard and metallic clanking to the floor. The sound is not terribly loud, yet the witch reacts like a bomb's gone off, her chair shooting back and her hands flying over her head.

The room freezes, and someone mutters, "Sorry."

The witch continues to cower with her elbows pinned to her ears and her body bent so her chest is on her thighs.

The woman who had touched her shoulder leans forward as if to comfort her, but the judge's sharp shake of his head stops her.

The witch trembles, her rib cage moving with her breaths.

Softly, the judge says, "Davina."

She nods, letting him know she heard him; then, after another long minute, all of us watching, she pulls her hands from her head and straightens. I can't see her face but know by the hitch of her shoulders and the way her head tics side to side that her eyes are still scanning and that she's ready to dive beneath the table again.

"Do you need a recess?" the judge asks with concern.

"No," she says, the word so tight it's difficult to hear. "I'm okay. Thank you . . . I mean, thank you, Your Honor." She scoots her chair in, and everyone breathes.

"I could clear the gallery?" the judge offers.

She cranes her head to look at the people behind her. Her supporters smile encouragingly. A few wave. One woman blows a kiss. Another mouths the words "We love you."

She turns back. "No, Your Honor. I'm fine. I appreciate them being here. Thank you."

"Ms. Lister," the judge says, reverting to her last name, "do you have representation?"

"Just myself, Your Honor."

"Okay then, let's proceed."

Our lawyer presents our side of the case. There's not much to say. The property is ours. We have a deed to prove it. The cabin violates all sorts of rules regarding the river and the fire codes. Which means the witch needs to leave, period, end of story.

When the lawyer retakes his seat, the judge asks, "Ms. Lister, do you have any evidence to refute this?"

She stands and says, "Only the word of a dead man."

The audience murmurs, and the judge raps his gavel.

The witch goes on, "Colonel Polster, who owned the property until he passed, said the cabin was mine to live in long as I needed."

"Darn right!" someone shouts.

The judge raps his gavel again and says, "If you can't hold your tongue, you and your tongue will be escorted from my courtroom." He turns back to the witch. "Do you have any proof of that?"

She shakes her head, and the judge sighs.

"Thank you, Ms. Lister. You may be seated."

She retakes her seat, and the judge rubs his jaw, then folds his hands in front of him. "Based on the evidence before me, the court has no choice but to rule in favor of the plaintiff." He frowns at my mom, letting her know that though he's issuing the verdict in our favor, he's not at all happy about it. "The defendant will vacate the premises immediately."

There's a sharp intake of air.

He turns back to the witch. "Ms. Lister, unfortunately, due to the unusual circumstances of this case, technically this is not an eviction but rather an injunction. There is no lease, and therefore, you are not considered a tenant, and that means you do not have any of the legal rights or protections normally afforded to someone in your situation. Which means if you are found on the premises, you will be guilty of trespass. Do you understand?"

"That's bull!" someone says. Others murmur in agreement, rage rippling through the room as Mom shifts uncomfortably in her seat.

The witch cocks her head. "You're saying I can't go back?"

"I'm afraid not," the judge answers. He looks again at my mom. "But perhaps Mrs. Egide would allow someone to collect your things?"

Mom nods eagerly. "Of course," she says, then stupidly blurts, "And they're welcome to use our driveway."

I tense, feeling like we're a hair trigger away from a full-on mutiny.

The judge, sensing it as well, says quickly, "Jim, please escort Ms. Lister out."

The man in uniform opens the door through which the witch entered, and, realizing he's opening it for her, she stands.

Instantly, the room quiets, anger shifting to worry over upsetting her again.

Pulling her shoulders back so she again looks like a soldier, stiffly she walks across the room, her posture straight except her head, which remains off kilter, as if she is still confused.

The door closes, and the man in uniform says, "Please rise."

We stand, and the judge leaves.

As soon as he's gone, the audience also funnels out, several making their displeasure known by hurling insults and barbs our way as they go. Bravely, the man in uniform stands in the aisle, creating a human barrier between them and us.

When we're alone, our lawyer mutters a sour "Congratulations," making it clear I was right, and that he, too, wishes we had lost.

He leaves, and the man in uniform says, "Probably best if you leave out the back as well." He nods to the door the witch used.

Mom's voice trembles as she says, "Thank you. Yes, I think that's a good idea."

We follow him down a long corridor, and when we reach the door that leads outside, he says, "If you give me your keys, I'll bring your car around."

"That's very kind of you," Mom says, eyes on the floor and jaw locked tight.

"Two sides to every story," the man says; then he walks into the noon-bright day, leaving us alone, silent and stunned, terrified that we won.

27
MARIE

I'm in the living room, staring at my laptop. Our satellite internet was installed yesterday, which I'm starting to believe might not be a good thing. We've been home less than two hours, and somehow, in that short time, our legal battle has exploded into national news, every station in the country reporting "breaking news" about the ruling against the wounded war hero who has been cruelly evicted from her home.

At the moment, CNN is discussing Davina's service and sacrifice. They have on a psychologist who specializes in PTSD as a consultant, and with great sympathy, he speculates on how difficult this must be for her, then goes on to explain the disorder and its various manifestations, including a detailed analysis of what happened in the courtroom and how sharp noises and unexpected stress can be triggering for someone as traumatized as she's been.

I can't believe this is happening. The hearing was so much worse than I expected, all those people hating us and that awful moment when the reporter dropped his recorder and Davina cowered under the table. Why did she put herself through it? She must have known how hard it was going to be.

"We reached out to the heiress, Marie Egide, who inherited the property, for comment," the CNN reporter says, "but she has not responded to our requests."

It makes me want to hurl the laptop across the room. *Heiress.* Ha! Leo and I have worked for everything we have. We've fought and scrabbled and saved. I inherited an eighth of this property when I was twenty-two, and we bought the rest with hard-earned money. From the time I was sixteen until two months ago, I've had a job, sometimes two jobs. Perhaps to the outside world it appears our good fortune was handed to us on a silver platter, but that's not how it was. My parents provided me an education for which I am incredibly grateful. Beyond that, we earned this life. What would our detractors have us do? Ignore the potential liability and allow Davina to stay? Never sell the property at all, leaving us in a deep hole of debt we might never claw our way out of? Would any of the people who are so quick to judge do that? It's easy to cast stones when you're not the one being asked to make the sacrifice.

I close my eyes and rub my temples between my fingers, a headache forming, unable to believe the nightmare this has become. The judge was right to be worried for our safety. I now have a dent in the driver's door of my car, along with a broken taillight, both from rocks hurled at us as we pulled into our drive.

Brendon stormed into the house as angry as I've ever seen him, steam practically blowing from his ears as he muttered "Jerks" and slammed the door behind him.

I called the sheriff, and he has posted a deputy on the road, but the mob has grown so large a single deputy doesn't seem like enough. It's as if a great Woodstock revival has landed in the cornfield across the street—music blasting from trucks and speakers, meat grilling on spits and barbecues, kids running around with sparklers—a grand menagerie of people united by their shared repulsion toward money and greed, with Leo and me the perceived embodiment of it.

"You okay?" Leo asks, poking his head into the living room.

I close the laptop so he won't see what I'm watching. "Yeah. You?"

"Dandy," he says with a sideways smirk.

He looks exhausted, his face drawn and unshaven. Since Brendon and I got home, he hasn't stopped pacing, moving through the house like a prowling lion as he checks and rechecks the locks and mutters aloud to himself. He ordered the kids to their rooms and has told me at least a dozen times to stay away from the windows.

"I spoke to the sheriff," he says. "He's going to keep a deputy posted through the night."

I nod and pray one night is all it takes for this to end. Leo and I have already discussed hiring a moving company to deal with Davina's things. She just needs to tell us where she wants them moved. In the meantime, until she finds a place, the girls will look after her chickens and cats. We left word of the plan with the sheriff so he could communicate it to Davina. The last thing we want is to cause her more stress.

I was stunned when the judge announced the verdict, then said she couldn't return. I thought he was going to tell her she had a certain amount of time. It made the ruling so much harsher. It wasn't what we wanted. None of this is what we wanted.

I jump at the sound of glass shattering, and Leo lunges from where he's standing to get between me and the noise. I look around him to see shards of glass on the floor with a rock the size of a cantaloupe in the center.

"No, Leo!" I shout as he runs for the door and flings it open.

"Come near us again," he screams, "and I'll blow your bloody brains out!"

His fury is more frightening than the rock. I've never known my husband to yell like that, and he's as nonviolent as a man can be.

He slams the door, then marches to the door that leads to the basement. When it closes behind him, I walk to the rock. Painted on it are the words "Romans 12:19, It is mine to avenge; I will repay."

The basement door opens, and I look up to see Leo with a shotgun at least as old as he is, a relic that belonged to my grandfather.

"Leo—"

His fierce look stops me. "They come near us again," he says. "I'll blow their bloody brains out." Storming past, he walks out the door, and a moment later, I hear the porch swing creaking as he swings and waits.

28

DAVINA

I'm in my boat on the river, my mind drifting dangerously in and out of focus. Though I'm motoring upriver toward home, I know that's not where I'm going. I'm going to Linda, Al, and Rock's to stay with them until I can figure out another place to live. The judgment went against me, as expected, but the ruling that I couldn't return at all has thrown me for a loop.

I shake my head to try and clear the sticky cobwebs that have formed, gummy and thick, like the signals can't quite get through. Today was too much, and I regret not listening to Leo. Stubborn and mulish. Trying to make a point? For what? Out of spite toward Marie?

All those people and the commotion: I should have realized how impossible that would be. It's been more than twenty years since the explosion, and yet I still can't handle sharp noises . . . or crowds . . . or conflict.

My limbs tingle, a pins-and-needles sensation in my fingers that radiates up my arms. I open and close my hands, hoping it will help, my body having a delayed reaction to the stress. *Too much.* All of it too much.

My breath is shallow and my head dizzy. I want to open the collar of my uniform to get more air, but there are strict rules about that. A uniform is to be worn with respect, the seams pressed, your nylons straight and without runs, and your shoes polished. Everything buttoned and tucked. I'm in my dress uniform and know there's a reason but can't quite reach it. And when I look down and see there are no ribbons or medals, I find myself more confused. Where are my stripes and my name badge and my medical corps lapel pins?

The dizziness is getting worse, so I steer to shore, put my elbows on my knees, and drop my face to my hands, pressing the heels of my palms to my eyes until dots spin. Sucking air through my nose, I force my thoughts back, spiraling through time until I'm at the most horrible day of my life. Though it's counterintuitive, I've found remembering the worst of the past the quickest antidote for stilling the panic of the present.

Hot.

It's always the first thing I remember.

The morning of that day, I woke at dawn already soaked in sweat and my throat dry like sandpaper. Afghanistan hot is different from New England hot. Afghanistan hot is like sucking in furnace dust while a scorching Martian sun leaches every ounce of moisture from your skin. New Hampshire hot holds life, verdant and moist, almost refreshing if you remain still.

The day started the same as most. I dressed quickly, then called Rose, the time difference making it homework time in New York. She always saved her math problems for us to do together. That morning we were working on matching numbers to words: 45 is forty-five; 99 is ninety-nine. She didn't need my help. Rose was whip smart, and the exercise was easy. But she did it out loud for my sake, saying the number, then spelling out the answer.

We were almost finished when the corporal who was the assistant to our major walked into the barracks. He gave a nod and head flick, which meant I was needed.

"Sweetie, I have to go," I said as Rose said "Thirteen," then began to spell it: "T-h-i . . ."

She cried, "No!"

"I'm sorry, but I have to." Already, I was pulling on my boots.

"We're not done!"

Rose had a temper, a red-hot spirit she inherited from her father, and perhaps a little from me.

"There are soldiers who need me," I said.

The night before, we'd gotten word of a convoy that had been ambushed as they traveled north toward Kabul. Badly outnumbered, they had abandoned their vehicles and taken cover in a trench beside the road where they were pinned down and waiting for air support. Three soldiers had been killed, and eight were wounded and in need of medical attention.

"I need you!" Rose screamed.

"Yes, but the soldiers are hurt, so they need me more."

Those were the last words I said to her: "They need me more."

She hung up without a goodbye.

I hurried to headquarters. As lead trauma nurse, I would be responsible for informing my team of our orders. Already our logistics sergeant, Bill O'Timley, and my commanding officer, Tim Reich, were in the tent, standing at ease in front of our major, Jeremy Pinkter.

I saluted, and the three casually saluted back. Other than the major, who was new to our unit, we were friends.

Bill held my eyes an extra half second before turning back to the major. "We need to wait," he said. "I get that you want to help, but we won't be helping anyone if we end up ambushed as well."

The major's face was flushed, and drops of sweat beaded his forehead and upper lip. He was young, late twenties, making me believe he came from some deep pedigree that had moved him up the ranks quickly.

"Those men are wounded and need our help," he said.

"And they'll get it," Bill said calmly, "as soon as air support arrives."

"By then it will be too late," Pinkter said, the flush on his neck growing. "Some of those men won't make it."

Tim spoke next. "Sir, all due respect, but if we lose our medical team, we'll lose a whole lot more, present and future, than the soldiers you're trying to save."

To some that might have sounded cowardly, but I knew Tim to be one of the bravest men I'd ever met. He was the best trauma surgeon I'd ever had the privilege to serve under, and he knew better than anyone how hard it was to get doctors and nurses to enlist.

"We're not going to lose anyone!" Pinkter nearly roared, which showed how naive he was. Soldiers die every day, and commanding officers have very little say over it. "Get your teams ready. We leave at oh seven hundred."

He sounded like a little boy saying "Charge!" and I knew right then we were in trouble. War isn't a game. It isn't paintball, where if you get hit, you get to go again. In real life, if you make a mistake, that's it, game over. But all of us were soldiers, and an order was an order, so we saluted, then left to inform our teams.

Fifty minutes later, I was in the second truck of a three-vehicle convoy headed north. An hour after that, the Humvee in front of ours somehow missed the IED planted in the road, and three seconds later, our truck hit it. The deafening explosion is the last thing I remember.

I was blown clear of the truck and was the only one to survive. The only reason I was seated where I was, in the back beside the tailgate, was because I'd forgotten to grab Rose's charm, a small gold talisman in the shape of a rose my second mother had given me when Rose was born. I had needed to run back to the barracks for it, so I was the last one to climb in.

Lucky? Unlucky?

Hard to say. At the time, I thought the latter. It took years before I could appreciate the blessings of each new day.

The rose is in my shoe now, so worn it no longer resembles a flower but instead looks like a small gold nugget. Yet each night, I admire its beauty, knowing it's the reason I lived, my second mother and daughter joining forces to protect me.

I woke three months later in an army hospital in Kabul, over 30 percent of my body burned, my lungs damaged, unable to talk and barely able to breathe. Without knowing it, I'd survived more than sixty surgeries and had nearly died three times. The doctors said I was a miracle.

My first question was about Rose. I wrote it on a whiteboard: *My daughter? Is she here?*

It is not uncommon for the family of a severely injured soldier to relocate so they can be close during a long convalescence. When the doctor shook his head, I was not really surprised. I'd chosen poorly when I decided to marry, an impulsive choice based more on timing than love.

Moz and I met on my second tour. He was handsome and brilliant, and I mistook infatuation for love. He was a consultant from Iran without US citizenship, so the only way for us to be together was to get married.

It was only after our nuptials that he revealed his true nature, a selfish man who was immature and flared at the slightest insult. By the time I realized my mistake, I was pregnant, and though I didn't love him, I didn't want my child to grow up without a father, so I stayed.

It was a few days after I woke that I discovered he had not only not relocated to help me through my recovery, but he had taken Rose and disappeared altogether. The news nearly destroyed me. I stopped eating and became unresponsive, my only thought: escape. A letter from my second mother, reminding me of what had been sacrificed when I was a child so I could have the life I had, brought me back.

I need you! It's always Rose's angry voice along with the simultaneous replay of the explosion that startles me back. With a gasp, my eyes fly open, and I blink several times, trapped between past and present.

I scan the shore, my breath coming in gulps. In front of me is a bramble of honeysuckle, and to the left, a thick patch of saw grass. With a shuddering breath, I restart the motor and return to the river, knowing there's something I'm supposed to be remembering but unable to focus.

When I reach the beach, I pull the boat to shore, stumble to the cabin, climb to the loft, and collapse exhausted on the bed.

29
PENELOPE

Hannah and I sneak out the back door, quiet as mice, to take care of the cats and chickens. We don't tell Mom and Dad we're leaving, knowing if we did, they wouldn't let us go.

Last night was a very bad night. Dad was so upset after the rock was thrown through the window, he slept on the porch with a gun. And Mom was so upset I don't think she slept at all. Both forgot to mention we were no longer allowed to leave the house to take care of Davina's animals.

I feel bad for them, but I'm also mad. We should have just left Davina alone. I don't see why we need to move to Farmington. If they'd have asked me, which they didn't, I'd have told them I don't want to move. I like our house. I like my school and my friends. And I like that Bee was a part of it.

As we walk, I'm jumpy. Maybe it's because so many people hate us, or maybe it's because of the rock, but the woods, which never felt unsafe before, suddenly feel strange, the trees too quiet, as if the birds and animals are hiding.

"Hannah, do you think someone's out here?" I whisper, eyes darting.

She scans around us as well. "I don't think so," she says but picks up the pace just the same, and when we reach the clearing for the cabin, both of us sigh in relief.

"Morning!"

My face snaps sideways to see Davina at her worktable.

"Davina!" I run to her and wrap my arms around her waist. "You're here!"

"My. That is quite a greeting. Where else would I be?"

I peek at Hannah, who is still standing at the trail, a worried look on her face. "Didn't the judge say you couldn't come back?" she says.

Davina tilts her head, looks at the dried leaves on the table, then back at Hannah, her brow furrowed as if the question is confusing.

"You don't remember?" Hannah asks, stepping closer.

Davina frowns, then blinks several times. "I'm afraid yesterday's a bit of a Pollock."

"A Pollock?" I ask.

"A splatter mess in my brain I can't quite make sense of."

"You went to court," Hannah says slowly. "And the judge said you weren't allowed to come back. My mom and dad were going to have your things moved for you."

The confused look remains; then she looks again at the leaves. "Need to get this tea made," she says. She picks up a leaf and starts tearing it to bits; then, glancing at me, she says, "Pen, would you like to help?"

I shoot Hannah a look, begging her to let it go. The past day's already been bad as a day can be, and Davina is here making tea, and we're not even supposed to be here, so no one will even know that she's here.

Hannah's mouth is screwed tight to the side as her eyes squint, deciding what to do.

"Here you go," Davina says, handing me a pair of gloves.

I put them on and step onto the milk crate beside her, silently still praying as I lift a thorny stick to pull off the leaves. Finally, I hear Hannah walking toward the river and nearly cry out in relief.

"What kind of tea are you making?" I ask.

"Poop tea," Davina says, the twinkle returning to her eyes. She gives a wink. "Helps with the runs."

I giggle, and the twinkle brightens.

It makes me want to hug her again. I don't care what the stupid judge said. I'm just glad she's here.

"How come you're not wearing gloves?" I ask as I continue pulling off leaves.

"These old hands are tougher than any thorns," she says with pride. She's about to say something else when her phone rings. It's an old phone, the kind that flips open.

"Hello."

Pause.

"Yes. Of course I remember." She blinks rapidly, making it clear she forgot whatever it is she said she remembered.

"I'm at home." Beat. "Yep, the cabin."

More rapid blinking as she listens to the person on the other end.

"Nine would be fine. My beach is just south of a large willow a couple miles into the timberland."

She chuckles at something the other person says.

"I look forward to it. I've been a fan since she started on your show."

30
HANNAH

I swim until I can't get a breath, then turn on my back and let the current carry me back. When I get to the shore, Teddy is waiting.

He's the biggest cat I've ever seen and definitely has the most swagger, the Casanova of cats. At the moment, he's stretched out in the shade, his yellow eyes slitted open as he watches me make my way to shore. I drop into the lawn chair and pull the tincture from the hidden pocket of my backpack.

As it dissolves beneath my tongue, I close my eyes and let the rising sun warm me. The bitter taste is awful and comforting, the worst thing I've ever tasted and the most wonderful for the promise it offers of another headache-free day.

"Hey."

I nearly leap out of my skin at Rock's voice, then turn to see him behind me.

I'm in my swimsuit, my bare, fleshy stomach exposed, and I really wish I'd thought to wrap a towel around myself.

"Hey," I manage, craning my neck to look at him so my back is still to him. "What are you doing here?"

"My ma asked me to check on Davina. We figured, when she didn't show up at our place last night, she must've come home."

"Oh. Yeah," I say, wishing I could figure out a way to put my clothes on without needing to stand up.

He shakes his head. "I knew this was going to be too much for her."

"She does seem a bit rattled."

The truth is, it was more than a bit. Her confusion was alarming, like she had no idea how she'd gotten to the cabin or what had happened at the hearing. My first instinct was to call my dad and tell him she was here, but Pen gave me that look, a desperate plea that felt like a wish, and all I could think about was Bee.

While I don't believe, like Pen does, that Bee still exists in manifestations such as butterflies and birds, since she's been gone, constantly I'm aware of the imprint she left behind, like she's in each of us and still weighing in on things. And in that moment, I saw her in Pen and felt her inside myself, a strong urging to leave things be.

Rock walks to the edge of the water, picks up a stone, and flicks it sideways. It skips three times across the surface, leaving rings.

I take the opportunity to shimmy into my shorts and yank my T-shirt over my head.

"It's not right," he mutters, not so much to me as to the air in front of him.

I nod. It's not. But that's life. Not fair a lot of the time.

He flings another stone, and it hops five times.

"You probably wish we never came here," I say, my heart heavy with how much we unintentionally ruined things.

Rock stops and, for a moment, says nothing. Then softly, his voice barely a rasp and his eyes still on the water, he says, "The opposite. It's like I wished for something too hard, and this was what happened because of it."

It's the most awful, beautiful thing I've ever heard, and my heart tightens and bursts at once.

As if only just realizing what he said, he gets embarrassed. His ears turn red, and he picks up another stone and flings it for his best skip yet, eight bounces almost to the middle of the river.

"How do you do that?" I ask.

He looks from the fading ripples to me, and our eyes lock in some new terrifying and wonderful way. "If you want, I can teach you."

31
LEO

This whole thing has gotten completely out of hand. Last night, I slept on the porch with a shotgun. *Me*, a proclaimed pacifist who regularly petitions for gun control and has even done an economic study on the monetary impact of gun violence on our society.

I rinse the razor in the sink and return to shaving the shockingly gray stubble from my chin, trying to avoid looking too close at the rest of my face and the toll the past two months have taken. Stress can take years off a life. It's why presidents look so much worse after they've served. I cannot believe how much we are hated and how quickly it happened. Before we came here, we had always been well liked. The sort of people others referred to as "good folk" or "a nice family." I was the kind of guy people knew they could count on, often called on to volunteer in the classroom or coach or chaperone a school trip. Marie was admired and respected and constantly asked to serve on boards and committees because she is smart, reliable, and fair.

The gun is back in the cabinet in the basement. I woke this morning feeling incredibly foolish. It wasn't loaded. I couldn't find any shells. Even if I had, I wouldn't have known how to load it. I didn't even have any idea if the gun still works. But when that rock smashed through the window, something came over me, a primal instinct to do whatever it took to protect my family. I became possessed with uncharacteristic rage that made me want to seek out the evildoers and exact vengeance. The whole thing ludicrous.

I shake my head and rinse off my face.

At some point, I must have dozed off because I woke at dawn to a helicopter circling, a cameraman in the open door with the lens aimed at me. I dropped the shotgun beneath the swing, which I'm certain only made things look worse. And now, I'm incredibly embarrassed and wish there was some way to undo it.

Marie spoke with the sheriff about the rock, and he promised to speak to the landowner across the street about kicking the protesters off his property in order to disband them. He assured her, one way or another, he'd get it done. He's a good man and seems to understand our side of this fiasco.

The front door opens, and I hear Marie snap, "Are you kidding? Where have you two been?"

Quickly, I wipe my face with a towel and hurry down the stairs.

"You left the house?" Marie says. "After what happened? Do you know how dangerous that is?"

Hannah and Pen stand just inside the door. Hannah's hair is damp, her head bent and her eyes on the floor. Pen, on the other hand, glares angrily up at Marie, her arms crossed defiantly over her chest.

"We needed to feed the chickens and cats," she spits. "Otherwise, they'd starve."

Marie startles at Pen's anger, her harshness like a lash.

I step beside Marie and set my hand on her shoulder. "I should have told you it was too dangerous," I say to Pen. "I didn't think of it. Until things settle down, it's best if everyone stays in the house."

"Like prisoners?" Pen says, turning her anger on me.

"Sweet Pea," I say, calmly as I can manage, "I know this is hard—"

"No!" she snaps. "You know who this is hard on? Davina. I don't want to move to stupid Farmington! And I don't want you to kick Davina out of her home! It's not right. And you know it!" She races past and up the stairs.

I feel Marie quiver.

Looking at Hannah, I ask, "Did something happen?"

Hannah's face grows pink like a thermometer dipped in a vat of boiling water, and I feel her wavering, torn by the dilemma and whether or not to tell the truth. Finally, she says, "Davina was there. At the cabin." She looks up at us through her lashes. "But not on purpose. It was like she was confused. I don't think she even remembered that she wasn't supposed to be there."

I tense, and my heart tightens. PTSD. My father and grandfather struggled in distinct but equally troubling ways. My grandfather raged at everything around him, while my dad buried his feelings so deep it was impossible to know he felt anything at all. Both often seemed lost and disoriented, as if a step behind and stumbling to catch up.

Marie's head lolls back and forth. "That woman is going to be the end of us."

"I'll talk to her," I say.

Marie looks back over her shoulder, her crystal-blue eyes red rimmed with exhaustion and from a night of tears. "No," she says. "I'll go. You need to stay here with the kids."

32
MARIE

I walk toward the cabin feeling like my legs are pinned on backward, the world off kilter as I struggle to stay upright. I can't believe she came back. It's like we're living in a nightmare that won't end.

I hear a helicopter overhead and move off the path and out of sight, cowering like a fugitive on the run. *Like prisoners?* Pen's angry voice replays in my head.

My heart aches with how upset she was, her eight-year-old heart not able to grapple with the adult reasons for why this is happening. Meanwhile, Brendon is firmly planted on the other side.

He was there as I pulled on my shoes, standing halfway down the stairs.

"We're still moving, right?" he said.

I glanced into the kitchen, where Hannah and Leo had started to make breakfast, my heart torn in a million pieces. "Of course. Pen's just upset. This has been hard on all of us." I finished tying my laces and straightened. "We've already put the deposit on the new house. We just need to get this thing with Davina straightened out, then we'll have the cabin removed and sell the property like we planned."

The words were as much for me as for him. Nothing's changed. Forward, forward, forward . . .

Sweat leaches from my skin and soaks my shirt. I forgot how brutal New Hampshire summers can be, the most punishing days larded with such humidity it's like sucking oxygen through a straw. I trudge on, limbs leaden and thoughts muddled.

I see the tip of the A-frame through the trees and stop to wipe the wetness from my brow and to take a minute to consider the best way to approach this. Davina and I are not on the best of terms, and the last thing I want is to trigger another episode like the one in the courtroom.

I'm still thinking about it when I hear voices coming from the direction of the cabin—a woman who is not Davina along with several men. I crouch-walk to a fallen log to the left for a better view and, through the trunks, see a blonde woman standing with Davina near the chicken yard, a television crew around them. There are two cameramen, a woman with a clipboard, and another with a boom microphone.

My blood heats up, and I look closer at the camera nearest me to see a CBS insignia on its side. I turn back to the blonde woman and do a double take as I realize who she is—Lesley Stahl, the *60 Minutes* reporter I've idolized since I was a child.

Davina laughs, and a blaze of fury surges through my veins. PTSD! My foot! Davina knows exactly what she's doing, same as she knew what she was doing at the hearing. She came back here for no other reason than to do this interview, a grand play for sympathy and her best shot for staying in the cabin. Lesley Stahl points to the satellite dishes on the roof, and Davina's hands move with her words as she gestures and answers. Lesley Stahl smiles wide, delighted by the response, and they move on toward the river.

My eyes sear into Davina's back, watching as she jauntily walks along, and things suddenly become clear. This isn't about the cabin. It's personal. She is exacting revenge for what I did to my grandfather. She made it clear the first time we spoke. *You were his favorite, though you left him like the rest.* I abandoned him, and this is her way of paying me back.

I get it now—the reason she refused to leave; the reason she went through with the hearing despite knowing she was going to lose; the Oscar-winning performance she gave of being traumatized in the courtroom. She probably even planted the accomplice in the audience to drop the tape recorder. All of it planned to make me out to be a money-grubbing heiress and teach me a lesson.

My heart screams as I march back toward the house. She's cunning; I'll give her that. She has the whole world fooled. But this is not only me she's hurting; it's my family. And she should know better than anyone not to mess with a mama bear who is looking out for her cubs.

33
HANNAH

I lie on the couch staring at the ceiling, afraid to blink for fear I'll wake up and discover it wasn't real, that I never left the house this morning or swam in the river or sat in the lawn chair on the shore; that Rock never appeared and that I never had my first kiss on the bank of the Merrimack with a flock of geese flying overhead.

If it's a dream, I want to go on sleeping.

I sigh out happily and think of the letter to Juliet I will write recounting my own wondrous first encounter with love.

"I still don't think I'm holding it right," I said after my third attempt to skip a stone ended with it kerplunking ungracefully into the water.

Rock stopped skipping his own stones and came over to help. He tried to get my fingers in the right shape but couldn't quite manage it. So he stepped behind me, his body so close I could feel its heat; then, reaching his right arm around my shoulder, he moved the stone into place. I can't remember how it was positioned or a single thing he said, my entire focus on the warmth and the thousand watts of electricity running down my spine.

He felt it, too, and fell back as if shocked. "Now try," he peeped, his voice oddly high.

I liked his nervousness. It made me feel better about my own.

Clearing his throat, he said, "Don't throw it. Flick it." He demonstrated, slinging his arm sideways and snapping his wrist.

I tried to imitate him. Kerplunk.

I looked at him, and he laughed, and I laughed. A great release. And we went back to throwing . . . flicking stones—his dancing and mine sinking. Until finally, by some miracle of physics and chance, I tossed one, and it skipped three times. I squealed, and he turned, his face lit up.

Then I don't know what happened. Either he stepped in, or I did, and as if it was the most natural thing in the world, our lips touched, a graze so light that, when we fell apart, I wondered if it happened at all. But then I saw his stunned face and knew it had. He smiled, and emboldened by the grin, I stepped in and kissed him again, longer this time, my lips lingering, just like I'd imagined all my life.

At the sound of footsteps, we jumped apart.

"Whatcha doing?" Pen asked.

I was quite certain my blush would give us away, but Pen didn't seem to notice, and Rock recovered impressively, saying, "I was teaching your sister to skip rocks."

"I wanna learn," Pen said.

So Rock went about teaching her, and the three of us spent another glorious hour on the bank, Rock and I stealing glances that made my insides buzz.

When we walked back, Rock accidentally-purposely touched my hand four times, causing my heart to skip as jauntily as the rocks we'd thrown.

Voices outside startle me from my thoughts, and I push myself up, hoping it's not more reporters looking for interviews or protesters here to harass us. Careful to stay out of sight, I peek out the window, and my heart seizes.

I race down the stairs. "They're arresting her!" I yelp to my dad, who is working at the kitchen table on his laptop.

He looks up and blinks in confusion.

"Davina!" I point to the door. "Now! They're arresting her!"

He leaps to his feet, and I race after him out the door.

We get there too late, the sheriff's car already halfway down the drive, the back of Davina's head visible through the back window.

My dad pivots, and I follow him upstairs to my parents' room. My mom is on the bed, her arm draped over her eyes.

"You had her arrested?" my dad says.

My mom pushes up on her elbows and meets his glare. "I called the sheriff and told him the situation."

"You said you were going to talk to her, not have her arrested."

"I went to talk to her, but when I got there, she was too busy to talk." My mom's voice is ice cold, and I feel her anger pulsing. "She was giving a tour of the cabin to Lesley Stahl from *60 Minutes*. You know Lesley? The one who's always so nice to the people she interviews."

"She was giving an interview?" my dad says.

"Yup. Showing her around. Laughing. But don't worry"—she nods to the computer on the bed beside her—"it's only a small viewership, something like ten million."

My dad startles.

"Do you know what's going to happen when that episode airs?" my mom goes on. "The whole world is going to see it, and rather than being a blip on the evening news, we're suddenly going to be dinner conversation for all of America, the name *Egide* synonymous with Dahmer, Putin, and every other infamous horrible human *60 Minutes* has publicly crucified. So yes, I called the sheriff. At this point, what do we have to lose? She wins. She destroyed us just like she wanted."

My dad opens his mouth to say something, then closes it.

"She's not trying to destroy us," I say. "She was confused."

My mom turns her frosty glare on me. "Right," she says. "She just happened to be at the cabin she wasn't supposed to be at on the morning she had an interview with *60 Minutes*, and just coincidentally had neatly braided her hair and decided to dress in her best clothes?"

I shake my head, not willing to believe it. Davina would never do what she is saying. I saw her. Rock saw her. She was there by accident, unsure what was what. Wasn't she?

34
BRENDON

"Stay!" I say to Banjo, who is looking at me expectantly, his cone cocked to the side. I hold my hand out like a stop sign to reinforce the command and slip out the back door.

All night, I couldn't sleep. It's been five days since the trial, four days since the witch was arrested, and I feel like we are living in a pressure cooker, waiting for it to blow. Last night, the stupid *60 Minutes* episode aired, and almost immediately after, Mom's and Dad's phones started ringing with calls from unknown numbers, and twice—once at eleven and again in the middle of the night—people pounded on the door.

It was awful and scary, and entirely unfair. The interview made us out to be these horrible people who only care about money, and the witch as this innocent, helpless victim with no blame at all in what's happened. At the end of the story, they showed her in jail, sitting on a cot, her scarred face looking at the camera as she said, "All I want is to be left alone, to go back to my woods and my home."

It was all I could do not to hurl the laptop across the room. That's not all she wants. What she wants is to ruin us. There are other places she can live, places where she's not mooching off others and making them look like the bad guys.

Last night, I heard my parents talking. Dad was saying we need to leave and go back to our old house, and I could tell Mom was wavering, seriously considering it and giving up on Farmington altogether.

No! I wanted to scream. *She doesn't get to win!*

I wipe my nose with the back of my hand and realize, with frustration, I'm crying, and I hate myself a little more. Until Bee died, I never used to cry. Now it seems the smallest thing sets me off. It's pathetic. I'm pathetic.

To make matters worse, yesterday was Father's Day.

I didn't even realize it until I walked down the stairs.

"We're making breakfast for Dad," Hannah hissed quietly so Dad, who was upstairs, wouldn't hear. She ushered me into the kitchen. "It's Father's Day."

"We're making pancakes shaped like spiders," Pen said. "The bacon will be the legs."

She was standing on a chair, measuring pancake flour into a bowl. And as always happens when I first see her, all I could see was Bee, turning my skin hot and making me want to switch direction and run.

"Spiders?" I managed.

"Dad's on an arachnid kick." She did a strange wavy thing with her arms.

"It's the mating dance of the male spider," Hannah explained.

Then Pen did it again, her arms flailing in what looked like a spider rendition of the "Y.M.C.A." dance. It was so dorky it was impossible not to smile. It was also very Pen, and very not-Bee, which settled me down.

"Fine," I said. "What do you want me to do?"

"You can crack the eggs," Hannah said and slid a basket of odd-size brown and white eggs toward me.

I stared at them, then, realizing where they came from, seethed, "Whose side are you on?"

Hannah's eyes widened, and her head started to shake, while Pen fisted her hands on her hips and said, "Davina's."

My face snapped to hers, and the next words flew from my mouth before I could stop them: "Why did you have to be the one who—" I stopped the last word from escaping, but it didn't matter. We all knew what I intended to say.

Hannah stared, her mouth open and the knife she was holding stopped midslice through an orange. Pen's hands dropped, and so did her eyes.

I spun and fled. It was the worst thing I'd ever said.

All day, I wanted to apologize, but what could I possibly say? *I didn't mean it. I take it back.* Some things are just too awful to fix.

The rest of the day, I stayed in my room, only coming down for dinner, where we all ate in silence before watching *60 Minutes* on Mom's laptop. I didn't look at Pen, and she didn't look at me.

I went to bed so irritated I didn't even try to sleep, my mind spinning until finally the sun came up and I knew what I needed to do. As Dad says, "There's nothing you can do about what's done, so you might as well spend your energy on what's still possible."

The sun's heat rises as I march closer, my resolve hardening and hope growing. The past is behind me, so instead, I will focus on what is to come and the single thing I can do to fix it.

35
HANNAH

"Stripes or dots?" Pen asks. Before I can say neither, she exclaims, "Or hearts?" then she puckers her lips and makes several kissy sounds.

"Just pink," I say, frowning at her, though I'm certain my Irish skin is betraying me as I think, *Hearts, hearts, hearts!!!* Just the thought of Rock turns me into a lobster. It's very embarrassing, and Pen is having a field day with it, bringing him up every chance she gets.

"Oooh," she says, "or rocks? I could totally paint rocks."

I stick my tongue at her, and she sticks out her tongue back. Then I return to fretting over what to wear for my first date ever. Rock didn't say it was a date; he posed it as an offer to give me a tour of Franklin. I suggested a picnic beside the barn instead, knowing there was no way my dad would let me go to town, things being what they are.

Of course, that was yesterday. Before the *60 Minutes* episode. And I keep looking at my phone, certain Rock's going to text and cancel. The interview was very unfair despite everything that was said being true. The story focused on Davina, her backstory, her health, and her predicament and left out everything about the cabin not being up to code and that it is a great liability. They played up my great-grandfather's role, making it sound like his intention to leave the cabin to Davina was much clearer than it was. And they spoke of us like we were heartless, greedy outsiders with no attachment to the property at all and whose sole objective was money. They made it sound like we blindsided her on purpose and took her to court, aware she would lose and then wouldn't be able to return for her things, then lay in wait, knowing she'd come back to care for her cats and chickens, which gave us the opportunity to have her arrested. They showed the animals a lot. Teddy was a superstar.

The entire time I was watching, I thought of Rock, my insides flip-flopping as I wondered what he made of it. Already he had quit working for us, so angry at my mom for calling the sheriff.

"So, rocks?" Pen says, stopping the mental spinning.

"Fine," I say. "One rock."

"One rock for one Rock," she says excitedly, then starts rummaging through the nail kit. I'm about to suggest using the light blue when a shout from outside stops me.

"Was that Dad?" Pen asks.

Walking on my heels so as not to smudge the polish, I hobble to the window and look down to see my dad on the lawn. He glances up and yells again, "Fire!" then points toward the woods before taking off into them. I look where he was pointing to see a billow of black smoke rising from the spot of Davina's cabin.

"Oh! Oh no!"

"What?" Pen asks.

I whirl and grab my sneakers. "Stay here!"

"Your nails!" she yelps as I yank them on, not bothering with socks.

"Call 9-1-1," I say as I race from the room. "Tell them there's a fire."

When I step through the front door, my mom is stepping from her car.

"Fire!" I scream as I run past.

I hear her footsteps behind me and her breathless voice on the phone. "There's a fire." She rattles off our address. "Not the main home. Davina Lister's cabin, down near the river."

I'm certain she's unaware she just referred to the cabin as Davina's.

I smell the smoke, then taste it, the ash growing thick in the swampy air and making it difficult to see and nearly impossible to breathe. I suck air through my nose as my mom yells, "Cover your nose and mouth with your shirt."

I do as she says, my eyes stinging as I peer into the darkening haze.

We reach the clearing to find the cabin engulfed in flames, a great spire whipping and swirling toward the sky.

My dad races from the river trail and heaves a plastic bucket of water at it. A small spot fizzles while the rest of the fire continues to rage.

"Bat it down," my mom says. "Keep it back from the trees."

She pries a leafy branch from a bush and charges at a flare-up near the garden. She slaps it down, then moves on to another. My dad and I follow, the three of us tearing off branches and circling and swatting at any ember that leaps outward.

Water leaches from my pores and evaporates instantly, my skin so hot it feels as if it's crisping to leather as my eyes and throat burn. Somewhere to my left, my dad coughs, and it makes me flinch with concern. He's being far less cautious than me and my mom, charging very close to the flames and pushing us back from any flicker larger than a candle.

I see a carved sign that says **WITCH HOLLOW** and try to get close enough to grab it, but the heat pushes me back. Then my dad is there, one arm pushing me away as he continues to whack at the fire with the other. When I look again, the sign is gone, incinerated to ash.

I continue to circle and swat, my arms so tired I'm certain they're going to fall off and my throat so parched I can't get air. My mom looks up, perhaps sensing it, and for the briefest second our eyes connect, and somehow, that small glance gives me the strength I need to go on.

After what feels like hours but is probably only minutes, sirens, thread thin, reach us from the direction of the house. We continue to swat at the flames for what seems like another eternity, and finally the firemen appear. There are eight of them, their faces beaded with sweat and their chests heaving from running through the woods in their gear. Each carries an axe with a sharp end and a flat end. One carries a chainsaw.

The captain, a celery stick of a man with a large brown mustache, runs his eyes once over the situation, then barks, "Team A on a firebreak behind the structure." He nods toward the cabin, which is also the direction the flames are blowing. "Keep it from the trees. Everyone else form a brigade." He points his axe toward the buckets Davina uses to hold her leaves beside her worktable. "Douse the garden and chicken yard. Let's try to save what we can."

A lump forms as I realize that he's saying the cabin is a lost cause.

"We need a runner to relay the buckets back to the river."

My dad steps up, and the captain gives a nod of respect. The four men on the first team trot toward the backside of the cabin, and my mom and I follow the others toward the river.

The captain positions us near the water with two dozen feet between us, and bucket after bucket, we work. Each bucket is incredibly heavy, and quickly I grow exhausted, my shoulders aching and blisters forming on my hands. I see how exhausted my mom is as well, the deep breaths she takes to steel herself for the next load and the tremble in her arms. Meanwhile, tirelessly, my dad races back and forth, shuttling each empty bucket back to the river, then returning to the start for the next one.

Just when I'm certain I can't do it, convinced I'm going to drop the next handoff and reveal I'm the weak link in the chain, the captain shouts, "Last one!"

The fireman in the river scoops the bucket he's holding through the water, runs up the beach, and hands it to me, and I stagger forward to give it to my mom. She stumbles away, and I bend over my knees, my body trembling.

"Baby?" I look up to see my mom's ash-stained face. "You okay?"

I manage a nod and watch as she draws several ragged breaths through her nose.

"Stay here," she says, and staggers up the trail.

I watch her go, then drop my face and cry.

36
MARIE

I stare in disbelief. The cabin—there my entire life—gone. Reduced to ash and char. Only the potbellied stove remains, a blackened sentry on its concrete plinth, smoldering rubble around it.

How?

Davina wasn't even here.

My legs go weak. Her clothes, her things, the book she was reading the first day I saw her. Tears try to form, but there's no water left in my body, so instead it is only a hard ache in my eyes, the familiar throb of loss. *Incinerated,* I think. *Nothing left.* The fire so incredibly hot.

What would you like for us to do with the body? It's the last thing I remember the hospital administer asking before the world went black. I found out later, Leo had her cremated. Burned. I hated him for it, which was unfair; it was what he thought we believed in.

"Hey."

I turn to see him beside me, his face streaked black. Beneath the soot, his skin is singed, red like he fell asleep in the blazing sun without sunscreen.

"Drink," he rasps and holds a bottle of water toward me.

"You're hurt!" I yelp.

He follows my eyes to look at the white-and-red blistered skin on his hands as if only just noticing it.

"We need help!" I scream, my voice like gravel.

The fireman closest to us, the man who carried the chainsaw, turns.

"My husband, he's burned!"

"Jags—" Leo starts.

I shake my head hard and turn back to the firefighter. "Please, we need a medic!"

The man speaks into the walkie-talkie on his shoulder, and seconds later, another fireman jogs toward us.

"His hands," I say and nod toward Leo as I take the water bottle from him.

Almost embarrassedly, Leo lifts his hands. Gingerly, the man takes hold of the fingertips and turns the palms up, then down. The left hand is worse than the right, the skin broiled red and bumpy, with blackened bits around the thumb and forefinger.

"Let's get you back to the bus," the man says in a calm but serious way that tells me it is in fact bad.

Leo hesitates, looking at me with worry.

"Go," I say. "We're fine."

Still he doesn't move.

Please, I plead silently as the paramedic says, "You need to get these burns looked at."

Leo swallows once, then reluctantly turns and walks with the man toward the trail.

I watch them go, then sink to the ground and drop my chin to my chest. My heart aches, and I rub my knuckles against my sternum, hoping to relieve the pressure. Realizing I'm holding the water, I bring it to my lips. My throat struggles to open, but when it does, I guzzle the water down.

When the bottle is empty, I drop it to the dirt. And since I am already on my knees, in a pose of supplication, I offer up a prayer. First, for Leo to be okay, and second, for forgiveness.

Though I didn't start the fire, I feel like I'm to blame.

When I saw the *60 Minutes* episode, I realized I was mistaken. Hannah said Davina came back because she was confused. I should have believed her. It was obvious, when I watched the interview, she wasn't herself. Several times she lost track of the conversation or forgot what she'd said only minutes before. Then, as if realizing it, she would apologize. A psychiatrist came on and explained that a triggering event such as the hearing could cause an episode of PTSD that might result in disorientation or memory lapses that last days, possibly even weeks. When Lesley Stahl asked Davina why she had returned to the cabin after the judge told her not to, she said she didn't really know. She thought she might have done it for the animals. Though watching her, it was clear she wasn't sure of the answer at all.

When the show ended, I felt terrible for having called the sheriff, and I made the decision to do what I could to make things right. Which was why, this morning, I drove to town to meet with the judge. I was hoping to get the charges dropped and have her released.

It was a good, productive conversation. The judge grew up with Davina and knows her well. He suggested we leave her put, which surprised me until he explained he believed jail to be a good place for her to recover. He assured me she was being well looked after and that he and several others were discussing solutions for alternate places for her to live.

I said I wanted to help, and he promised to keep me in the loop. I drove home excited to tell Leo and the kids what I'd done.

"Mrs. Egide."

I blink my eyes open to see the fire captain in front of me. His helmet is under his arm, and his bald head glows in contrast to his ash-streaked face. He holds out his hand to help me up, and shakily I get to my feet. He was remarkable during the fire—brave, decisive, and calm—and watching him reminded me of my grandfather.

"Your husband's on his way to the hospital to have his burns looked at."

I think of Leo leaping around at the flames, his devotion torn between keeping the fire from escaping and protecting me and Hannah.

"Mrs. Egide?"

I blink and realize the captain said something else.

"I asked if you have any idea who might have started it."

The question takes a moment to register.

"Oh," I say, realizing what he's saying. The fire wasn't an accident. *Someone* started it. And he thinks that someone might have been me.

I shake my head, denying it as well as answering the question. The small motion causes a wave of dizziness, and I stumble. He catches me by the elbow, then guides me to a lawn chair at the edge of the woods that somehow survived.

Over his shoulder, he hollers, "Jake, I need a bottle of water over here."

I close my eyes to still the wooziness and suck air through my nose to keep down the bile that's risen in my throat.

"Mom?"

I blink my eyes open to see Hannah and, with strength I didn't know remained, push to my feet to pull her into my arms. She is wet and beautifully clean, and I realize it's because she went in the river—her skin cool and her body solid, real, and whole.

"You were so brave," I mumble into her hair.

"So were you," she says. "You were amazing."

37
DAVINA

"Morning," I say to the sheriff. "Here to get your keister whooped again in rummy?"

Since I was arrested four days ago, Cory's made a habit of stopping by in the afternoons. Mostly we play cards. Once we watched a silly movie on his laptop about time-traveling aliens. But today, his weather-beaten face is serious, a deep frown carved in place as he unlocks the cell and steps inside. For a moment, he stands rocking heel to toe, eyes fixed on some invisible point three feet from his toes.

"Well, spit it out," I say. "Haven't got all day. I'm a busy woman; places to go, people to see." I smile at the joke, but he doesn't smile back, letting me know how truly bad whatever he's come to say is.

"Is Al okay?" I ask, my first worry going to Rock's stepfather and his long recovery from the stroke he had a year ago.

Cory shifts his weight. "Everyone's fine."

I sigh with relief.

"It's about the cabin."

I roll my eyes and blow out a frustrated breath, irritated with all the fuss being made over an issue that's already been settled. While I appreciate everyone's support, it's over. I lost. The cabin isn't mine, and I'm here because I wasn't supposed to be there and I was. Plain and simple. I screwed up, my brain on time delay that day and not working right.

The time in jail has been good for me, has allowed me time to rest and process things. It reminds me of my days in the military, everything planned and orderly so I don't have to think—three meals a day, a set time to wake up, go outside, turn off the lights.

I'm the only inmate in the women's cell, which is in the original part of the building and a good bit away from the men's cells, so it's very quiet. And people have been dropping in nonstop since I got here, so I haven't had time to be lonely. I've also been given all sorts of things to make me comfortable—quilts, pillows, books, pies, bread, casseroles, cake. I've got more food than I can eat, and the deputies are pretty happy about it.

Rock is looking after the cats and hens, and Linda promised to take care of delivering the tinctures and teas to my patients. The only worry I have is figuring out where I'm going to live when I get out of here. Linda says I'm welcome to stay with them, but their house is small, and I don't trust myself sleeping in such tight quarters with others, my nightmares still unpredictable.

"It's bad news," Cory says, and rocks back and forth again.

"Well, based on that hangdog face, I assumed you aren't here to tell me I won the lottery."

Cory and I have been friends since we were kids. We even dated a bit. But then I went to nursing school in New York, and he went to the police academy in Concord.

"I hate to be the one to tell you this. But there's been a fire."

The final word sets every nerve buzzing, a thousand-watt jolt down my spine. I've heard it been said that we can't actually remember pain. Anyone who believes that has never been burned.

Seeing my expression, he adds quickly, "No one was hurt." Then amends it to, "Well, almost no one. It isn't serious, but Leo Egide's suffered some burns to his hands."

"Leo?" I ask.

"He and his wife and daughter tried to save it."

"Save what?" I say, my mind still tripped up on the word *fire*.

"The cabin."

My eyes flicker side to side, the words suspended and not making sense.

"I'm afraid it's gone," Cory says. "All of it but your garden, the coop, and your shed."

"How?" I ask. I wasn't even there and haven't lit a fire since the rabbit stew I cooked over a week ago.

Cory looks down again. "Pete thinks it was intentional. He says someone doused it with one of the gas canisters you keep for your outboard."

"They burned it down?"

"Not the Egides," Cory says. "At least Pete doesn't think they had anything to do with it. He says what they did trying to put it out was nothing short of heroic."

I lean my elbows on my knees and shake my head as I try to process it.

"The town's taken up a collection . . ."

He's still talking, but I've stopped listening, my brain gone sticky and my fingers starting to buzz. I lay back and drape my arm over my eyes. A moment later, the cell door clicks closed. *Fire*, the great destructor of my life.

38
LEO

I'm in an exam room at the hospital doing my best not to flinch as a nurse large and ripped as Dwayne Johnson delicately applies salve to the blisters on my hands. His name is Sam, and he sympathetically winces each time I jolt.

"Sorry," he says again and again, making me try that much harder not to react. Though I find it impossible. The skin on my left hand is far worse than the right, the flesh around my thumb seared raw and bits missing from where the charred pieces needed to be tweezed from the wounds.

The doctor who examined me offered morphine, but I turned it down, adrenaline and stupidity making me believe it wasn't that bad. Now, I am regretting the choice. It hurts like nothing I've ever experienced, and each stab of pain makes me think of Davina and how much worse she must have endured.

"Almost done," Sam says, dabbing the cotton swab ever so gently on the delicate webbing between my thumb and forefinger.

I squeeze my eyes tight as sweat drips from my brow. My left hand was lower on the branches I used to bat back the fire and therefore closer to the flames. The idea of swatting out the embers was brilliant and worked remarkably well. Marie never ceases to amaze with the things she knows. Tears spring to my eyes with the thought of her . . . and of Hannah . . . how brave they were and the danger I put them in.

"You okay?" Sam asks.

I manage a nod. Until you get married and have kids, you don't realize how far you will go to protect another. I'd have dived straight into the flames if it meant saving them. I didn't even notice my hands, not until Marie said something.

The salve hits a nerve, and I recoil, my arm yanking from Sam's grip.

"Sorry," I croak, my vocal cords as singed as my hands.

"You're fine, man. It's a hell of a thing you did."

I nod numbly, feeling no pride. The cabin was destroyed, and I put my family in danger, running at it the way I did. *Stupid. Irresponsible and stupid.*

"Now I need to wrap them," Sam says.

He starts with the right, which isn't burned nearly as badly, the skin mostly just red with only a few small blisters. It hurts as he twines the gauze around it, but the pain is bearable.

"Do you know Davina?" I ask.

Keeping his focus on his task, he says, "I think everyone in Merrimack County knows her or at least knows of her. She's been helping people far back as I can remember, and her mother and grandmother were doing it before her."

The comment makes me feel worse. I think of what she did for Hannah the day after we arrived, leaving cures without us asking and not expecting anything in return.

"We didn't mean for any of this to happen," I mutter.

Sam nods to my hands. "I'd say these burns prove that. Like I said, it was a brave thing you did, trying to save her place."

I hope the rest of the world sees it that way. While all this started with us moving here, I feel like we were only a flutter of wings that somehow managed to alter the entire ecosystem—Edward Lorenz's butterfly effect.

Lorenz's theory was that a small change is capable of causing very large consequences. A speck of dirt in an assembly line in China causes a pinprick hole in the seam of an arm floatie. A little girl drowns in a pool in Connecticut. A family is destroyed. A New Hampshire woman's world is decimated. All for a speck of dirt on the other side of the world.

"Time for the left," Sam says.

I look down to see my right hand mummified into an oven mitt of gauze. I try to wiggle my fingers, and they barely move.

"How am I supposed to use my hands?" I ask.

"You're not," Sam says. "The skin needs to heal."

He blows out a breath as if steeling himself for battle, and I look up to see him sweating nearly as much as I am despite how cool it is in the room.

"Here we go," he says, and I try to brace myself as well. But as soon as the gauze touches the raw flesh, I nearly cry out for how much it hurts. *Davina. Davina. Davina.* Her face and scars blaze in my brain as I'm reminded again of how much she's endured.

~

An hour later, I'm in a cab on my way back to the house, so preoccupied I don't realize what's happening until it's too late.

"Crap!" the driver yelps, then slams down on the accelerator to gun the taxi into our drive and away from the insults and rocks being hurled by a mob at least three times the size of the one that had been disbanded after the trial.

"Damn, you're hated," the driver says as he pulls to a stop in front of the house, a note of glee in his voice.

I want to storm from the cab, indignant, but can't manage the handle with my mitts. So instead, humiliatingly, I need to wait for him to come around and open the door. Then, double humiliatingly, I need him to retrieve my wallet so I can pay him.

Begrudgingly, I give a large tip.

Pen runs from the house. "Daddy!" She throws her arms around me.

"Hey, Sweet Pea."

She crinkles her eyes at the sound of my voice, then notices my fried face and mummified hands, and her joy falls apart and her chin starts to quiver.

I kneel and pull her into my arms. "I'm okay," I say into her curls, breathing in the soft scent of the no-tears baby shampoo she refuses to give up. "Just a bit tattered at the moment, but I'll be back to my handsome-devil self in no time."

She nods against my shoulder as her tears soak through my shirt and straight into my heart, and again, regret pulses with how much I risked.

We walk into the house, where Hannah and Rock are in the kitchen, a plate of cookies between them. Seeing Hannah safe and healthy, I nearly lose it.

Both look up, then stand.

"Mr. Egide," Rock says, "are you okay?"

Based on their expressions—Hannah's full of concern and Rock's full of gratitude—I must look truly awful. Sam cleaned my face and arms before he tended to the wounds, wiping off the grime and ash, and I think it made my appearance worse.

I nod, hoping to minimize talking, each word like sandpaper raking my raw throat. Hannah, always perceptive, hurries to the sink and pours me a glass of water. I drink it gingerly, swallowing difficult.

"Where's Mom?" I croak.

"Still at the cabin," Hannah says, eyes dropping. "She's looking for things to salvage. I tried to get her to come back, but she wouldn't."

"We offered to help," Rock says, "but she said she wanted to do it alone."

I imagine her saying that, her guilt as heavy as my own.

"And Brendon?"

"In his room," Hannah says.

I rankle at the idea of him sitting on his bed playing his stupid games while the rest of us are in such distress.

"Do you want me to get him?" Pen asks as she grabs a cookie from the plate.

I hold the water glass toward Hannah. "No. Leave him. I'm going to help your mom."

"Do you want us to come?" Rock asks, his body coiled with desire to help.

"No. Best if I go alone." My eyes level on his. "But thank you." For the briefest flicker, I have the traitorous thought of how much more noble he is than Brendon. Blinking it away, silently I vow, when this is over, to find a way back to my son.

"Perhaps you can figure out what to do for dinner," I suggest, then hurry away before Rock can say something else that causes my thoughts to betray me again.

I walk toward the trail, unable to believe only half a day has passed since I saw the smoke billowing above the treetops. I still smell it, the same scent that lingers in my clothes after a bonfire at the beach, a smell that used to bring happiness but forevermore, like the smell of swimming pools and strawberries, will only bring sorrow.

I reach the clearing to find Marie sitting in the center of what had been the cabin, her body curled with her feet tucked beneath her. She is using what looks like a metal spoon to push around chunks of coal and ash. As I get closer, I see the small collection of her finds—several glass jars, a tin box, a copper plate, a hairbrush—all of it black with soot. The copper plate is deformed. The bristles on the brush are singed.

"Hey," I rasp.

She looks up, her blue eyes shocking against her ash-smudged skin. Dried tears stain her cheeks, and her hair is wild and also streaked black.

"Hey," she says, then looks at my hands, and fresh tears slip from her eyes.

"It looks worse than it is," I say, attempting to make my voice strong, which does the opposite, the effort inciting a coughing fit that causes Marie's jaw to slide forward in a heroic effort not to fall apart completely.

I step toward her, but she holds up her hand. "No," she says. "Please. I want to do this alone."

"Jags—"

She shakes her head harder and drops her eyes. "Please," she repeats, the word so full of pain it's like a thousand razor blades to my soul. "I need to do this."

I force myself to step back, though every part of me wants to do the opposite, collapse beside her and take her in my arms.

She returns to stirring the rubble, careful as an archaeologist looking for bones on a precious dig. For a moment, I watch, wanting to do something, while knowing, as so often has been the case since Bee died, I am powerless. So instead, I find myself wishing I could turn back time—a day, a month, a year—return us to whenever it was that I was ignorantly happy, going blissfully about my life with four healthy kids, a beautiful wife, a nice home, friends, entirely unaware how fragile it was and how easily it could all fall apart.

A chicken cackles, breaking me from the thought, and I look again at Marie, resigned to return to the house, when my eyes catch on the hairbrush.

"Jags, give me the brush."

She stops her sifting, follows my eyes to the mound of relics, then lifts her face to mine. "It's ruined."

I nod but keep my mitted hand extended. So Marie pushes to her feet and hands it to me. As I palm it between my mitts, our eyes connect—*devotion, love, apology, forgiveness*—can a single look hold all that?

"Jags, come back with me," I say.

The words, like a static shock, break the connection, and she releases the brush and returns to her dig.

When I'm on the trail and far enough away where Marie can't see, I look down, excited by the long black strands tangled in the bristles.

39
BRENDON

Banjo and I are deep in the woods, far away from the cabin, but still I smell the fire. Banjo smells it as well and is on edge, the scent upsetting to us both.

I did not mean for things to happen the way they did, for Dad to get hurt, for Mom to be blamed. Again, I've managed to ruin everything.

Dad was supposed to be gone. The night before, I heard him and Mom talking about going to talk to the judge. Dad said he didn't want her going into town alone, especially after the *60 Minutes* airing. It was supposed to only be me, Hannah, and Pen who were home. But instead, he was on the porch keeping watch.

Tears sting my eyes, and angrily I wipe them away.

Stupid! Stupid, stupid, stupid!

I only meant to burn the cabin enough so she wouldn't come back. I had no idea it would go up the way it did, explosive as a torch. As soon as I threw the match, I realized my mistake, leaping back from the flames and running for the house.

I was nearly to the back door when I heard Dad yell, "Fire!"

Terrified, I raced to my room and stared out the window as he ran for the woods. Then Mom pulled up, and Hannah appeared, and they, too, ran toward the billow of black smoke.

I didn't know what to do, whether to run and help or hide in my room and pretend that was where I'd been the whole time and that I didn't realize what was happening. I was still deciding when Pen knocked on my door. I kicked off my sneakers, yanked on my headphones, and jumped on my bed. She pounded harder, then opened the door.

"Brendon!" she cried. I pulled off the headphones. "The cabin is burning!"

I reached for my sneakers to put them back on, but she grabbed my arm and shook her head. "Don't go! Don't leave me!"

So I stayed, and together we watched from the porch. The fire trucks and ambulance arrived a few minutes later. The firemen raced into the woods, leaving the ambulance guys behind.

It was almost an hour later that we stopped seeing smoke. And a few minutes after that, one of the ambulance guys stepped toward us. He smiled kindly at Pen, then looked seriously at me. "Best if you take her inside," he said.

I looked at him curiously, and his eyes held mine, letting me know something bad had happened that it was best Pen didn't see. So I led her into the house and up to my room, where we stayed until Hannah came back.

When she said Dad was at the hospital because he'd been burned, I nearly lost it, my blood pumping so hard I thought my insides were going to explode—a feeling that hasn't gone away, so much pressure I can't get a breath.

I sit on a boulder beside the river, deep enough in the woods now we no longer smell the smoke.

Banjo plops beside me.

I took his cone off this morning, and he's much happier without it, the fight with the cat forgotten and his wounds nearly healed. It's been eight days. It feels so much longer.

I throw a pine cone in the river and watch as the current carries it away, and I think how I'd like to drift away with it.

For hours, I waited for someone—Mom, Dad, a fireman, the sheriff—to come upstairs and confront me, déjà vu from the day Bee drowned. But hours passed, and no one ever did. Dad went to the hospital, the firemen left, Dad came home, then went to join Mom at the burned down cabin, and no one said a thing.

When Dad came back and I heard him coming up the stairs, hurrying like he was in a rush, I was certain my moment of reckoning was upon me. But instead of exploding through my door, he went into his own room, where I heard him muttering aloud, almost as if excited.

Sometime around seven, Hannah brought me a plate of spaghetti, which I ate alone on my bed.

Mom came home when it was dark, and I heard the shower running and waited again for her or Dad or both of them to come in and ask me why I did it. But the shower stopped, and soon after, the house grew quiet.

I lay staring at the ceiling and, sometime around midnight, realized I'd gotten away with it . . . *again* . . . a sick feeling roiling in my gut.

And now, here I am, staring at the river and wondering what comes next.

Tears rise again, and Banjo looks up, concerned.

I scruff his ears. "It's okay."

My stomach rumbles. I haven't eaten since the spaghetti last night, and it's now well past lunch. I ignore it. Eyes on the water, I stare at the rushing current as my thoughts continue to turn. Finally they land on Bee and those last, awful moments, thinking of her underwater and wondering if she was crying or trying to scream. If she knew it was over or still believed it would turn out okay, knowing I was right there, certain I would save her.

Banjo sidles closer and nuzzles his head against my thigh, and I realize he's probably hungry as well. With a final glance at the water, I force myself up and start back for the house.

40
PENELOPE

"Girls," Dad says brightly as he walks into the kitchen where I'm helping Hannah make focaccia.

He looks happy, happier than he's looked since the fire three days ago. Though he still looks pretty bad with no eyebrows or eyelashes, his face a color between tomato and cinnamon, and his hands wrapped in gauze.

Hannah stops washing the dough bowl, and I stop using the star cookie cutter I was using to make the focaccia into shapes. Since Hannah started being all lovey-dovey with Rock, she's gotten even more into baking, each day making something new. It's funny and cute, and I like it since it gives us something to do now that we can't leave the house.

Since the fire, Dad's been even more freaked out about us staying inside. Even though the sheriff made the protesters go away, Dad doesn't trust that it is safe. "Someone started that fire," he's said more than once, his voice low and rumbly.

He and Mom have decided we're going back to Hartford. But until Dad's hands are healed enough for the gauze to come off, he can't drive, and we can't leave him here alone, so we're staying at least one more week.

"How do you feel about an adventure?" he says, his smile spreading out his cheeks.

I leap off the chair. "Where to, captain?" I say with a salute, excited by the prospect of anything that involves leaving the house.

It's then that I notice the envelope pinned to his side by his right arm. He glances at it, then back at me and, a twinkle in his eyes, says, "We're going to see Davina!"

"Really?" Hannah says with excitement that matches my own.

"Can we bring her some focaccia?" I ask, wishing we'd made something sweeter, knowing how much she likes sweets.

"I think she'd like that."

I step back on the chair to finish cutting the bread. I'm going to make a chicken to add to the circles and stars, and maybe even a cat. I'm also going to bring her something from the things Mom found after the fire. There are pots and pans, a few dishes, a tin with two beaded necklaces, a red clay aardvark, a mug with a cat handle, dozens of coins from all over the world, a small green marble toad, her collection of heart stones, and three doctor knives. Hannah and I cleaned all of it as best we could, though most of it's still stained black.

"Banana, do you think Rock can give us a ride?" Dad holds up his non-envelope-holding mitt.

"Let me text him," she says, her cheeks pinking.

I look into the living room at Mom on the couch. For two days, that's where she's been, unmoving as she watches movie after movie on her laptop. She hardly eats, and I don't think she sleeps. It reminds me of how she was after Bee died, like breathing was all she could manage. Dad says she'll be okay, that everyone deals with hard things in their own way and in their own time and that we just need to be patient. So that's what we're doing. But it's scary. It took a really long time for her to come back to us the first time, and there were moments I thought she might not come back at all.

Hannah looks up from her phone, a smile on her face. "He'll be here in fifteen minutes."

She bounces up the stairs to get ready, springing up them like Tigger from *Winnie the Pooh*. Her change in the past week has been the opposite of Mom's. With her headaches gone and Rock in her life, she's a caterpillar turned into a butterfly, flittering around, glowing and beautiful.

"Should I tell Brendon?" I ask.

"I'm sure he doesn't want to visit Davina," Dad says.

My brother hasn't been around much lately. I was with him during the fire, but since then, he's gone back to avoiding me. I think it's because of the thing he said on Father's Day. I want to tell him it's okay. I know he didn't mean it. He was just mad about the eggs, and I know that seeing me reminds him of Bee and that's hard for him.

Normally, Dad wouldn't let him hole up in his room and play video games all day, but Dad's mitts have been full since the fire, so he's let him be. I also think he might be mad at Brendon. When my dad's not happy, his left dimple tightens, and for three days, whenever Brendon's been near, his dimple's gone bonkers.

"He's here!" Hannah singsongs as she flies down the stairs toward the door, and Dad and I exchange a look and a giggle.

"Ready to make some magic," Dad says, the words causing my pulse to race. It's the phrase he uses when we're about to do something extraordinary, and I look again at the envelope and wonder what mystical power it holds.

41
HANNAH

My nerves are jumping as Rock and I follow Pen, my dad, and a deputy down a long hallway toward the cell where Davina is being held. Rock's hand is clammy in mine, his fingers gripped tight. He's already been to see her twice, and both times left him in a sour mood. Seeing her locked up is deeply upsetting, and I know he's struggling knowing it was my family who caused it.

I'm still not used to holding hands, but whenever Rock's around, constantly he is touching me in some way, nudging my shoulder, sliding his pinkie sideways on the couch beside mine as we watch a Netflix movie on my laptop, taking my hand when we walk. My parents aren't like that. Rarely do they hug or kiss in front of us. So it's strange, and I'm awkward at it. But each night when I go to sleep, it's those small touches that I drift away to with a smile.

I was certain, after the fire, he wouldn't want anything to do with me. But he showed up that afternoon with a plate of biscuits baked by his mom.

"Is your dad okay?" was the first thing he said, his chocolate eyes misty with concern. And I lost it. My dad was still at the hospital. My mom was at the fire site, rummaging through the ashes. And it was all too much.

Then he was holding me and whispering it was going to be okay as I sobbed against him, embarrassed but unable to stop. And since then, we've been inseparable, every moment spent in each other's company, the hug of comfort turning out to be far more poignant than our kiss.

"This is the original building," the deputy explains as we pass from a white-painted hallway into a wider one made of brick.

Instantly it gets cooler and brighter. To the right are a series of large arched windows that open to a courtyard of grass, and I'm glad Davina is here instead of in the new part.

I try to ignore the pulse of migraine that flares with the brightness. Despite still taking the tincture, without my morning swims, the headaches have crept back like a pulsing caution sign, warning what will happen if I don't continue my routine.

"Morning, Davina," the deputy says, and I realize we've arrived. "You have visitors."

I look past him and through the black bars to see Davina stand from the bunk she'd been lying on. There are two sets of bunk beds, and on the far wall is a sink with a small dividing wall beside it where I assume there is a toilet.

Rock's grip tightens, his anger pulsing, and I wonder if asking him to drive us wasn't such a good idea.

"Oh my!" Davina says, her eyes crinkling with her smile as she claps her hands in front of her. "Look who's here!"

The deputy swings open the door, and Pen shoves the Tupperware of focaccia she was holding at me and runs in. Davina drops to a knee and opens her arms to receive the eight-year-old missile, and Pen clings to her neck.

"Shhh," Davina says. "You're okay."

And I realize Pen is crying. It makes my own eyes well, and Rock's hand squeezes so hard I wince. He looks down, and realizing what he's done, his fingers spring open.

"Sorry," he mumbles, looking far more apologetic than he needs to be.

I retake his hand, and he's careful to hold it gently.

Davina looks up. "Well, hasn't this day just gotten a whole lot brighter?"

Pen releases her, and Davina stands with a small groan, reminding us she's not young.

She looks at my dad. "Oh, Leo," she says as she takes in his singed face, then drops her eyes to his bandaged hands. She shakes her head and returns her gaze to his. "It was only a cabin."

My dad nods as his Adam's apple bobs, and I realize he, too, is close to losing it.

"We brought you focaccia," Pen says, snatching the container back and thrusting it at Davina.

Davina peels back the cover and peeks in. "Chickens and stars. The earth and the sky made from pure deliciousness. How perfect."

"Davina," the deputy interrupts. He is still in the corridor, as if respecting Davina's space. "Perhaps you'd like to eat your focaccia with your visitors in the conference room?"

His deference is sweet and makes me feel a little better about things. Despite the accommodations, she is obviously being treated well.

"That's a fine idea!" Davina says with brightness that's almost jarring, her upbeat facade unconvincing given how thin she looks and the dark circles beneath her eyes that weren't there a week ago.

She touches my cheek as she passes, then looks down at my hand clasped in Rock's and gives him a wink.

We follow her back the way we came to a room with a fake wood table and eight plastic chairs. The guard leaves the door open and continues on his way.

"They really should do something about security in this place," my dad says.

Davina shrugs. "Where would I go?"

The humor thuds to the ground, and we all focus on passing around the focaccia and commenting on how good it is.

"I brought you something," Pen says.

From her pocket, she pulls out a small green marble frog my mom recovered from the fire.

"Oh," Davina says, lifting it carefully, her expression unreadable, and I realize what a terrible idea it was to bring it, the small trinket a painful reminder of everything she's lost.

She turns it in her palm, and a smile tugs at her eyes. "I got this in Afghanistan. At a bazaar in the town of Herat. There was a man there who carved them by hand."

"Frogs are lucky," Pen says.

Davina nods, and her eyes smile a little more as she continues to look at the immortalized little creature. "It was supposed to be for my daughter."

"Why didn't you give it to her?" Pen asks, her hand now on Davina's shoulder, the two of them admiring the frog together.

"Never got the chance," Davina says.

When we were helping Rock scrape the house so it could be painted, my dad asked him about Davina, and he told us her story. She used to be married and had a daughter named Rose. Rock said his mom had met the husband and Rose a few times when the family came home to visit Davina's mom for the holidays. But after Davina was hurt, the husband left with Rose, and Davina never heard from them again. Rock said our grandfather tried to find them, but other than to figure out that they'd gone back to the man's homeland of Iran, he didn't have any luck.

Davina plucks the little frog from her palm and holds it toward Pen. "You keep it."

Both my dad and I shake our heads, the idea of taking more from Davina impossible.

"The man who carved it also understood frogs are vessels of good fortune but . . ." Her eyes twinkle, and Pen is transfixed. "Only if received as a gift."

My dad and I stop shaking our heads and look away as Pen takes the little frog as if Davina has handed her the moon.

"Kids, I need a moment alone with Davina," my dad says.

We all look at the mysterious envelope.

"Say your goodbyes, and I'll meet you in the lobby."

42
LEO

I wait until I'm certain the kids are out of earshot, then turn to Davina. Despite the graciousness she's shown, I see the toll the week has taken, her shoulders stooped and her body thinner than the last time I saw her. It makes me think of the movie *E.T.* and how the wide-eyed alien's health and vitality faded the longer he was away from his world.

"You look terrible," she says, as if reflecting my thoughts back like a boomerang. "You need to get some rest and put some aloe on those burns."

I nod. I suppose the week has taken a toll on all of us.

"Davina, I'm so—"

She lifts her hand to stop me. "Don't apologize for things you can't control," she says. "I know you had nothing to do with the fire." She nods toward my hands. "And while stupid, I appreciate what you did to try to save the cabin."

I nod, though her words do little to assuage my guilt. In the end, we are the sum of our deeds, and I feel like I did far too little to stop everything that's happened. I look at the manila envelope on the table, hoping it's an ember of redemption.

I slide it toward her. "I have something for you."

Before she opens it, she takes a sip of water, tilting the bottle carefully as she tips her head back, like she did with the beer the first day I met her, and again my heart aches for the pain we've caused this woman who has already survived so much.

Setting down the bottle, she turns the envelope over, lifts the flap, and pulls out the four sheets I printed this morning. I watch, feeling like a parent at Christmas waiting for a child to open the present they've been hoping for.

Her eyes scan the first page, and I watch as her brow pinches, then as her expression freezes. Almost violently, she shoves the sheets back in the envelope and sets her fisted hands on top of it.

"Oh," I say as I realize what's happening. "You knew."

"Of course I knew," she says, her voice a hiss. "Where you come from and who you are are not things you forget."

My heart pounds as I process her anger, the reaction so different from the one I was expecting. I woke this morning excited to see the email I'd been waiting for. My brother is the analytics manager for a genealogy lab in Massachusetts, and on Monday, I overnighted him the hair sample from Davina's hairbrush. He rushed it through the lab, and this morning, I got the results. Rock told us Davina had a daughter who had been taken by the girl's father while she was recovering from her injuries. When I sent the hair to the lab, I was hoping to find a clue to the daughter's whereabouts. What I found instead was almost as wonderful . . . or so I thought. While the report didn't show any matches for potential children, under "Likely DNA Matches" were listed two paternal half brothers: Everett Dupree and Roger Dupree.

I stared at the names in disbelief—the two brothers famous, heirs to the great Dupree fortune. Their father, Stanley Dupree, had been a real estate developer who transformed his wealth into one of the greatest financial empires in the world as well as one of the greatest philanthropies. His foundation is responsible for funding all sorts of medical research, and universities all over the country have buildings bearing the Dupree name.

And Davina was a part of it. My initial thought was that her father had an affair. But then I remembered the scandal. It happened before I was born but lived on in infamy, as scintillating, unsolved mysteries of the rich and famous tend to do.

I punched *Stanley Dupree missing wife and daughter* into my computer and got over a million hits. I clicked on a story from two years earlier with a headline that read "Rebecca and Valentina Dupree: 50th Anniversary of Their Tragic Disappearance." The article included several photos, and there she was, a six-year-old version of the woman in front of me, the spice-gold eyes unmistakable.

"Have you told anyone?" she asks, eyes blazing.

I shake my head even as I realize it's a lie. I told Marie. This morning, as soon as I made the discovery, I ran downstairs to tell her. I thought it was wonderful news. Davina was Rebecca Dupree, which meant she was rich, richer than rich. Which meant she could move wherever she wanted, rebuild the cabin, build a hundred of them if she wanted.

Davina sighs in relief, her single nostril opening and closing. "I'll ask you to keep it that way."

I look at the envelope. "I don't understand."

"All there is to understand is my name is Davina Lister. My mother was Rosalinda Lister. And I've lived here long as anyone can remember."

I shake my head in confusion. "But you were kidnapped?"

Her face reveals nothing.

"Weren't you?"

Then I remember what she said about her first mother dying in the cabin.

"Oh," I say as I realize the other possibility. "You weren't kidnapped."

She doesn't answer, her ice-cold eyes holding mine.

"But he's gone," I say, "your father, and—"

"He's not my father."

The tremor in her voice sends a shudder through me, letting me know whatever Stanley Dupree did that caused her and her mother to flee must have been truly awful.

"He left a trust in your name in case you were ever found—"

"I don't want his money."

"But you could be rich, buy the property and do whatever you want with it."

A long beat passes, her eyes flickering as if considering something. Finally, she says, "Tell me, Leo, are you happy?"

No.

"Mostly," I lie.

"Let me rephrase the question. Before Bee died, were you happy?"

"Yes," the answer so instant it hurts. Before that awful day, I was content as a man could be and blissfully ignorant of how precarious it was.

She nods and stands. "So was I." She slides the envelope toward me, then stands and pivots away, leaving me alone and low as a man can be.

I think of Marie's reaction when I told her what I'd found.

"So she's rich?" she said, brows arching as she looked at the report. She was dressed in the same sweats she'd had on for days, her hair matted and her face gaunt from lack of sleep.

"But she doesn't know it," I said. "It happened when she was so young."

Marie tilted her head.

"What?" I asked.

"I don't know," she said. "I remember things from when I was six." She nodded toward Pen in the kitchen. "Pen certainly remembers things from two years ago."

I shook my head, certain it couldn't be true. If Davina knew, she'd have come forward when Stanley Dupree died. His final gesture of eternal love to his missing wife and daughter was an immense trust left in their names that was all over the news.

"Well, I suppose you'll find out," Marie said as she handed the report back; then she lay down again and curled on her side.

Now, here I am, a few hours later, and it turns out she was right. I was so sure I was doing something good, and instead all I've managed is to stir up old wounds and somehow, once again, make things worse.

43
DAVINA

I ball my hands tight and press them hard to my thighs to settle their tremble. Of all the bad things that have happened since the Egides arrived, this is the worst. I close my eyes and pray that, wherever Rose is, she is safe. Tears pool behind my lids, and I push them back. Crying doesn't solve anything, and neither does self-pity.

I can't believe this is happening. Already I'm at the center of a media spectacle I have no desire to be a part of. I can only imagine the uproar this would cause. Fifty-two years I've kept our secret, so long I started to believe I would take it to my grave. When the colonel passed, I was the last one who knew.

"You could be rich," Leo said, a question in his voice, bewildered that I was not thrilled by his discovery.

Pfft. I lie back on the mattress and drape my arm over my eyes. I know money. I know what it does to people and how easily it corrupts. Like a drug, it is addictive as heroin and the high as false. I know the power it gives those who possess it and how difficult it is to stand against it. I think of my first mother and the courage it took to escape. Eyes were everywhere, our home a gilded cage with a devoted staff paid exceptionally well to keep my father's secrets. Leaving was incredibly dangerous, and had we been discovered, we'd have never been left alone again. My first mother died, but I know, given the choice, she'd still have chosen to do what she did, knowing I survived. That's what you do for your children: you protect them.

Despite my efforts, the tears I've been fighting leak, as again, I think of Rose. It's why I never did a DNA test myself or searched too hard, knowing the Pandora's box I risked opening. While Moz was too selfish to take on the responsibility of caring for me after I was injured, I knew how much he loved Rose and always imagined, wherever they went, she lived a good life and was well cared for.

She's twenty-nine now, same age my first mother was when we fled. It's impossible to think of my daughter being the age of my first mother when she died, a grown woman with a life all her own. I wonder if she has children. The thought causes an intense ache. How I'd love to meet them and to see who my daughter has become. Though even as I think it, I pray it never happens and that our secret remains safe, knowing that the scandal of our discovery would blow up whatever life she's made. Suddenly, it would be all her life was about, her achievements diminished by money she didn't earn, her family thrust into a spotlight of fame they didn't ask for, and her name forever tied to the Duprees and our notorious past. I'd trade all my tomorrows to protect hers, and I hope I made that clear to Leo. He said he's the only one who knows, but someone ran the report. I can only hope the confidentiality those places promise is real.

"Davina?"

I move my arm to see Cory in the cell's doorway.

"Hey," I say, sitting up.

"Everything okay?"

"Hunky dory," I lie. I nod to the open door. "You know the security in this place is atrocious. A dangerous, wanton criminal could waltz right out."

"You're not a criminal," he says. "You're an honored guest."

"Then the accommodations are atrocious," I say. "Just look at this place." I wave my hand around the cell. "No mints on the pillow. No robe."

"Then you'll be happy to hear the news I have."

It's the second time in as many hours someone's offered a Cheshire grin like they're about to hand me the moon, and my blood goes cold, fully believing he's going to present the same stunning revelation as Leo.

"Seriously," he says, "you're not going to believe it."

"Try me." I lean forward with my elbows on my knees to brace myself.

"Someone's bought you a house."

I look up, tilt my head, and squint.

"And not just any house, your childhood house, the one you lived in with your mother."

"What the criminy are you talking about?"

"I just got off the phone with Bill."

Bill is the only real estate agent in Franklin, and he and Cory are good friends.

"He said some rich army vet saw the *60 Minutes* episode, and it pissed him off. So he did some digging, found out where you grew up, and made Emily and Bob an offer they couldn't refuse."

Emily and Bob Carver are the couple who bought my second mother's house when she needed to be moved to hospice. They raised their two children there and are now retired.

"Some stranger bought me a house?"

"Yep. Just when you start doubting humanity, someone goes and does something like this and restores your faith."

I think of my childhood home, a two-bedroom light-filled cottage with a large brick fireplace just south of the timberland.

"No strings?" I ask, a hot glow in my chest, almost painful from the promise it offers, the pull of my childhood home similar to that of the cabin.

"Except that he remain anonymous," Cory says. "Bob and Emily need a few weeks to move out. And until then, you're welcome to stay in these *atrocious* accommodations as our guest, or you can leave if there's someplace you'd rather be."

"What about my sentence?"

"I talked to Jeremy, and he agrees, since there's no cabin, he doesn't see any reason to keep you, so he reduced your sentence to time served."

"Nice to have friends in high places," I say, knowing the reason I was arrested wasn't about the trespassing but was so I'd be somewhere safe while I got my head screwed on straight.

"How about a game of rummy while you think about it?" he says and pulls a pack of cards from his pocket.

He sits on the mattress and starts to shuffle. I stare at the riffling cards and try to focus on the amazing good fortune about the house along with the promise it offers for my future. But no matter how I try, the alternative blares neon in my mind—my world blown up as headlines around the world shout "Dupree Mystery Solved!!!"

44
MARIE

I push myself upright, and my head swoons with dizziness from the sudden redistribution of blood. The family, except for Brendon, has gone to see Davina, Leo practically giddy with the news that she is rich.

I don't know how I feel about the discovery. When he first told me, my reaction was distinctly bitter, a sour taste on my tongue at the idea that the person responsible for destroying us, intentionally or not, was not the poor victim the world believes her to be but, in fact, rich as the Rockefellers or Hiltons—the rightful heiress to so much money she could have stopped all this from happening in the first place.

Leo was certain she has no idea. But how could that be? Six is not a baby. True, there could have been some sort of trauma that caused her to repress her memory, or perhaps even a physical cause for amnesia. But I don't believe it. I think she knows.

Which also upsets me. Why turn away from that sort of wealth, the kind that can buy a lavish life with any luxury you desire?

My stomach grumbles, and I look at the plate of uneaten toast left by Hannah on the coffee table hours ago. I know I should eat but have no interest. Instead, I drop my elbows to my knees and my face to my hands.

Davina is Rebecca Dupree, long-lost daughter of Stanley Dupree.

I think of the fuel this would add to this already raging media maelstrom around us. The only consolation I can think of is that a discovery this big might reduce us to a sidenote and allow us to get our lives back. Though I doubt it. Like the collateral damage of a catastrophic wreck, the destruction has already been done.

The day after the fire, I woke to an email from my boss in which he eloquently informed me that "in light of things," the board had decided to extend my personal leave "indefinitely." He said the "optics" of me returning were unfortunately "too unseemly." Twelve years I've given to that company, and that's the thanks I get: a kick in the teeth via email.

I press the heels of my hands to my eye sockets, regret pulsing. I never should have put the deposit on the Farmington house or bought all the things I did to furnish it. I press harder, wishing I could press it all away.

Since high school, I've worked tirelessly to get to the place we were—a comfortable life, a nice house, a future that was secure. Then, *poof*, just like that, all of it is gone, destroyed by the flick of a match I didn't throw.

"Mom?" I look up to see Brendon at the bottom of the stairs.

"Hey, buddy." I push shakily to my feet.

"I'm hungry."

"Right."

I shuffle to the kitchen and piece together a peanut butter and jelly sandwich along with some chips. I glance at the clock, surprised to see it's nearly three.

"Aren't you going to eat?" he asks when I slide the plate toward him.

"I'm not hungry."

He looks at his plate, then up at me. "So, now that the cabin's gone, we can sell this place, right?"

I blink, the words on time delay. *Cabin. Gone. Sell this place.*

"Not yet. The site needs to be cleaned up from the fire, and the house still needs to be painted."

My head spins with how much the quote was to dispose of the cabin's debris and to excavate and remove the septic system. Because of the cabin's proximity to the river, it can only be done by a special environmental remediation company, of which there is only one in the state, and the amount they want is exorbitant.

Brendon's shoulders sag, and he looks almost as defeated as I feel.

"We'll figure it out," I say, thinking again of Davina and her wealth, which creates a fresh wave of anger that dizzies me, and I steady myself on the counter.

"You okay?" Brendon asks.

I nod and lower myself to a stool. My head pounds like there's a monsoon in my skull, and I rub my temples between my fingers.

My eyes fly open, and I look at the sink where I poured the medicine Davina gave Hannah the day after we arrived.

When was the last time Hannah complained of a headache?

I look at Brendon, who has finished his sandwich and is trudging toward the stairs. "Bren, is Hannah still getting medicine from Davina?"

"How should I know?"

He continues, and I follow.

I walk into the girls' room, and it takes less than a minute for me to find the jar stashed in the inner pocket of Hannah's backpack. Betrayal pierces my heart, and the last of my sympathy runs out. The woman has destroyed my life, turned my daughters against me, given Hannah medicine I explicitly told her not to, and she is rich. For twenty-two years she has lived on our land rent-free. *Enough.* She is Rebecca damn Dupree, and the time has come for her to pay.

45
HANNAH

The drive home is quiet, each of us lost in our thoughts. Rock grips the steering wheel so tight his knuckles are white. He says he doesn't blame us, but there's no arguing we are the reason Davina's in jail, and seeing her there has put him in a mood.

My dad sits beside him, his excitement over what he came to share with Davina deflated. He still has the envelope, but it is cast aside on the seat, no longer prized, and again, I wonder what it contains.

I am sad. Pen is angry. And everything is so sideways I can't help but wonder how it got so out of whack. My parents are not bad people. Neither is Davina. Yet somehow, they've ended up on opposite sides of a battle everyone has lost.

The truck rolls to a stop, and my dad turns to Rock. "Thank you."

Rock gives a curt nod, and my dad climbs out.

"Hasta lasagna," Pen says, almost getting a smirk in the rearview mirror from Rock before she hops out as well.

The door closes, and I lean forward and hug him from behind. "Thank you. I know this was hard."

He reaches up and squeezes my arm but doesn't answer, and I wonder if this might be the final straw. After another excruciating second of waiting for some sort of reassurance, I release him and climb out, then watch as he drives away without looking back.

When I walk in the house, my dad and Pen are stopped in the entry. I follow their eyes to see my mom at the kitchen table, the jar of feverfew tincture in front of her.

A hard knot forms in my chest, and I wait for her to explode. Instead, she does the opposite. With a glance at the jar, then a devastating look at me, she pushes shakily to her feet and walks past.

"Mom," I say to her back. "I'm sorry."

She turns her head, her eyes red rimmed and filled with so much sadness it hurts to look at them. Her voice a rasp, she says, "It's fine. You made your choice." Then she looks at Pen and my dad, all of us shot through the heart.

Zombielike, she continues to the couch. On the table are the coffee and toast I set there this morning, and I wonder when the last time was that she ate, and my heart breaks a little more.

Pen looks up at me, and I wrap my arm over her shoulder.

"Girls, go on up to your room," my dad says, his eyes still on my mom and his once-proud shoulders slumped.

I turn Pen toward the stairs, but before we reach the first step, my eyes catch on the hidden door in the paneling that leads to the basement.

"Where are we going?" Pen asks as I steer her toward it.

"To do something good," I say with another glance at my mom.

As we walk down the stairs, I think of something Davina said the first day I met her. We'd been talking about Macbeth, and I said he was the worst protagonist ever. She chuckled and answered, "And therefore one of the best—evil and good—there's truth in that. The way I see it, we're all a bit like curdled milk, so the choice is, you either decide to make cheese or else let the whole thing go to rot." She smiled wide. "Personally, I like cheese."

I like cheese as well. And I love my mom. But I also love Davina. And awful as I feel about my mom finding out about the tincture the way that she did, I don't feel bad about caring about Davina. I didn't "choose," as my mom said. I simply opened my heart a little wider to let someone else in. Hopefully, eventually my mom will see that.

"Whoa!" Pen says, stopping halfway down as her eyes scan the treasure trove below.

The basement is filled floor to ceiling with all sorts of bric-a-brac. In front of us is a crystal chandelier the size of a car that looks like it came from *The Great Gatsby*. Suspended from the rafters is a canoe. And leaning against the wall are a dozen wooden carousel horses that make you wonder if, at some point, one of our ancestors owned a merry-go-round. There are dressers, bed frames, couches, and tables, along with baskets, trunks, and crates full of odds and ends. There's even a coffin.

"I figure we can look for a few things for Davina for when she finds a new place to live."

Pen nods eagerly, then bounds the rest of the way down the stairs, her heart open as an ocean.

46
PENELOPE

"Hey," I say to Hannah, who is across the room, sorting through a box of pots and pans. "Is this Mom?" I hold up a framed photo that looks a lot like Hannah standing beside a man I know is my great-grandfather.

Hannah sets down a skillet and steps closer.

"Wow," she says as she squats beside me, recognizing the likeness as well.

In the photo, Mom looks close to the same age Hannah is now, maybe a little younger. She's skinny, and her hair is long. Her faded gray T-shirt has a picture of Snoopy with sunglasses on it, and she's smiling wide as she leans her elbow on my great-grandfather's shoulder with her ankles crossed. My great-grandfather has his head tilted back and looks like he's laughing.

"They look so happy," Hannah says.

I agree. It's weird seeing Mom young and so unserious. And looking at my great-grandfather makes me think of Bee. He looks like a jokester. And I know I would have liked him very much.

"There's more," Hannah says as she pulls the plastic bin where I found the photo toward her. She plops to her butt, and for a long time, we look through dozens of albums and hundreds of photos.

There's an album dedicated to each summer the family came to visit. It looks like a lot of fun—my mom, aunt, and grandparents, along with dozens of people I don't know, playing, smiling, and laughing.

"Look," Hannah says. "It's Davina." She holds an open album toward me.

Standing in the snow is a girl with ink-black hair in two long braids and wide gold eyes the exact color of Davina's. Beside her is a snowman ingeniously holding its own decapitated head suspended from its stick arm.

"She was so pretty," I say, feeling a little jealous.

Hannah nods, then peeks at the cover to look at the date. "1974," she says. "This was before Mom was even born."

"Whoa," I say as an idea occurs to me. "Do you think our great-grandfather could be Davina's dad? Maybe that's why he gave her the cabin?"

Hannah's eyes grow wide. "Wouldn't that be crazy? That would make her Mom's aunt, and our great-aunt."

We both look again at the photo. She doesn't look like our great-grandfather or like Mom, but the idea is so wonderful I don't want to let it go. It would mean Davina is family.

We go back to looking through the albums, and a moment later, Hannah says, "Here's one of her older."

The photo is of Davina as a young woman holding a curly-haired baby in dungaree overalls.

"That must be Rose," I say, then notice a photo on the next page of the same little girl in the arms of a man with a mustache and thick black hair, Davina beside them. "And that must be her husband."

"Yep," Hannah says angrily, "that must be him."

47
BRENDON

I kick a pine cone hard, and Banjo, who is a few steps ahead, looks back. We're not moving to Farmington. We might not even still be a family.

Tears form, and I swallow them down. I don't deserve to feel sorry for myself. After all, I'm the one who caused it, all of it—Bee dying, Mom losing her job, everyone hating us, Dad lying so Mom says she can no longer trust him.

A blast of wind gusts, causing me to shudder. I left the house without grabbing a coat, and the night is cold and dark, a storm brewing. I don't care. The cold doesn't matter. Nothing does. I'm like the acorn that started the avalanche: I looked away for a moment, and the world hasn't stopped rattling since.

I reach the same boulder I sat on before and sit with my legs over the edge. Below me, the river rages, the wind creating small, angry waves as the current surges and swirls.

Banjo plops beside me, and I drape my arm over his neck.

I look at my sneakers over the water, stained and dirty. They were nearly new when Bee died. I remember how excited I was when I got them. All my friends were talking about the new Nike Airs, and our catcher, the coolest guy on the team, whose parents are megarich, had ordered them the day they were released. When I asked Dad if I could get a pair, he said, "Awful pricey for something you're going to grow out of in a few months." So I asked Mom, and she ordered them, right there on the spot.

When they arrived and Bee saw them, she wrinkled her nose.

"You don't know beauty when you see it," I said, pulling them on.

"And you don't know ugly when you see it." She wrinkled her nose again.

She was right. They are ugly—teal stripes with yellow suede on the toes and heels. They're loud and flashy and not my taste at all. And Dad was right: they were way too expensive for what they are. Another regret added to the incredibly long list of things I have to be sorry about. I can't believe I cared so much about a stupid pair of shoes.

Today was another awful day. This afternoon, Hannah, Pen, and Dad went to visit the witch in jail, and when they got home, something bad must have happened because no one was talking to anyone. We didn't even have dinner. Finally, at eight thirty, I went downstairs because I was starving. Pen was at the table eating cereal, and Dad and Mom were talking in the living room.

"She's not out to get you," Dad said in frustration, using a tone I'd never heard him use with Mom before.

"Well, whether she intended it or not, she's done a good job of it. She has you lying to me. Hannah lying to me."

"I'm sorry about that," Dad said.

I had no idea what lie they were talking about. But whatever it was must have been bad because Dad looked pretty broken up over it.

"And yet, you're still on her side," Mom said.

"It's not our secret to tell," Dad said.

"Fine, then. She wins. She gets to keep her secret, and we lose everything. Happy?"

Dad shook his head and looked miserable as I've ever seen him. They both did.

"I'll call the developer tomorrow," Mom went on. "Tell him we changed our mind and that we are forfeiting the deposit."

I wheeled for the back door, unable to listen to any more.

A shudder quivers my skin as I stare at the rushing water and again think of Bee and the last time I saw her.

Cold.

It's how she looked when I pulled her out, her face so white it was as if her freckles had been frozen away, her lips blue.

Her eyes were open, and when I laid her on the deck, I cried out in relief, stupidly believing it meant she was okay. But then I noticed her mouth, hung open like she was about to say something, but her body perfectly still, quieter than she'd ever been in life . . .

Peaceful.

Banjo's head pops up, and I turn with him toward a rustle in the bushes. His ears perk, and he takes off after it—a rabbit or a squirrel he won't be able to catch.

I turn back to the rushing water and look into the blackness, almost able to feel it—the silence, emptiness, and permanence . . .

Banjo howls, and my heart jumps.

48
DAVINA

After our game of rummy, Cory left, and after a nap and round of good-byes to the deputies, so did I. Not that I minded jail, but desperately I miss the river and woods.

The cabin is gone, but that doesn't concern me. I've spent many a summer night sleeping beneath the stars. In my boat is a sleeping bag, and I've taken the quilt and pillow Cory's wife dropped off at the jail. I also have the focaccia from the girls and a couple containers of other food generously dropped off by friends.

I keep my chin tucked in my jacket and my wool cap pulled low as I walk, both because there's a chill and because I don't want to be noticed. My scars startle those who don't know me, and I'm not in the mood to chat with those who do. There's been such a fuss made over the cabin, and I just want to get to the river without having to discuss it.

Rock moved the boat to the town dock after the fire, and I find it right where he said it would be.

"Hello, old friend," I say as I step into it.

The current is rough, with the promise of a coming storm. Wind gusts off its surface, creating small waves and making the ride rocky. I give her full throttle and let the cold rush over me as I bounce upstream, my lungs expanding and my muscles uncoiling.

It's almost nine and nearly pitch black: thick clouds obscuring the lingering daylight and covering the moon. I speed toward the timberland, hoping to get there before the rain starts in earnest so I can check on Teddy and the chickens and see for myself what remains.

I'm not worried about being arrested again. As Cory said, the cabin is gone. There's nothing for me to go back to, and I'm no longer addle brained from stress. I feel bad for the trouble I caused, but I don't control these things. They just happen, the scars within me as permanent as the ones that can be seen. It starts to drizzle, but I pay it no mind. Cory said the shed survived. If need be, I'll hunker down inside and ride it out.

As I drive past my second mother's property, I peer up the bank and am just able to make out the dark silhouette of the chimney. It makes me smile, and I send a silent prayer of gratitude to the anonymous soldier who gave it to me. Unlike Cory, I've known more kindness than greed in my life. Yet I never take it for granted, goodness and generosity commodities to be treasured. The house will hold ghosts, but I'm okay with that. I've grown comfortable walking alongside death, and I miss my second mother terribly.

I reach the beach as the first flash of lightning bleaches the sky. With my pack and sleeping bag, I head up the trail.

I've taken a dozen steps when the scent of char reaches me, and I freeze, my heart seizing as my scars light up and itch. Closing my eyes, I suck air through my mouth to still the panic and wait for the moment to pass. Rain seeps through my jacket, and the wet chill helps.

This is now. You are in the timberland. The fire has passed . . .

Over and over, I rationalize away the terror, and finally my heart settles enough for me to go on. Eyes on the ground, I continue up the trail, then stop again when I reach the clearing to give myself another minute. Then, with a deep breath, I lift my face.

Oh.

My fingers go to my lips, and my head shakes. Though Cory told me what happened, I wasn't prepared. Not a stick remains except the potbellied stove. The ground is black, and bits of char and ash stick up like tombstones from the soil, as if a giant black eraser came through and wiped away my life.

My books.

My clothes.

My furniture.

I stumble to the lawn chair beside my workbench.

Things, I tell myself as I lower into it, my chest tight with pain.

My rabbit-fur blanket.

My first mother's Bible.

Objects without heartbeats or breath.

My second mother's notebooks with her hand-scrawled recipes for tinctures and teas.

The letters and drawings from Rose.

No one died; that is what's important.

The consolations do little to help. Because what is life if not a collection of cherished memories? Fifty-eight years of experiences carefully curated and saved—mementos and treasures, knickknacks and gems—familiarity and love amassed day after day until I had created my own precious nest.

I shake my head again, unable to believe it, anger hot in my chest as I think about fire and all it has taken from me—my marriage, my daughter, my looks, my career . . .

And now—my home, my things, the life I'd built.

Through the drizzle, I continue to take it in, jaw locked tight as my eyes rove over the ruins.

They catch on the stove.

My kettle, the one with the rooster head, given to me by a young woman in payment for cramp bark. It was there when I left, ready to make my tea.

I squeeze my eyes against it, heart clattering as I try to get used to this new rhythm—a thought sparking a memory followed by a sharp stab of pain. Remembrance, longing, grief, and back again. A scent, a flash of color, a word—and a shock of anguish will slam into me, stunning me for a second until I can move past it.

The chatter of the chickens startles me from the thought, their frantic clucking a warning of the storm getting close. Pushing to my feet, I grab my things and hurry to the shed. I pull out the wheelbarrow and propane tanks, then lay out a tarp and then my sleeping bag. As I crawl into it, the first heavy drops begin to fall, and I look up at the tin ceiling, grateful that Lloyd, true to his word, came by last weekend and put on a new roof.

Small graces: they are what gets you through. As I listen to the dance of the rain above me, I think of the garden and send another prayer to the firemen and Egides, who fought so hard to save it. A few of the plants were scorched, but if there's life in their roots, they will come back and should be okay. The rain will help. *God washing away our sins,* my second mother used to say whenever there was a storm, believing rain to be a baptism of sorts.

For a long time I lie with my eyes open and think about all the things that need to be done—the cuttings I need to take to create a new garden at my second mother's home, the workbench I need to build, the tinctures and teas my patients need most. But as the storm continues to grow, the thoughts overwhelm, and my mind drifts from future to past, and instead I think of Rose.

We used to come home each Christmas to visit my second mother and the colonel—"Grandma" and "Papa." The colonel pretended the name was no big deal, but his cheeks pinked each time she said it. His own grandchildren were no longer in his life, and it made him cherish Rose that much more.

Rose loved it here. My second mother taught her to garden and cook. The colonel taught her to fish. I smile at how upset Rose was the first time they caught a trout. She was four and had never seen an animal die. Her fish came in the shapes of sticks and stars, coated in breading with a mound of ketchup on the side. She refused to eat it, completely inconsolable over the death. After that, she never ate "animals" again. It's how she put it. "I won't eat chicken or meat or fish because they're animals, and I like animals." Moz, a big fan of meat, was not happy about it, but since I was the one who did the cooking and always made a portion of "animals" for him, he put up with it.

I wonder if she remained vegetarian, or possibly even became vegan? Though growing up with Moz in Iran, that would have been hard.

A clap of thunder crashes overhead, Mother Nature unleashing her fury, and I shudder against the cold and reach outside the sleeping bag to zip it up farther at the exact moment something wet touches my cheek. I jolt upright and look down to see a soaked Teddy rubbing against me.

"Theodore!"

He mews his hello, then moves farther into the shed.

I open my pack and rummage through it until I find the small sausage that came with one of the baskets I was given. I pull off chunks, and he gobbles them up.

"I'm so glad you're here."

When half the sausage is gone, I rewrap it in its wax paper and return it to my pack. Exhaustion catching up with me, I settle back in the sleeping bag, and Teddy curls comfortingly against me.

My eyes have just closed when, in a brief silence between downpours, there is a howl—the distinct universal cry of terror and pain.

Teddy bolts from the shelter to run opposite the danger, while I leap to my feet and race toward it. Rain pelts me as I trip blindly in the dark, and I swear at myself for not thinking to grab the flashlight or my phone from my pack.

Damn bastard, I think as another howl cuts through the night. The cabin's been gone less than a day, and already Danny's back at it, claiming the timberland as his own.

I trip on a fallen trunk, stubbing my toe and nearly going down. "Dang it!" I hobble on.

"Help! Someone please help!"

I stop in my tracks, the voice unexpected and changing things. It is the boy from the house, which means it is not a wild animal caught in a snare but the dog. I continue toward them and, when I'm several yards away, stop.

My brain spins to come up with the boy's name. Unable to think of it, I say, "Mr. Egide."

Silence.

I repeat myself louder, "Mr. Egide?"

"I need help," he whimpers. "My dog, he's caught in a trap."

"Okay. I'm here. I'm walking toward you."

I blink through the wetness dripping in my eyes and step into a narrow hollow of birch. In the hazy blackness, I'm just able to make out the dog is on his side and the boy beside him. The boy looks up; then, realizing it's me, his eyes dart away.

"Let me take a look," I say, stepping closer.

I crouch beside them and lean closer to try to see the trap clearer, but the rain and darkness make it impossible. The boy uses his phone to shine his flashlight on it. The screen is lit up with the words "Call failed. No service."

The dog's right forepaw is caught in a leghold trap, the blades smooth, not toothed.

"I need a stick," I say. "Thick, at least an inch wide."

The boy scrambles into the woods.

While he searches, I do my best to assess the injury. The jaws caught the leg about an inch above the paw. I feel the sticky warmth of blood, but it doesn't feel excessive. The dog whimpers but doesn't snap. He's a smart animal who trusts humans and seems to understand I'm a friend trying to help.

"You're okay," I soothe, feeling his fear.

In case the wound is bleeding more than I think, I pull off my left boot, then my sock, then put my boot back on and use the sock to make a torniquet above the wound.

"Shhh," I say in a low rumble as I stroke the dog's trembling fur. "We're going to get you out of here."

"Will this work?" the boy says, reappearing with a three-foot-long red maple branch.

"Let's give it a try."

I push to my feet and pull off the twigs as he shines his light on it to help.

"I'm going to pry it open, and you pull him out."

He nods, then kneels on the ground and wraps his hands around the dog's leg above the tourniquet. I wedge the branch between the blades in front of the paw.

Straightening, I grip the branch near the top where I will have the most leverage. "On the count of three," I say as I set my feet and tighten my grip.

The boy nods again.

"One, two, three!"

I bear down with all my strength. . .

The branch snaps, and I fall hard to the ground, and the wind goes clean out of me.

The dog yowls, and the boy drops to his knees. "You're okay!" he cries, stroking the dog's head. "I'm so sorry. You're okay. You're going to be okay."

I push myself up, rub my bruised elbow. As I recover my breath, I look again at the trap. In war, you learn quickly that sometimes snap judgments are all you have time for. There will be times you are wrong, and regret will live eternal in your soul. But doing nothing is worse, and the consolation of that understanding is what allows you to live with it and go on. This is one of those moments. The dog's breathing is now rapid and shallow, signs of distress, and if we don't get him out soon, he will go into shock, and we could lose him.

"Brendon," I say as the name comes to me, "we're going to try again." I'm amazed how calm my voice is, considering what I'm about to suggest. "Same plan, but I'm going to pry it open with my hands."

He looks at the trap, then at me and, realizing what I'm suggesting, shakes his head.

"It's the only way."

I see the wetness on his cheeks that has nothing to do with the rain, his bottom lip quivering and his face white with fear.

"You need to pull him out before it slams closed," I say.

His eyes flick side to side as he considers it, and he shakes his head harder.

"It's going to be okay. I'll get my hands out in time," I lie, the statement more hope than any promise I can guarantee.

In order to pry the trap open, I will need to wrap all eight fingers around the blades, and once the paw is free and I release my hold, it will be a race between retracting my fingers and the trap slamming shut.

"If you don't do this," I say, my cadence even and measured, "your dog will go into shock, and that could be very dangerous. We need to get him out, and we need to do it quickly."

The dog whimpers as if confirming it, and Brendon looks at him. He looks terrified, and I'm afraid he might lose it. Which can't happen. I need him to keep it together.

"Brendon," I say, lowering and hardening my voice.

He lifts his face back to mine.

"You can do this."

Tim, my commanding officer, had been brilliant at calming nerves in the most calamitous of situations, and I learned from him that low, slow directness works well.

"Take hold of his leg just above the trap."

Brendon does as I say, his fingers wrapping over the knotted sock.

I slide my right hand in front of the paw and my left hand behind it as every atom in my body screams at me not to. Curling my fingers around the blades, I dig my knees into the ground to steady myself and say, "Same as before. On the count of three."

I feel Brendon's body coil as his hands clench and his muscles tighten.

"One, two, THREE!"

With every ounce of will and strength I possess, I wrench the blades apart.

The springs give barely half an inch, but it's enough. Brendon falls back with the dog, and I yank my hands out . . .

Almost getting them out in time.

"He's out!" Brendon cries, elated. "We did it!"

I nod as my brain spins with dizziness, the wooziness that comes after a stun.

"Now I need you to do something for me," I say, the shock fresh and the pain on time delay.

He looks up from where he's squatted beside the dog. I keep my left hand lifted but slightly behind me. I feel the blood dripping down my arm and mixing with the rain. I can't see the missing finger but feel its pulse and imagine the trap caught it just below the first knuckle.

"I need you to give me your shirt," I say.

He tilts his head; then his eyes move to my arm, and I watch as his mouth drops open and his head starts to shake.

"Brendon."

He stares.

"Brendon, look at me."

He shifts his gaze, and our eyes lock.

"We're going to get through this. Now, give me your shirt."

He nods numbly and pulls his rain-soaked T-shirt over his head.

I wrap it around my left hand and hold it in place with my right.

"Now, I need you to use the light on your phone to look for the top part of my pinkie."

The words alien, he blinks, then blinks again.

"Brendon, we need to move quickly." My voice is tight, the pain catching up to my brain. "It should be near the trap."

Almost as if on autopilot, he drops to his knees and shines the light on the ground. His face very close to the dirt, he scans. Silently, I pray he finds it. If we get to the hospital in time, there's a chance it can be reattached.

"Got it," he says. He stands, an inch of finger in his palm.

I send a small prayer of thanks to the heavens. "Put it in my shirt pocket."

Carefully, he pulls open my left pocket and drops it inside.

"Carry the dog and follow me."

I lead them to the boat.

"We're taking a boat?" he says.

"It's the quickest way to town. Put him in the bow."

He takes a step toward the stern.

"The front," I clarify, the pain making it hard to focus.

Brendon lowers the dog in front of the first bench. I climb in after, so the dog is at my feet.

"You need to drive," I say. "Push us out, turn the boat around, then climb in beside the motor."

"I've never driven a boat."

"Well, you're about to learn." I brace my elevated arm against my head for support, but the muscles still quake.

With the grace of an athlete, he turns the boat into the river and vaults over the side.

"Lower the propeller."

He puts the outboard in the water.

"Keep your hand on the tiller and start the motor."

He turns the key, and the engine purrs to life.

"The knob is the throttle. Push it forward."

He does it too fast, and the boat jolts, then stalls. He throws up his hands.

"It's okay. Try again. Ease her into it."

I practically feel his heart racing as he starts the motor again.

"Gently," I encourage.

Carefully, he pushes the throttle forward, and the boat starts to move.

"A little more."

He throttles up the slightest bit, so we're moving at a very slow cruise, and though I want him to go faster, I know he is terrified, so I let it be. We're moving and going with the current, and the town is only a dozen miles away.

"It's opposite of driving," I say. "You pull the tiller right to go left and left to go right."

He tries it out, moving us left, then right, his brow furrowed in deep concentration; then he lifts his face and gives me a nod, letting me know he's got it.

The rain has lightened, and there's now black sky beyond the clouds, along with a small bite of a moon. I see Brendon is shivering from the cold, his left arm wrapped across his bare chest for warmth.

The dog whimpers, and I stroke him with the toe of my boot.

Brendon, hearing the dog's distress, mercifully increases our speed.

When I'm certain he's comfortable, I say, "Keep one hand on the tiller, but with the other, I need you to call 9-1-1 and put it on speaker."

He wrangles his phone from his jeans and sets it on the bench beside me. His quaking fingers struggle to dial, but finally he manages it.

"9-1-1, what's your emergency?"

"Sheila, it's Davina."

"Hey, Davina. Aren't you in the cooler?"

"Not anymore. I got out, and I'm heading into town with an injured dog and a missing finger. I need an ambulance to meet me at the dock along with a vet, if you can find one."

"A missing finger?"

"It's a long story. I'll tell you some time."

"Oh dear. First your cabin burns down, now this."

"I'm hanging up now."

"Hank will be waiting."

Hank is Sheila's husband and the best paramedic in town.

I return my focus to the river, peering into the darkness to be sure we don't run into any obstacles, boating after a storm at night not usually the best idea.

"You're doing fine," I say to Brendon.

He nods but keeps his eyes on the water, his jaw locked forward as he purposely avoids looking at me, and I wonder what's changed.

Oh, I think, recalling Sheila's comment about the fire, and a shudder that has nothing to do with the cold runs through me.

I return my eyes to the river, unsure what to do with the revelation.

49
LEO

I lie in bed staring at the ceiling, thinking how I miss my wife, her warmth, her body, her smile, her laugh. The guilt of my betrayal haunts me. We promised to always be honest with each other. How did I lose sight of that? I feel like, since Bee died, I am bumbling my way forward, and bungling every step.

Outside, a storm rages, making the room chilly and especially lonely. The burns on my hands itch beneath the gauze. The healing has reached the uncomfortable stage, the dead skin sloughing off as new cells form. *Regeneration.* I've always liked that word, the promise it holds. I tuck the gauze mitts beneath my thighs so I won't rub at them. With luck, the bandages will come off in a few days, and finally we can go home.

Tell me, Leo, are you happy? Davina's words from earlier return.

No. I'm so unhappy it hurts.

She has turned her back on a fortune and seems content. Meanwhile, Marie and I have chased the "American dream" for decades and are drowning in debt, and I wonder if money could be the root of our unhappiness?

No. Loss is the root—deep, horrible, soul-eviscerating loss.

We started out with nothing, so I know we can be happy that way. I come from little, and Marie comes from "earn your own way," so when we first got married, we lived in a tiny one-bedroom apartment close to campus that only allowed for a full-size bed. I didn't mind sleeping close; it made it easy to know when Marie was in the mood or when she just wanted to cuddle. I like both. Though lately, I miss the first. Since Bee died, we've only made love once, the night we vowed to move forward, but instead of bringing us closer, it seemed to create a strange force field between us that neither of us knows how to bridge.

We always had such a good sex life, easy and uncomplicated, often funny, sometimes beautiful, and sometimes nothing special but still satisfying. I feel like years with a person does that: the self-consciousness falls away, and you're able to simply enjoy each other.

My phone buzzes on the nightstand, and I glance at the clock to see it's after ten. My first thought is to ignore it. There's no one I want to talk to, and most likely it's another reporter looking for an interview. But when it buzzes again, I look at the screen, then jolt upright as I fumble to answer it before it stops buzzing.

"Brendon?"

"Dad"—his voice is thin and strained, identical to when he called to say Bee was on her way to the hospital—"you need to come to the animal hospital in Franklin. Banjo's been hurt."

"You're in Franklin?" My eyes dart to the door that leads to the hall. *He's in his room. He should be in his room. Did I check? I always check. I poke my head in the rooms and count heads. I always used to check.*

I squeeze my eyes tight as regret lodges like a hard stone in my throat.

"He got caught in a trap in the woods." The words hiccup, and his distress brings me back to the moment.

"I'm on my way," I say, already out of bed and pulling on my jeans. I'm about to say "Hang tight" when another thought occurs to me. "Wait. How'd you get to town?"

There's a beat of hesitation; then very quietly, he says, "The witch. In her boat."

Witch?

"Davina?" I ask.

"Yes."

My head spins in confusion. "Okay, I'm coming."

I race down the stairs. "Jags!"

She sits up groggily from the couch and looks over the backrest.

"We need to go. Brendon's at the animal hospital with Banjo."

She squints and tilts her head. "Huh?"

"Now!" I practically screech.

Unsteadily, she pushes to her feet. "What are you talking about? Brendon's upstairs."

"No. He's not."

"He's not?"

"He was in the woods, and Banjo got caught in a trap. Davina drove them in her boat to the animal hospital."

"Davina? She's in jail."

"Apparently not."

"She came back?" Marie says, the words sharp.

"Jags!"

She shakes her head as if to clear it, but the frown remains. "Tell Hannah we're leaving," she says as she bends down to pull on her shoes.

I race back up the stairs. When there's no answer to my mitt's thump on the door, I open it and step inside. The girls sleep cocooned together, a larger butterfly enveloping a smaller one, and seeing them, my heart stops for a second.

I jostle Hannah's shoulder, and she squints her eyes open. "What?" she groans.

"Your mom and I need to go to town."

She nods and doesn't ask why, and I envy the ease of it. Despite all that's happened, her life is still secure enough for her to sleep peacefully, a small miracle for which I'm grateful.

I race back down the stairs to find Marie beside the door, her hair brushed and her rain jacket on. I realize I forgot to grab my own rain jacket but don't bother with that now. Brendon is waiting.

50
MARIE

I'm frustrated Leo didn't ask Brendon more questions but keep the irritation to myself. We've fought enough for one day, and I feel like one more nudge could tip us over an edge from which we might not recover.

Davina. Why does everything seem to begin and end with her? Why is she out of jail? And why was she in the woods . . . with Brendon?

I look at the clock to see it's nearly eleven and wonder how we didn't notice he was gone. But I know why. Since Bee's death, we've been living in a fog and only half functioning as parents.

"Here!" Leo barks.

I blink to realize I didn't hear my car's navigation and slam on the brakes in time to manage the turn. Silently, I promise to do better, pay more attention, be present. But even as I make the vow, I feel it being broken, my mind seemingly incapable of prolonged attention toward anything.

The Franklin Animal Hospital comes into view, the parking lot empty except for a lone truck beside the entrance. Leo jumps out before I've put the car in park, and I watch as he hurries inside.

With a heavy sigh, I climb out as well, knowing once again, impossible as it seems, things are about to get worse.

The lobby is blindingly bright—white light, yellow walls, and a dozen lime-green chairs. Brendon sits with his head hung and his elbows on his knees. Leo has taken the seat on his right, and his mitted hand rubs circles on his back. I take the seat on his left.

Brendon's jeans and shoes are wet, but the oversize sweatshirt he wears—emblazoned with a Franklin Sheriff's Department logo—is dry.

"Hey," I say softly.

To the floor in front of him, he says, "He went after a squirrel." Then he brings his hands to his face, releases a shaky breath, and starts to cry, great heaving sobs that convulse his body and unnerve me. Even as a baby, Brendon wasn't a crier, and I don't think I've seen him shed a tear since he was two. Even at Bee's service, he sat frozen and dry eyed as a statue. But now, a great exorcism of grief consumes him, anguish so violent I think it must hurt—his lungs, his gut, his spine. It's the most painful sound I've ever heard, so wretched I know it comes from someplace deep and broken, much greater than what happened tonight.

I miss her too, I want to say at the exact moment he wails, "I couldn't get him out!"

"It's okay," Leo says, continuing to rub his back.

Brendon shakes his head, his hands pressed to his face. I agree, the comment is stupid. Because it's not "okay." None of this is "okay," and it feels like none of it will ever be right again. I also hate *It will take time, but you will find a way through this* and anything resembling *She's in a better place.*

No! No! No! I miss her, and I want her back. I just want her back.

I'm hurting, and Brendon is hurting, pain you can't imagine, and no one can understand. And though I want to help, I also know there's nothing to be done. Loss is personal and belongs solely to the person experiencing it. So I sit silent as he keens, aching with him and my mind on fire, the moment almost unbearable.

In front of him, his sneakers swish like windshield wipers, a habit he's had since he was little. I fixate on the movement, watching as they wave back and forth and as the sobs run out of him, quieting to hiccups, then sniffles, and finally to silence. His head remains bent, his hands over his face, and the sneakers continue to swish.

They are hideously ugly, a strange combination of aqua, mustard, and white. I remember how badly he wanted them, telling me how they were the coolest shoes ever and that all the guys on his baseball team were getting them. It seems like a lifetime ago.

They're dirty now, and there's splatter on the toes, a speckling of spots two shades darker than the wetness from the rain. The day of the hearing, when we were waiting to be let into the courtroom, he was swishing them as he is now, but there was no splatter, and I wonder what made it.

He releases a final trembling breath, and I ask, "Why did you go to meet Davina in the woods?"

He looks up through his tear-soaked lashes, a question on his face.

"Dad said she drove you to town in her boat."

"I didn't meet her," he mumbles, looking back at the floor. "She heard me yelling for help and found us."

"Oh," I say, trying to process it.

Leo looks over Brendon's back at me with confusion that matches my own.

"So then, why were you in the woods?" he asks. Since the fire, Leo's been adamant that we stay in the house, terrified of the danger around us.

"I don't know," Brendon mutters. "I just needed to get out."

The shoes swish faster, and again, I look at the spatter, the small specks taking on new significance as I realize what they mean.

The day after the fire, the fire captain returned with an arson investigator. The investigator confirmed an accelerant had been used to start the fire, which was why the cabin burned so quickly. He said it had been "doused in gasoline, then lit."

Gasoline that splatters and stains.

No! No, no, no!

I try to push the treacherous thought away, but the waving stains sear into my brain.

"Bren, do you know how dangerous that was?" Leo says.

The swoosh kicks into high gear—left, right, left, right . . .

"I told you. I needed some air."

Oh, Brendon.

"Jags, you okay?" Leo says.

I lift my face to see him looking at me with concern.

"I need to make a call," I say and, before he can ask another question, push to my feet and hurry out the door.

My phone is out before I reach my car.

"Franklin Sheriff's Department," a woman answers as I climb into the driver's seat.

I explain who I am and that I'm trying to locate Davina. Half a minute later, I'm racing toward the trauma hospital in Concord, every other second glancing at my pinkie, amazed how I continue to get it wrong, each time believing things are bad as they can get only to discover there's still farther for us to fall.

51
DAVINA

I wake up groggy and disoriented, the brightness of the fluorescent lights along with the beeping of machines spiraling me back to the darkest time of my life, and I need to remind myself this is not then.

My left arm is suspended in a sling to keep my hand elevated, and I feel the pulse of my pinkie but not yet the pain.

"Morning!"

I turn my head to see a nurse in lollipop scrubs, and my first instinct is to ask for someone more serious. When I chose nurses for my trauma unit, I looked for a certain somberness that spoke to underlying grit. You need it when dealing with the wounded and dying. And though my injury is not mortal, I'd appreciate a little of that now.

I look at my hand, relieved to see purple skin running the length of the aluminum brace.

"The surgery was a success?" I say, half statement, half question.

Her eyes go a little misty. "Dr. Reynolds did a remarkable job."

The pain emerges with her words, darts of red-hot fire shooting down my arm. Gritting my teeth, I lean into it—pain an old, familiar friend.

"You have a morphine pump," the nurse says. "On the rail beside your right hand."

Blindly, I reach for it and give it several pumps, then close my eyes and wait for the drugs to take effect, relishing the promise they offer of hazy, thoughtless oblivion until the worst has passed.

"I'm going to take your vitals," the nurse says.

I barely notice as she takes my blood pressure, measures my pulse, and checks my temperature.

"Everything looks fine. Rest now, and the doctor will be in soon to check on you."

"Sheriff," I mutter.

"Huh?"

"I need to talk to the sheriff," I say, the words distant but certain, a vague but determined urgency glowing like a warning light through the fog. Something about the fire, the trap, Danny, and Brendon.

52
HANNAH

I sit with my feet in a bucket of hot water and an ice pack on my head. Without my morning swims, the headaches have returned, not as bad as they were but a constant throb that starts midmorning and continues until I go to sleep. The ice and foot baths help, but I really wish I could return to my routine.

As I wait for the hot and cold to work their magic, I think of Banjo. He is still at the animal hospital, where he will need to stay for the next several days. He lost a paw and part of one of his front legs, an idea so horrible I can't get used to it.

When I came down this morning, my dad told me the news. I can't believe I slept through it, stunned and dismayed that somehow, once again, just like with Bee, someone I loved was suffering and I didn't sense a thing.

My mom is also gone, in Concord at the hospital waiting for news on Davina, who lost her pinkie when she pried open the trap to free him. I still don't understand how it was Davina who saved him. It makes no sense. I thought Davina was in jail. Dad doesn't know either. He just said we were lucky she was there.

"God watching out for us," he said, then cocked his head and added, "or Bee."

I've never known my dad to be religious, but since Bee died, he refers to God or things like God a lot more often. I think it's his way of dealing with it, believing there was a reason for what happened or at least something waiting on the other side now that she's gone.

I don't see it that way. Since it happened, I think of it more as the opposite and that there was no sense to it at all, and instead it was only simple, awful bad luck—a pinprick hole in a floatie at a moment Brendon wasn't watching. Horrible and life altering, but no more meaningful than that. For me, it's easier that way, lays less blame and feels less terrifying. I don't want to believe Bee was chosen or that God had anything to do with it.

"Hey."

I drop my face, and the ice pack falls from my head.

"Hey," I say to Pen, who is in the archway, dressed in her denim shorts and rainbow-striped T-shirt.

"We need to go to the garden," she says, her face serious. "I want blueberry pancakes, and that's where the blueberries are, and you need to go for your swim."

I start to shake my head, but it hurts too much. "Dad says we can't leave the house."

"Yes, we can. The guy they think started the fire was arrested."

"He was?"

She nods. "Dad just got a call from the sheriff. He thinks it was the guy who set the trap. He doesn't have proof but is pretty sure it was him. The guy didn't like Davina because she was always throwing his traps in the river and she gave him poison ivy."

I almost smile at the idea of Davina doing that but then think of the fire and the price she paid, and the tickle of humor stops before reaching my lips.

"Dad said we can go?" I ask.

Her eyes slide away as she shrugs.

"Pen?"

"It's safe!" she practically shouts. "He only said we couldn't go because of the fire guy! And now he's in jail! And your head hurts!" She's worked up in a way that makes me feel bad for her. This has been a lot for everyone. And Pen is only eight.

"Okay," I say, pulling my feet from the water.

Her chin still trembles, but she keeps it together and nods. "I have your swimsuit," she says. She swings her backpack from her shoulder so I can see she's packed and ready to go, and I don't know if I've ever loved her more. Of everyone, I think she hates my headaches the most.

We head out but only make it a few steps before the sound of scraping stops us. I turn, thinking it's Rock, and my heart jumps with the idea that he's forgiven us. But when I squint up, it's Brendon I see on the ladder. He's halfway up, a fierce expression on his face as he scrapes at the remaining section of flaking paint. I look at the progress he's made and realize he's been at it for some time. It's strange to see. As far as I know, my brother is averse to work, especially manual labor that requires boring, monotonous physical effort.

"Come on," Pen says, taking my hand and pulling me forward.

We're almost to the cabin when Pen stops. I stop as well and look with her through the trees to see my mom sitting in an aluminum chair beside the potbellied stove.

"What's she doing?" Pen hisses.

I shake my head. I have no idea. Her hands are on the armrests, her feet planted in front of her, and she appears to be looking at the trees. The only movement is the repetitive tapping of her left finger on the aluminum.

Pen looks up with concern. I agree. It's very disturbing. I put my finger to my lips, and slowly we back away, careful not to make a sound.

53
BRENDON

I'm almost finished with the scraping when the girls walk from the woods. Pen sees me, and her eyes go wide with guilt. I pantomime locking my lips and throwing away the key, and she smiles wide. Hannah offers a thumbs-up.

I return to work, the exchange adding to the surprisingly bright morning. I was certain today would be like when Bee died, the weight of what happened so heavy it was impossible to breathe. But instead, last night, I fell into the deepest sleep I've had since the drowning and woke hours later, lighthearted, nearly giddy.

He lived! The thought made me almost loopy with relief.

I think it has to do with Davina and what she said on the boat. We were nearly to the town's dock. I could see an ambulance and fire truck waiting along with several men. I was shivering, chilled to the bone from being on the river without a shirt and soaked through from the rain. My only thought was to get us safely to the pier.

"Hell of a night," she said.

I didn't answer, my eyes fixed on the pylon I was aiming for. Boats don't turn like bikes. They're slower to react and go the opposite of how you think they should steer.

"Damn lucky," Davina went on.

I tilted my head, nothing about what we'd been through feeling the least bit lucky at all.

"You being with the dog when he got snared and me being nearby to help."

"Oh," I said, looking up, then quickly away, unable to look at her.

"Aim a bit more right, then cut the motor and let our momentum and the current do the rest."

I did as she said, and we glided in perfectly, the boat kissing the first pylon, then locking in against the second. A paramedic went down on his belly, reached into the boat, and grabbed the rope, then tied us to the dock. Another held out his hand for Davina, but she stayed in her seat. Her injured finger was in the air, the arm pinned against her head, and her body quaked from the exertion.

"Davina?" the man said.

She ignored him, and her eyes locked on mine before I could look away. "A night like this makes you take a minute."

I sat trembling and paralyzed, my guilt unbearable.

"Makes you think about things. What you've done right, and the things you might want to fix."

Her eyes narrowed, and I knew she knew.

"Hey, kid!"

I looked up to see a deputy at the edge of the dock. He held up a sweatshirt, then tossed it down, and I caught it and held it in my lap.

"Put that on," Davina said, so I did.

As soon as it was over my head, I lifted my face to hers and opened my mouth to confess, to tell her how sorry I was and that I didn't mean for things to happen the way they did.

But she got there first. "The way I see it, tonight is a night of reckoning. A reminder of what's important, and perhaps a bit of a kick in the butt to take an inventory and settle some scores."

I dropped my face, and my head reversed direction, some scores so large they can't ever be squared.

"Is that right?" she said. "You think once a person does something bad, that's it? They're bad forever with no chance for redemption or ever making things right?"

The warmth of the sweatshirt caused an uncontrollable shiver, and I folded my arms across my chest and thrust my chin forward to keep from crying in front of all those people.

"Davina," the paramedic said more forcefully.

"You should go," I muttered.

Again, she ignored us. "Pfft. Nonsense," she said, sounding almost irritated. "I'll admit, some things are a bit tougher to make up for than others, but it's still possible."

A bright light hit us, a spotlight from one of the cars, and I glanced up to see my shirt blood-soaked around her hand.

"Please," I pleaded, "go."

"Davina!" the paramedic snapped, obviously seeing it as well.

Davina's eyes pierced mine as if looking straight into the back of my brain. "In my experience," she said, "it's a ratio somewhere around five to one."

So desperate for her to let the paramedic help her, I nodded, willing to agree to anything so long as she'd get off the boat.

"You say something mean," she said, "you need to say five things nice to make up for it. You do something wrong; you need to do five things right. It's not an exact science, but in my experience, it's close." She gave a nod as if confirming she had it right, then stood, wavering so dangerously the paramedic lunged for her, getting hold of her shoulder and steadying her.

She looked from him to me. "The way I see it, tonight, you put three in the plus column." She counted them off. "You saved your dog. You found my pinkie. You got us here."

235

She gave another succinct nod, then stepped on the bench so the paramedic could help her onto the dock. As soon as her feet hit the boards, her knees went weak, and she crumpled. Half a minute later, she was on a gurney and being wheeled toward an ambulance.

The rest of the night is a blur. Banjo was lifted from the boat. I was ushered into the back of a van. And Banjo and I were driven to the animal hospital.

When I was alone in the lobby waiting for my parents, I thought about what she said and wondered if it could be true, if it was possible to make up for things. And this morning, I woke with her voice in my head. *He lived. We were lucky. It's a ratio somewhere around five to one.*

The three thoughts propelled me from the bed and straight outside, where I set to work scraping the house. It turned out to be strangely satisfying. I liked seeing the progress I was making and knowing it was number four: *I saved Banjo. I found the pinkie. I got us to the docks . . . I finished painting the house.*

"Can we help?" Pen asks, looking up at me.

"Sure," I say, surprised how happy the offer makes me, and I realize how lonely I've been. "Rocking the rainbow look," I say with a nod to her T-shirt, which I know is her favorite.

She beams.

One, I think. *Ninety-nine to go.* Some things will take more than a five-to-one ratio to make up for, and the comment I made on Father's Day is going to take a lot of making up for.

"Tape or scrape?" I ask. "Dad's taping because it's all he can do with his mummified hands."

Dad came outside an hour after I started, and when I told him what I was doing, he looked genuinely proud and offered to help.

"Tape," Pen says as Hannah says, "Scrape."

"Dad's out front," I say to Pen. "He has the tape."

I turn to Hannah. Her brow is squinty, and I know it's from a headache. "You sure you want to do this?"

She nods, so I climb down to look for another scraper, finding one just as Rock's truck rumbles down the driveway toward us.

Hannah hurries away, and I see Pen run toward him as well. He steps from the truck and sweeps Pen into his arms, then swings her round and round, making her legs fly. He sets her down dizzy and giggling, and seeing how easy it is between them, I wonder why I never think to do things like that. Perhaps I should give it a try, see if I can lighten up and take myself a little less seriously.

Mom's car pulls up behind Rock's truck, and all of us watch as she staggers from the driver's seat. She's wearing the same clothes she had on at the animal hospital, and I realize she didn't come home last night.

While we were still waiting for news about Banjo, she went to see Davina at the hospital in Concord, which is the closest big town to Franklin. It turns out you need a special kind of surgeon to reattach a finger. Dad called her on the cab ride home to find out how Davina was doing, and Mom said she was still in surgery.

I wondered if, when she woke, she would tell my mom or the sheriff what I did. But this morning, when Dad came outside, he said the sheriff had called and told him they believed the fire had been set by the same guy who set the trap. Which stunned me, knowing it wasn't true. It also meant Davina hadn't told. Dad said they didn't have any proof, so they weren't charging him with it, which was a great relief. But they are going extra hard on him for everything else, which I don't have a problem with. Banjo lost a paw, and Davina lost a finger.

I watch Mom talking to Rock. I can't hear what she's saying, but his reply shatters the air: "Are you freaking kidding me?"

Dad is there in a flash, stepping between them, his hands lifted. "Rock, it's been a rough night for all of us."

"Really?" Rock says, glaring down at him. "Looks to me like you all still have your fingers and toes . . . and your homes."

Though Dad's half a head shorter and fifty pounds lighter, he stands his ground, looking Rock in the eye as he says, "We didn't set the trap, and our dog lost his leg."

This seems to affect Rock, and he takes a step back, then runs his hand through his hair, raking it so hard it looks like he's trying to pull it out by its roots. "Where is she?"

"Concord Memorial," Mom says, "but she doesn't want visitors."

"Is she okay?" I ask, stepping closer.

Mom turns, and when she sees me, her eyes drop.

"They reattached her finger," she says, eyes roving the grass between us, then sticking on my shoes a moment before returning to the grass—looking everywhere but where I am. "But it will be some time before they know whether it was a success."

And I know she knows.

54
PENELOPE

Rock drives off, upset, his truck kicking up dirt as he races too fast toward the road. Hannah stares after him, her arms crossed and her eyes squinting painfully into the brightness. Chin quivering, she shuffles inside. Dad wraps his arm around Mom's shoulders and steers her up the steps as well. They're halfway to the door when Mom stops. I watch as she blinks several times as if trying to remember something that popped into her brain, then fluttered away.

"Jags?" Dad says, trying to coax her forward.

"Oh." She turns back to Brendon, but her eyes fall somewhere in between. "Bren, Davina wants to see you, and she wants you to bring her things from the shed. I need to get some rest, but I'll take you this afternoon."

"I thought she didn't want visitors?" I say.

"She doesn't. She only wants to see Brendon."

I look back and forth between them, something going on they're not saying. Brendon's body is rigid, and Mom's is slumped, and neither is looking at the other.

Dad tugs Mom forward, and they disappear into the house.

Brendon starts for the trail, leaving me alone. I'm about to start taping the window where Dad left off when I hear, "Hey, Pen."

I turn to see Brendon stopped. "You want to come?"

"Really?" I say and drop the tape on the railing.

I hurry to catch up, and almost silently he says, "Two."

He looks at me slightly cockeyed, as if considering something, then awkwardly reaches out and tousles my hair.

I didn't realize he was going to do it, since he never does things like that, so I rear back, and his fingers get tangled. His eyes go wide, and my eyes go wide, and I'm quite certain this is the moment he gets mad and tells me to forget it. But instead, to my amazement, he tousles my hair even more, as if my curls are a wild serpent that has captured his hand and won't let go. He thrashes and yanks at his wrist with his other hand as if trying to get it loose, and I play along, shaking my head like it is swallowing the limb, and we laugh and laugh until both of us are busting up, hysterical.

Finally, he pulls it free, falling away and gasping, his hand held out like a mangled claw.

Breathless and smiling, we continue toward the trail, and almost silently, he says, "Three."

While he goes to the shed to get Davina's things, I go to the garden to collect blueberries. A moment later, he joins me. He sets the stuff on the ground, then offers his baseball cap to hold the berries since I didn't bring a basket or bag, and together we fill it almost to the brim.

As we start back for the house, I think *Four*, not sure what we're counting but fairly certain we reached another number in the game.

55
MARIE

I was so done in I barely noticed Leo leading me up the stairs. He helped me into bed and took off my shoes. I thought he was going to leave, return to whatever he was doing—taping the windows, I think. But instead, he lay down beside me, then reached over and took my hand.

I closed my eyes and focused on the sound of his breath, listening as it grew slow and heavy and he drifted off to sleep.

Despite my own exhaustion, I can't turn off my thoughts, my brain spinning so wildly I wondered if this is what is meant by "losing your mind." It's how it feels, like my rational mind is lost somewhere beyond reach.

Turning onto his side, Leo drapes his arm over my hips and snuggles close.

The embrace steadies me, and I close my eyes and take deep, slow inhales and try to focus on the moment. *I am here. Safe. My family is here and safe.* Over and over, I repeat the words.

Leo's snores tickle my neck, and I drift into the languid in-between state before sleep, my eyes flickering behind my lids as the morning replays in my mind. The surgery was complicated, and after, Davina needed to rest, so I spent the night in the waiting room, my mind numb with worry and my heart heavy with everything that had happened. It was a little after nine when the nurse finally came out and said I could see her.

When I walked in the room, I was stunned. Hannah had mentioned that Davina had lost weight while in jail, but I was not expecting the frail woman in front of me. Her left arm was suspended by a pulley, the hand and wrist encased in a thick foam cast wrapped with an Ace bandage, and her eyes were bruised and her cheeks sunken.

"Oh, Davina. I'm so—"

"The nurse said you have news about the dog," she said brusquely, cutting me off. Her cheek twitched, it seemed from pain, and it caused a knot in my chest.

"Is there anything I can—"

"The dog," she said, clearly not wanting my condolence or pity.

I dropped my eyes. "The vet said he'll be okay. He lost the paw, but the tourniquet you made . . . and what you did"—my voice caught— "saved him."

"Dogs do fine on three legs," she said matter of factly. "Adaptable creatures." Her brow was moist with sweat, and her skin nearly glowed with how pale she was. "And your son?"

It was very slight, the smallest shift of her eyes from mine, but it sent an ice-cold stream of fear through me as I realized she also knew what Brendon had done. Terrified, I opened my mouth to say something, but she got there first.

"He did a good job last night."

"Davina—"

"Now, if you don't mind, I'd like to get some rest."

She closed her eyes, letting me know I was being dismissed. But I didn't leave. I stood there frozen, panic and confusion coursing through me. "So a secret for a secret?" I said, believing I had puzzled it out.

Her eyes snapped open, then blazed, and I realized instantly I had gotten it wrong. "So your husband is a liar as well," she said, and I realized she hadn't known I knew about her being Rebecca Dupree.

"I . . . he . . . I'm his wife. I'm sure he didn't think about it."

Eyes storming, she said, "Have Brendon come see me."

I couldn't tell if it was a threat, and I wished desperately I could take back what I'd said.

"He's a good kid," I muttered, feeling stupid as I said it. After all, he'd burned down her home.

"And tell him to bring my things from the shed." She closed her eyes again, her single nostril opening and closing violently.

I drove home, my brain on fire, and when I reached our drive, continued past. The prospect of seeing my family . . . especially Brendon . . . too much.

I parked at the edge of the timberland and walked to the site of the cabin, then sat beside the potbellied stove and looked at the woods. It was quiet, the trees and animals tuckered from the storm the night before. I could hear the river on my right and faint birdsong in the treetops. I thought about Bee, then Brendon, and wondered how it was possible how little I knew my son.

Or my daughters. Or my husband.

Perhaps all of us are not who we seem, each of us altering the narrative to portray nobler versions that make us appear better than we are.

Sensing I was not alone, I opened my eyes to see a butterfly in front of me, floating on the gentle breeze.

"Hey, Honeybee."

Its wings were midnight blue, and when they opened, there was a vivid slash of white. It flittered close, keeping me company or trying to tell me something. Then a shift in the wind, and it fluttered away.

A moment later, the cat appeared. He strutted past, then returned and deigned to greet me with a nuzzle. He was a handsome fellow— gray with yellow-green eyes. I assumed he was the one who attacked

Banjo, but I didn't hold it against him. As Davina said, he was just defending what was his.

Like Brendon, I thought as I scratched him behind the ear.

Tears formed: I know the reason he did it was for me. He knew how much I wanted the house in Farmington and believed the cabin was the thing standing in the way.

My grandfather's voice played in my head: *Marie, only when you lose the desire for the things that don't matter do you start to have fun.* He said it with a wink, then stripped to his boxers and ran laughing like a lunatic into the river. I turned crimson seeing him nearly naked before busting up laughing, then tearing off my sweatshirt and shoes to splash in after him.

I lost sight of that simple, eternal truth—deluded myself into believing a house would bring relief, when, if there's one thing I should know, it's that nothing not of flesh and bone ever satisfies the soul but briefly and superficially. I leaned forward, elbows on my knees. The rain had washed away the ash, leaving the earth black and dank. A foot from my sneakers, a single green bud had sprouted. I stared at it and imagined how different the place would be in a year.

Eventually, I stood and staggered back toward my car. For a while, the cat walked with me but, about halfway there, turned and, head held high, haughtily walked away, proud of himself, as if he'd done his job magnificently, which almost made me smile.

When I got to the house, my family was there, along with Rock. I told him the news about Davina, and understandably, he didn't take it well. He's hot tempered with a short fuse that ignites easily and burns out quickly, a lot like my mom.

And like Bee.

My eyes snap open, and I stare at the spot in front of me where the butterfly had been.

Nothing is there, but the chimera lingers, tugging at me, my mind suspended between past and present as it struggles with a thought it can't quite reach. Squinting my eyes, I imagine the fluttering of wings and the blinking blaze of white, and like a ship rolling through a mist, it comes to me, an idea that wasn't there before, growing brighter until it glows clear in my mind.

I turn to tell Leo, but he is sleeping so soundly I don't want to wake him. Even in sleep, he looks tired, aged a dozen years from two months ago. Yet still handsome. And I'm reminded why I fell in love with him—good and brave, noble and devoted. I lean in and brush a kiss across his lips, and he stirs.

"Hmmm," he mumbles, then pulls me close and, with no preamble at all, starts to undress me.

His gauze mitts make a comedy of it that sends us into a fit of giggles. I give him a hand . . . two hands . . . and still laughing, we come together. It's familiar and foreign and like a great inhale of oxygen straight to my lungs.

He rolls off, smiling. "Hey," he says.

"Hey."

Then he closes his eyes and, in minutes, has fallen back asleep. I envy it all the way to my bones and, for a moment, watch him, then, with a contented sigh, sidle from the bed, pull on a fresh set of clothes, and hurry to the kitchen. I start a pot of coffee, then settle at the table with my laptop. One of my kids is in trouble, but this time, there's something I can do. First and foremost, I am a mother. So is Davina. So that is where I begin.

56
LEO

I wake grinning. *Wow! Pow! Zip-a-dee-doo-dah!* For weeks, I've been struggling to figure out a way to bridge the growing chasm between us, dreaming of a profound reconciliation that would return us to who we were before our lives derailed. Then, *wham!* Just like that, she was kissing me, and we were laughing, my mitts making a mockery of any sort of seriousness, which was far better than the deep solemnity I had envisioned.

Peanut butter and jelly, tomatoes and cheese, wine and crackers—Marie and I just work.

I suck in a deep breath, then blow it out, tears stinging my eyes from the relief of it, like I've been pulled back from the precipice of something truly terrible. Always after sex, I sleep. Soundly. It's one of the most pleasurable things about it, the dreamless, content moments after. And today, it was especially satisfying.

Invigorated, I tie on my sneakers and bound down the stairs, excited to go for a run.

Marie is in the kitchen, along with Pen. Marie stares intently at her laptop, while Pen uses a frosting tube to decorate a pan of muffins.

"Hey," I say to Marie.

She looks up and blushes, our playful secret between us, and I feel another rush through my veins.

"What are you doing?" I ask, thinking she might be looking for a new job.

Instead, she shocks me with "Finding Davina's daughter."

I freeze. "Did she ask you to find her daughter?" I hope she doesn't hear the uneasiness in my voice, thinking of Davina's reaction when I showed her the DNA results. All she's asked since we came here is to be left alone, and we've done a magnificently terrible job of it.

"It's turning out to be quite difficult to find someone who's left the country."

"Perhaps it's not our place—"

"But I have an idea," she says, interrupting as if I wasn't talking. And I realize, looking at her—her eyes red and her hair wild and unbrushed—it's possible she is deeply sleep deprived and not operating on all cylinders. "His name is Mozaffar Taheri. At least that was his name—"

"Jags—"

"He was a drone consultant for the military, which is how he and Davina probably met."

I have no idea how she knows all this, but Marie's always been extraordinary at research.

"I assume he didn't give it up," she goes on. "So that's where I've started. There are only a handful of companies that specialize in drones."

"I'm sure Davina's already done that."

"Nu-uh," Pen says, causing me to look up in surprise, having forgotten she was there.

"Nu-uh what?" I ask.

"Davina didn't look for him. Or Rose."

Marie and I both startle. What parent doesn't search for a child that was taken from them?

"She said she didn't want to mess up Rose's life," Pen says, her brow pinched.

"Mess it up?" Marie asks.

"Davina said when she got out of the hospital, she couldn't be a mom and that it took a long time for her to get better, and by the time she did, Rose was already mostly grown up, and she didn't want to mess things up for her." Pen looks down at the frosting tube, then at Marie. "I'd want you to find me no matter what."

Marie holds her arms out, and Pen climbs from the chair and walks into them.

"I'd never not find you," Marie says into her curls. "I'd walk to the end of the earth and back again."

I blow out a hard breath, my opinion changed. "Okay," I say. "How can I help?"

"Well," Marie says, releasing Pen. "I've made a list of every drone company in and around Iran, which is where Mozaffar was originally from. I figure I'll go through each company's directory, looking for a Mozaffar. Though if he changed his name, which is possible, then I don't know. Some of the websites have photos, at least of the executives, so if we knew what he looked like, it would help."

"We do!" Pen says. She hurries away and disappears through the hidden door that leads to the basement.

Lickety split, she's back, a photo album in her hands. She sets it on the table and pages through it.

"There," she says, pointing. "That's Rose. And that's the dad."

Staring from the album is Davina as a young woman beside a man holding a curly-haired little girl—a stunning little family frozen in time.

"Wow, look how beautiful Davina was," Marie says.

She's right. Davina was a stunner, graceful and slender with a flirty smile that captured the lens. The man is handsome and serious, with olive skin, thick black hair, a shadow of a full beard, and a distinctive mole in the shape of a comma below his right eye.

Brendon walks in, freshly showered and dressed in his nicest jeans. He has Davina's backpack over his shoulder and a sleeping bag under his arm.

"Mom, can you drive me to the hospital now?"

I want to tell him Marie needs to rest, but I see how intense his expression is and how Marie is looking at him, and I know it would be a waste of breath.

Instead, I turn the computer toward me. "I've got this," I say.

Pen reaches past Marie and carefully pulls the photo opposite the one we were looking at from its corners. It's a shot of just Davina and Rose.

She holds it toward Brendon. "Give this to her." Then she skips to the counter, pulls four muffins from the pan, and puts them on a plate. She brings them back to Brendon. "And these."

Brendon smiles at her as he takes it. "Good job, Pendulum."

Marie and I look at each other. It's been a long time since Brendon has called Pen by the pet name he gave her as a baby, and even longer since he was so kind.

I watch as they walk toward the door, a vestige of who we were trailing behind, and my eyes slide to the album and Davina's radiant smile as she stood with her beautiful family, thinking how, only two months ago, I, too, was entirely unaware how easily it could disappear.

57
HANNAH

I stare at the screen until the words blur. I've reread the email so many times the letters are permanently etched in my brain. It's the most beautiful, painful thing I've ever read. He starts off apologizing for not being a good writer or knowing the right way to deal with this sort of thing. Then he tells me how much I mean to him before going on to say he can no longer see me. He cares too much for Davina and seeing her continually hurt is killing him, and while he knows none of it is my fault, being with me feels like a betrayal of her.

Heartbreak. The word makes sense, like my heart is being torn in two, the blood in my veins not flowing right so I can't think and barely have energy to move. Though we'd only been seeing each other a short time, already he was constantly on my mind, and my world had begun to revolve around him.

With a ragged sigh, I click the window closed and turn to the worries of others. A new Juliet letter arrived last night from a young woman in Alaska.

Dear Juliet,

I recently met a man, and I have fallen in love with him. He is kind and generous and makes me laugh. He says he feels the same way and tells me I treat him better than anyone ever has. The problem is, when it comes to intimacy, he says he doesn't find me desirable because of my weight. I'm a plus size lady with ample curves. In the past, he has always dated thin women, and he doesn't think he can get past it. I don't understand how you can love someone and not desire them. Should I stay or should I go?

Sincerely,
Amanda

The response that comes to mind is *Love sucks.* I type it, then erase it, then stare a long time at the screen before beginning in earnest.

Dear Amanda,

Thank you for your letter. Relationships are certainly complicated. There are so many facets, and it sounds like you and the man you believe you are in love with click on many of them—intelligence, thoughtfulness, humor. But he does not love you the way you deserve to be loved. I recently met a woman who was in a horrible accident when she was young and suffered burns over thirty percent of her body. When I first met her, her scars were all I saw. But after only a short time, my admiration and affection grew so strong, not only did I no longer immediately see her scars, I started to see her as beautiful, her unmarred eyes windows to a remarkable soul I simply wanted to be near. Beauty comes in all shapes, sizes, and forms, and if he doesn't desire you as you are, he doesn't truly see you, and you deserve to be seen. We all do.

All my love,
Juliet

I hit send, sigh, and lean back against the headrest of the bed, my brain throbbing as much as my heart. Rock *saw* me, and I don't know if I will ever meet anyone who sees me as clearly again.

58
DAVINA

Brendon sits in the chair beside my hospital bed, my backpack and sleeping bag on the floor beside him. He looks nervous, his eyes sliding to my cast again and again.

I let him stew. What he did is no small thing, and he needs to know it.

The photo he brought of me holding Rose is on the side table along with the blueberry muffins. I remember the moment the photo was taken, my second mother laughing as Rose squirmed uncooperatively in my arms. "Payback's an itch," she said. According to her, I had been a high-spirited, willful child, and there was no doubt Rose had inherited my temperament.

I'd asked her to take the photo so I could give it to the colonel for his birthday, a photo of just me and Rose without Moz. The colonel had never taken to my husband, perhaps sensing his lack of character from the start, which obviously I failed to notice myself until it was too late.

Rose was around one, and those early years of being a mom were the happiest of my life. After my maternity leave, I requested a transfer to domestic service and was assigned to the VA hospital in Queens. Moz was lead engineer on a new exploratory moon drone project headquartered in Manhattan. We had a two-bedroom apartment in Greenwich Village, and we were busy and mutually over the moon about Rose, which made our tumultuous relationship tolerable.

It wasn't until my mom got sick, a few years later, that things began to unravel. Moz resented my frequent visits home and wasn't happy about the financial toll her care was taking. It was because of his constant haranguing about money that I signed up for another tour. It was clear my mom would need to be moved to a full-time hospice facility, and I knew Moz wasn't going to offer to pay for it. Returning overseas came with a promotion and a substantial pay hike. I only needed to serve a year, and then I could return home, the promotion and raise still in place. It was almost three months to the day I deployed that the truck hit the IED.

"Should I call a nurse?" Brendon asks, and I realize I'm wincing.

"No," I say, as I suck air through my gritted teeth. The pain is a good sign, proof the reattachment is working, the nerves regenerating and the ligaments healing, though it hurts like a son of a gun. "Just give it a second."

Brendon shifts uncomfortably, his hands fisted on his thighs. It's hard to watch someone in pain, especially if you feel responsible for it.

When the worst is over, I say, "I need you to do a couple things for me."

He looks terrified, afraid of what I might ask. Which is good. He should be scared.

"First, I need you to ask your mom to take you to Franklin so you can drive my boat from where we left it to my new house."

"You have a new house?" His surprise is followed by a gulp that gets stuck in his throat, guilt radiating as he realizes how much worse his crime is for how unnecessary it was.

"I do. It used to belong to my second mother. The property is the first one south of the timberland. There's a dock barely big enough for a single boat that juts out from a bank of saw grass. Do you think you can manage it?"

He nods slowly, and I watch his spine straighten with the responsibility.

"Second, on your way to the docks, you need to stop by the sheriff's office."

His eyes widen.

"They need a statement from you about last night."

He opens his mouth, but before he can say anything, I go on. "You need to tell them about the dog getting caught in the trap. They have the guy who did it. Believe he's also the one who started the fire."

Unwittingly he shakes his head, his mouth still open.

My eyes hold his. "Hopefully, he learns his lesson."

His head reverses direction, nodding almost eagerly, and I work to hold back my smile.

As Marie said, he's a good kid who made a terrible mistake, believing he was doing it for the right reasons. I made my decision not to tell Cory my suspicions before we reached the dock. Marie and her stupid threat had nothing to do with it. What I saw last night was a kid who stepped up and did what was needed to save his dog and who deserved a shot at a second chance. Danny Canton's had plenty of second chances and has blown every one.

"The key for the boat is there." I nod to the side table.

He stands and, as he takes it, mumbles a strangled "Thank you."

When the door clicks closed behind him, I blow out a hard breath and hit the morphine pump, completely done in from the exchange. Mercifully, the drugs do their job quickly, and I drift away to thoughts of Rose in my arms and my second mother laughing.

59
BRENDON

I'm on the river in Davina's boat. It's different, driving against the current. I need to throttle more and keep the rudder angled left to counter the tide that continually pushes me toward the bank. I remember my dad telling me when we were driving here that the Merrimack got its name from the Native American words "merruh auke," which means "strong place." I agree, the river possessing awesome, almost mystical power.

The day is incredibly bright and clear, like the storm from last night washed the world clean. I pass several small boats like the one I'm in, along with a pair of kayakers and a college rowing team. Each gives a nod or a wave, and I nod and wave back, happy to be a part of it. On the banks are fishermen, people lounging on patches of beach, kids playing in the water, and I gain a new appreciation for this place and the things I never noticed.

I'm careful not to look away too long. The storm washed branches and other debris into the water, and I don't want to mess up. Mom was nervous letting me do this alone, and it took a lot of convincing to assure her I could manage it.

Though she still hasn't said anything about the fire, I feel the change between us. The drive to the hospital was awkward, as if both of us were afraid to speak. Finally, she turned on the radio and cranked it up loud. And when I climbed back into the car after seeing Davina, she didn't even ask how it went. I told her what I needed to do, leaving out the part about needing to stop by the sheriff's office, and we drove to Franklin in silence, the loud music filling the void.

She dropped me at the dock, then stayed a moment as I pretended to walk to the boat. When she finally drove away, I waited another ten minutes to be sure she was gone, then walked into town. Luckily, when I got to the sheriff's office, only a single deputy was there. He asked a few questions about the trap—where it was, what time it was when Banjo got snared, and whether I'd seen anyone in the woods. I answered with a lot of nods and *Yes, sirs* and *No, sirs*, and that was it. He never brought up the fire.

A large branch drifts toward me, and I release the throttle and carefully steer around it.

Catastrophe avoided. So easy, yet also entirely reliant on chance. A goose flying overhead or a distraction on shore, and it's possible I would have missed it. I'm starting to learn we have less control over things than we believe.

It's quiet now, this part of the river remote, so I am alone on the water. I spot a beaver den built into the bank and marvel at the ingenuity. High in the trees, birds squawk and trill, and I'm curious what the sounds mean. I cruise along slowly, not in any rush, the colors startling in the blazing afternoon sun—vivid blue sky and verdant green grasses—*smaragdine*, as Bee would have said. She claimed it was her favorite color, I think more for the name than the color.

I spot the small dock Davina described—worn gray and barely visible in the long grass. I throttle down as I aim north of it, then cut the motor and let the current and momentum do the rest, just as Davina taught me. I miscalculated slightly and end up clunking instead of gliding in, but it wasn't a terrible landing, and I exhale in relief, glad I made it with the boat and me in one piece.

I tie the boat to a pylon and climb out. Beyond the steep bank, I can just make out a brick chimney and part of a wood-shingled roof. I hike toward it, and when the rest of the house comes into view, I smile. It looks like a cottage from a fairy tale—light yellow with white shutters and a red-flowered hedge. To the left is a garage with two trucks parked out front. One I recognize; the other I don't.

I scan for Rock, but the only person I see is a large man in a plaid shirt kneeling on the roof, swinging a hammer. He notices me at the same time I notice him, and our eyes lock, causing a bad feeling to run through me.

Lowering my head, I hurry for the road.

I'm still a hundred yards away when a deep voice behind me says, "Looks like we have ourselves a *trespasser.*"

I freeze. Then, knowing I can't outrun him, turn.

Well over six feet, the man glares down at me, his right hand fisting the hammer like a weapon.

"Brendon!" Rock jogs toward us. "What are you doing here?" He says it brightly, as if we are old friends, though we've barely said two words to each other.

"Davina asked me to bring her boat," I say, then stupidly hold up the key as if to prove it.

"You saw her?" Rock says, hurt in his voice.

"She needed her things from the shed, and I guess she figured I owed her." I risk a glance at the man with the hammer. "Which I do. I owe her my dog's life."

"And a pinkie," the man mutters, the hammer gripped so tight it trembles.

I clench my left hand, unsure if he means it literally.

Rock sets his hand on the man's shoulder. "Chill, Lloyd. The kid wasn't the one who set the trap, and their dog lost his leg." The words are an echo of what Dad said this morning, and I'm incredibly grateful for it.

Lloyd doesn't look like the chilling type but, mercifully, with nothing but an angry huff, pivots and walks back toward the house.

Rock blows out a breath.

"Thanks," I mutter.

"Come on. I'll give you a lift. Bad idea, you walking around here alone."

As I climb into his truck, I nod at Lloyd, who is back on the roof. "What are you and Lloyd doing?"

"Fixing the place up so it's ready for Davina. The people who lived here agreed to move out early on account of what happened so Davina will have someplace to recover when she gets out of the hospital. Good people."

I nod. I'm coming to discover there are a lot of good people in this town.

"Lloyd's fixing the roof and building a chicken yard, and I'm trying to make a garden."

"Trying?"

"Running into more rocks and stumps than I expected, so it's turning out to be more work than I thought. It'll get there, but it might start out a small garden."

"Can I help?"

He looks sidelong at me, letting me know the encounter with Lloyd wasn't a one-off and that it's better if I stay away.

We drive a bit longer in silence.

When we're almost to our driveway, I say, "My sisters found some furniture and things in the basement for her."

He nods, makes the turn, then, trying to sound nonchalant but doing a poor job of it, asks, "How are your sisters?"

I know he's asking about one particular sister, and I shrug noncommittally. Hannah's not doing well. All morning, she's been holed up in her room, and several times I heard her crying. I glance at Rock to see his jaw clenched, looking almost as miserable as she sounded.

"Maybe you should talk to her?" I say.

His frown sets deeper, and his head shakes. "You all are leaving, and I still need to live here."

I get it. After my encounter with Lloyd, it's pretty clear he's in a tough situation.

He pulls the truck to a stop in front of the house.

"Thanks," I say as I climb out.

He doesn't answer, his eyes on my sisters' window above.

60
PENELOPE

We're going home in two days. Dad's bandages were removed yesterday, so finally he can drive. We just need to finish painting the house.

His hands still look bad, the skin blistered red with bits of yellow peeling around the fingers. It hurts when he uses them, and several times, he's muttered "I don't know how Davina did it" as he winces in pain. I try not to wince with him, but it's hard, like not yawning when someone else yawns.

Hannah and I are in the kitchen. Hannah is making a cake for Davina's welcome-home party, which is tomorrow but which we're not invited to because everyone in Franklin still hates us. Which isn't fair. The stupid guy who burned down the cabin is in jail, and it wasn't us who set the trap that made her lose her finger. We never wanted any of this to happen, and we love Davina at least as much as they do.

While Hannah bakes, I sit at the table, going through the albums from the basement. I'm looking for three perfect photos to put in three carved black frames we found. It's going to be my gift for her new house.

I already chose the first one, a photo of our great-grandfather and Davina in front of the cabin when Davina was around Hannah's age.

His arm is slung over her shoulder, and he is laughing as she smiles mischievously up at him.

I know I want one of her and her second mom and, of course, one of her with Rose. But there are a lot to choose from, and I want to pick the perfect ones that I know will make her smile.

Banjo sits alert beside me, his ears perked and his head cocked. I've been sharing my Cheerios with him as I work. He's doing great with only three paws. It took him less than a day to figure it out, and now he's hopping around as if it's the most natural thing in the world. He doesn't even seem upset about it, his tail wagging happily as if nothing's happened at all.

Brendon is far more concerned. He's done all sorts of research on fake legs and even talked to Dad about getting him a surgically attached paw to turn him into "Bionic Banjo." Dad likes the idea but said we can only do it if we're able to sell this place. It seems a lot of things depend on that. It's weird. Before we came here, my parents never talked about money, but lately, it seems to be constantly on their minds.

I toss a Cheerio in the air, and Banjo goes up on his hind legs, snatches it, then lands easily on his single front paw. "Good boy," I say, proud of him.

"Taste," Hannah says, holding out a beater coated in white frosting. "Too sweet?"

It's a little sweet, but Davina has the biggest sweet tooth of anyone I know. "Nope. Perfect."

Hannah returns to the mixer, and I open a new album, this one filled with photos of my great-grandfather when he was serving in a war. He looks important—lots of uniformed men and women around him, with him always in the center. In one, he looks like he's pacing in front of a great number of soldiers with guns strapped to their belts and slung over their shoulders. Their eyes are glued to him, and his mouth is open as if caught midsentence. I wonder what he was saying, thinking how hard it must be to come up with words to lead people into a fight.

I hear Dad outside ask Brendon something. Dad and Brendon have been working like crazy to get the painting done. They start as soon as it's light and only stop when it's too dark to see. It's weird how close they've become, like a common mission was all they needed.

I pull a photo from the album and set it in the "maybe" pile. It's a picture of Davina at her high school graduation. I like it because her second mother is in it and they are both dressed up, but they look a little stiff, and I think I can probably find another that's better.

At the exact moment I think it, a warm breeze blows in from the window, causing the pages to blow, and I look down to see the album open to a photo of Davina around my age. She is sitting on a rock, a fishing pole in her hand and her eyes looking off into the distance. As I look at it, I think of Bee. She and Davina look nothing alike, but something in the picture captures me—the tilt of her head, or maybe it's the way her bare feet are crossed. The first day we came here, Bee led me to Davina, tangling us together and changing our lives forever.

61
DAVINA

At least two dozen people stand outside my second mother's house as Cory drives us in his sheriff's car down the long drive.

"Well, would you look at this," I say, the words catching in my throat. It's quite something when you realize how much you're loved.

Cory's two little girls hold a hand-painted banner that says **WELCOME HOME DAVINA!** with the *N* backward.

Bob and Emily moved out early just so I'd have a place to go when I was released from the hospital. Good people. It's why my mother sold the house to them instead of others who offered more. Some call it karma. Some say you're paying it forward. My second mother would say, "It's the good deeds that make you who you are and paint the future in ways you never imagined."

"Ready?" Cory asks with a grin.

"Let the festivities begin!" I say and hop from the car.

My pinkie pulses with all the jostling, but mostly what I feel as I walk toward the crowd is comforting warmth on my spine, my second mother here and encouraging me on.

I hug everyone, moving person to person, almost like it's a receiving line at a wedding.

When I reach Bob and Emily, I blubber a tear-filled "Thank you," my feelings overwhelming me and turning me into a sniveling fool.

Bob shrugs, and Emily waves her hand like it was no big deal. But I see Emily's blush and how straight Bob stands and know they feel good about what they've done.

"Any idea who bought it?" I ask, pulling myself together.

"Not a clue," Bob says. "It was all very mysterious and hush hush."

Emily adds, "Whoever it was made a big deal about no one finding out who he or she was. They paid cash, and the deed's in your name. I figure it's someone famous, like Donald Bren or Ralph Lauren."

Both Mr. Bren and Mr. Lauren served, Mr. Bren in the marines and Mr. Lauren in the army. But whether it was them or someone else, whoever it was, I hope they're blushing as bright and standing as straight as Emily and Bob.

Lloyd and Arleta are next.

"Who's this?" I say, admiring the bundle of pink cradled in Lloyd's arm, his hand nearly palming the baby's entire body.

"Sadie," Arleta says proudly.

"Ah, Sadie, which means princess, a title worthy of royalty." I wink at Lloyd, and he smiles so wide I think his cheeks must hurt.

The name is perfect. Already, it's clear she has her father wrapped around her little finger. Big lug. Never met a man so tough on the outside and soft in the inside. Cory said he and Rock have been working on the house all week. I hope he and Arleta have a brood more children so eventually I can repay them.

I move on to Rock, Linda, and Al, and seeing Rock, I nearly lose it again, knowing he's the one who organized all this.

"Ready to eat?" he says before I can manage a thank-you.

Linda smiles, and Al laughs. Since he was born, the kid's liked food.

"You betcha," I say.

We walk to a tent set up on the lawn with a buffet beneath it, so much down-home deliciousness on the tables I know I'll be remembering it in my dreams for years. Since this whole brouhaha started, I haven't had much of an appetite and have lost so much weight my clothes hang loose. But looking at the spread before me, I'm certain I'll gain at least half of it back in this single meal.

I hold my plate balanced in my right hand and point with my cast at the things I want.

"Good to know you haven't lost your appetite," Rock says with a chuckle, my plate heaped so full food is being piled on top of other food.

"Load her up," I say pointing to a tray of macaroni and cheese, my mouth watering. "And a piece of that." I point to the welcome-home cake beside it.

"Hannah made that," he says, his voice dropping.

"That girl is *sweet*." I titter at the pun. "How is she?"

The serving knife stops midslice before he shrugs.

"You don't know?" I ask.

He returns to cutting the cake and doesn't answer.

"What'd you do?" I say.

"Who says I did anything?"

"Rock?"

"Fine," he huffs. "I got mad."

"Got mad? At who?"

He dumps the cake on top of the mac and cheese, my plate now a dangerous teetering mountain and my arm struggling to balance it.

"At them," he says.

"Because I was a dang fool and stuck my hand in a steel-jaw trap?"

He grumbles, grabs my plate, and marches toward the tables on the lawn.

"You're an idiot," I say to his back as I follow.

His shoulders hitch up around his neck; then he slams the plate down on the table, causing the cake to topple. Marching to the other side, he plops down on the bench and drops his face in his hands.

I shovel a forkful of the cake in my mouth, sickly sweet and wonderful. Dessert before dinner: it was something the colonel and I did all the time. I take another big bite.

"So fix it," I say as I chew.

"Why?" he mumbles into his palms. "She's leaving."

I continue to shovel alternate bites of cake and macaroni and cheese into my mouth and let him stew. I've found saying nothing is often far more effective than haranguing.

The cake and macaroni and cheese gone, I dig into the rest—barbecue ribs, beans, collard greens with bacon, cornbread.

"She probably wants nothing to do with me," he says, dropping his hands and looking up with so much regret I almost show sympathy.

Keeping it in check, I say, "If it were me, I certainly wouldn't."

"Yeah, well, she's nicer than you," Rock says.

"She certainly is." I suck the last bit of meat off the final rib and stand. "I'd say that girl's too good for both of us."

"Where are you going?"

"To the house. All this food has made me tired. And I'm old. And my pinkie hurts."

I'm halfway to the door when I hear his truck driving toward the road, and I smile knowing he's on his way to make either a fool of himself or a knight. Hopefully it's the latter, but knowing Rock, it could easily be the first.

I walk into the house, and a strange vertigo comes over me.

Leaning against the wood, I wait for the dizziness to pass, the feeling like I've stepped back and forward in time at the exact same moment. I stare at the grain of wood at my feet, the same pine floors of my childhood, and inhale the smell of fresh paint and Windex.

Through the door, I hear people gathering their things and saying their goodbyes. Then one by one, the cars drive away.

When there is silence, I take a deep breath and lift my face.

Oh.

I blink, then blink again. It's like a magic trick happened while I was standing here, and the house entirely transformed from what I was expecting. Gone are the dark wood paneling and lemon wallpaper I grew up with, the walls now the color of summer wheat, and the baseboards and trim white. The kitchen has new cabinets, and there's a round pine table with four chairs and a crystal vase in the center bursting with daisies. In the living room is a gold velvet couch that looks like it belongs in a palace, an overstuffed leather chair, and a magnificently carved coffee table.

I marvel at how pretty everything is and am once again overwhelmed by the blessings in my life. My gaze stops on the wall beside the hall. Neatly hung in a column are three framed photos. I step closer, and my eyes fill as I look at the captured moments. The first is of the colonel and me in front of the cabin when I was a teen. We're dressed warmly, and the trees are orange, so I know it's late fall. I don't remember the photo being taken or why we were there, though judging by the grins on our faces, we were having a grand time.

The one below is of my second mother. She is bending over an elderberry bush bright with fruit as she clips a cluster with her shears. I almost forgot how beautiful she was, soft and silver and made for love and laughter. I touch my fingers to my lips, then to the photo.

The third is of me and Rose. We are in the boat on the river, either just coming in or just going out. Rose is around five, her wild curls long and her body lean, the last remnant of baby in her round face. We are sitting side by side, my hand on the tiller, our eyes so alike it could almost be me and my first mother a generation before.

I stare so long the photo blurs, and only when I hear the rusty creak of the mailbox opening and closing do I break my eyes away to look out the front window, turning just in time to see Marie's car driving away.

Curious, I go to see what she's left.

The envelope is small and cream colored and has my name scrawled in blue ink on the front. I carry it inside, sit on the gold couch, and set it on the coffee table. For a long time, I look at it—premonition, good or bad, stopping me from tearing it open.

The shadows grow long as the sun begins to set, and finally, with a deep breath, I pry open the flap.

Inside is a three-by-five index card, and in very precise handwriting, it reads:

Dear Davina:

Please accept this as a parting gift to do with as you wish. It does not make up for the pain we've caused you, but sometimes all we can offer is what we have. Your daughter's name is Dr. Nasrin Rendon. She lives with her family in Hoboken, New Jersey.

Dr. Nasrin Rendon
NRendon@humc.org
www.humc.org/nasrin-rendon

Best,
Marie

P.S. If you were my mother, I would want you to find me.

My pulse pounds out of rhythm, the feeling akin to the moment before I stuck my hand in the trap, knowing to reach out is to risk losing another part of myself, a piece I might never get back and from which I will not recover.

62
HANNAH

I wake to the sound of something hitting the window. At first, I think it's a bird pecking to get in, and in my languid in-between state of asleep and awake, I think of Bee.

The rap sounds again, and I stumble from the bed, my head a dull throb. Pulling back the curtains, I look down to see Rock on the lawn, his round face illuminated by the moon and his arm paused midthrow, a pebble in his hand.

He smiles wide and waves for me to come down.

I let the curtain drop as a dozen thoughts ping in my head. *Why is he here? I look awful! I should have pretended I didn't hear him. I can't believe he's here.*

Another pebble hits the glass.

If he breaks the window after all the work we've put into getting this place ready to sell, my mom is going to kill me!

I pull the curtain aside and nod so he'll stop throwing pebbles, and he smiles again. I glare, letting him know he's not forgiven, and the grin drops from his face.

I yank on some clothes and brush my hair. And my teeth. Then, embarrassed that I'm already considering the idea of reconciliation and possibly a kiss, I throw the lip gloss I was about to apply back in the drawer.

With a glance at Pen sprawled on the bed, I tiptoe from the room and down the stairs.

"Where are you off to so late?"

My head snaps sideways to see my mom on the couch, her laptop open in front of her.

I consider making up a lie but instead surprise myself by blurting, "Rock's outside."

A smile tickles her lips.

"He threw pebbles at my window to wake me," I say with a blush.

Her smile grows. "Very Shakespearean."

My thought exactly. In the original play, there is no balcony, only a window in which Juliet appears when Romeo comes to the orchard under the cover of night. I don't know if that's what Rock was thinking when he came up with his plan, but I like the idea so much I choose not to disillusion myself by asking.

"You should go down to the river," my mom says. "It's especially beautiful under the stars."

My heart swells, grateful she trusts me enough to walk with a boy to the river alone at night. I blow her an air-kiss and continue out the door.

Rock waits beside the steps, a bouquet of daisies in his hand and a tail-between-the-legs puppy dog look on his face. "Sorry," he says. "Really, really, really sorry." He toes the dirt. "I almost came earlier, straight from Davina's party, but I know how much you like the Juliet thing, so I thought this would be better." Even in the thin light, I see his blush. "Not that I'm any sort of Romeo, but still, I figured you'd like it."

I do like it. I like it so much my hurt has melted away. Taking the flowers, I bring them to my nose. They have a grassy smell, but I don't mind. It reminds me of Davina's garden and the woods.

"Davina says I'm an idiot," he goes on.

I nod. He was. But I also know the reason he was an idiot, and it's hard to be mad at someone for their devotion.

I set the daisies on the railing, then step down and take his hand. "What do you say we go to the river? I'd like to see it one more time before we leave."

"Leave?" His voice pitches high. "You're leaving? I thought you were staying until the end of summer?"

"Change of plans. My dad can drive now, so we're leaving tomorrow."

His face drops. "Davina was right. I am an idiot."

I nod again. Time wasted . . . even a minute . . . is a great loss, and because of his choice, we lost eight precious days of happiness.

"We still have tonight," I say, then lift up on my toes and brush a kiss across his lips.

He releases my hand, and his arms slide around my waist to pull me into a much deeper kiss, our mouths melting together. He tastes like sugar and peppermint, and I know I will forever associate frosting and toothpaste with this moment, the most remarkable ending to the most remarkable summer of my life.

When we pull apart, he says, "So this is it?"

"No," I say. "This is only now," and I kiss him again.

63
MARIE

Yesterday was the twins' ninth birthday. Since we arrived home a week ago, the day has loomed foreboding in all our minds, a test of sorts.

Leo overcompensated, of course. The day started with a breakfast of all Pen's favorites—lemon-ricotta pancakes, overcooked bacon, and strawberry-banana smoothies. Then we went to his parents, where they spoiled her rotten with too many gifts. And after, we went to a park for a bike ride followed by dinner at Pen's favorite pizza restaurant.

Our gift to her was a garden. Leo and Brendon worked all week to build it. They removed the grass in a small area of lawn beside the pool, installed rail ties and an irrigation system, then topped it with mulch. My gift was a dozen different seed packets and saplings. Hannah gave her a wind spinner made of rainbow butterflies. Pen said the garden was her favorite gift ever, and her smile almost made the day worth it. Ceremoniously, we all planted the bee balm cutting at the southwest corner, where it would get the most sun, and we all wished a happy birthday to Bee.

I went to sleep exhausted but also relieved. Somehow we made it through. Two months ago, I don't know if I'd have been able to get out of bed. Slowly, impossible as it once seemed, we are healing. My journey is slower than the others', but the sticky gauze that has enveloped me since Bee's death is not thick as it once was and, at moments, even loosens enough for thin rays of brightness to break through.

The house is haunted, Bee everywhere, but I'm growing used to it. The memories are not as jarring, and at times, I even find myself seeking them out, leaning into the pain if only to feel her and relishing the ache.

It helps that Pen is growing like a weed. She's a head taller than she was when summer began, and though echoes remain, when I look at her now, I only see the whole rather than the half that's missing. She still talks to her sister—often sitting in her room with Bee's old pirate chest open, telling stories and having conversations as if it is alive. Leo says it's okay. We all deal with grief on our own terms, and Bee was Pen's twin, and therefore will always be a part of her.

Three, not four. Three-quarters. Seventy-five percent. I close my eyes and do the math for the millionth time, the rhythm like a mantra, upsetting and comforting at once. While a piece is gone, so much remains.

When my heart settles, I open my eyes and return to staring at the job listings on my computer. I am determined to find work. The problem is there is not much out there for an ex-CFO whose name search results in over two thousand unflattering posts about how she evicted a wounded veteran from her home, had her arrested, and was suspected of burning down the home while the veteran was in jail.

I lean back and take a sip of my now cold coffee, then turn to watch Hannah through the sliding glass doors as she does laps in the pool. Each morning, soon as she wakes, she swims. She says it's the reason her headaches have gone away, though I know she is also still taking Davina's remedy. I haven't brought it up, and neither has she. At some point, I'll tell her it's okay. The betrayal still hurts, but I'm just happy the headaches are gone.

"How's it going?" Leo asks, walking in dressed in his running clothes.

His eyebrows have grown back, and his hands are mostly healed, so he almost looks like himself again except the pepper of gray in his sideburns, which I don't think will ever go away.

"Okay," I lie.

"You'll find something." He drops a kiss on my head before continuing out the door.

Several times, he's brought up the idea of us starting our own firm. We talked about it in college, offering financial planning to companies not large enough for a full-time CFO. I like the idea, but to do it we would need start-up money, which means the property needs to sell.

It went on the market the day we left, and there have been a few showings, but it's not turning out to be the easy sell the real estate agent led us to believe it would be. The house is too large for most families and the property too expensive for the timber companies. Yesterday, a couple looked at it as a possible bed-and-breakfast but decided it was too far from Concord.

I think the kids are hoping it doesn't sell. All three have talked about going back. Brendon wants to get a boat and take up fishing. Pen wants to visit Davina and learn about plants. And Hannah, of course, wants to see Rock.

Part of me feels the same, a pull I can't explain. Tragic and awful as our weeks there were, it also reminded me of the summers of my youth. And secretly, I've wondered if it would be possible to recreate them, if my sister and cousins might step away from their busy lives a few weeks each summer to reconnect and enjoy each other's company.

Funny how Davina is always part of the thoughts, there among us, the cabin where it was and her boat on the bank.

I think of her often, wondering if she did anything with the note I left. It was surprisingly easy to find her daughter once I found her ex-husband. As I guessed, he continued his career as a drone engineer. He is the lead technology officer for a manufacturer in Tehran. His name is now Ashraf, not Mozaffar, but his last name is the same, and the photo on the website was unmistakable.

Once I knew his name, the rest was easy. Rose, now Nasrin, grew up in Tehran but went to college in the US. She got her undergraduate degree at UCLA, then went on to medical school at Princeton. She married a fellow student with the last name Rendon, and they are both finishing their residencies in her husband's hometown of Hoboken at the University Medical Center.

Her Facebook profile picture is of a pretty, intense-looking woman with curly black hair and spice-gold eyes unmistakably her mother's. In the photo with her are two little girls. Based on her posts, her life looks full and happy. She's big on decorating for the holidays, and she and her husband seem to enjoy hiking and camping.

I wonder if Davina has cyberstalked her as well and what she makes of it, if seeing her daughter so content makes her more or less likely to reach out. I imagine her torn between the two, her longing to be a part of it warring against her selfless desire not to disrupt her daughter's life.

Hannah climbs breathless from the water, and as I watch her, I know, for me, it wouldn't be a choice. Having my daughter so close but not in my life would be impossible.

The day is breathtakingly beautiful, the rosebushes that line the yard in full bloom and the sky blindingly blue. I think how I might want to paint it. Eisenhower painted. So did Winston Churchill. Both suffered the loss of a child. I wonder if there's something to that. I think of the words I saw in the Churchill War Rooms in London posted beside a slideshow of his paintings:

HAPPY ARE THE PAINTERS,
FOR THEY SHALL NOT BE LONELY.
LIGHT AND COLOUR, PEACE AND HOPE,
WILL KEEP THEM COMPANY TO THE END,
OR ALMOST TO THE END, OF THE DAY.

They hold such promise.

I wonder if one of the kids might want to paint with me. I could see Hannah as an artist. She's such a romantic and has such patience. Though it's Pen who has become obsessed with drawing, carrying a notebook everywhere she goes so she can sketch leaves and plants and make notes to research later. Leo and I are convinced someday she will be a great botanist who discovers a cure for some rare disease, a modern-day Marie Curie or Alexander Fleming.

Hannah walks in, a towel around her waist. She grabs a banana and, as she walks past, chirps "Morning, Mother," and continues on her way.

The comment is nothing special, just a bright morning greeting said in passing, yet feels remarkable for how normal it is. A stunning little moment, a pearl in a broken necklace, beautiful in itself.

64
DAVINA

I'm nervous as a newborn colt. I shake out my arms and legs and tell myself to relax. Not that it does any good. What do you say to a daughter you haven't seen in twenty-three years? Or to two granddaughters you've never met at all?

I am in my garden, tending to the transplants Rock and I moved from the timberland. Most have taken root, and by next year, I should have a decent crop.

My pinkie pulses, and I open and close my hand several times to work out the cramp. The finger is healing well and looks surprisingly normal. The only sign of the trauma is a thin, jagged white line you need to look close at to notice. The surgeon did a remarkable job. I'm lucky he was so skilled, God smiling down and offering an artist, not a butcher, the night I was hurt. The pinkie doesn't curl completely but works well enough, and I'm still able to do everything that needs doing, which is a great relief.

It was important that the finger was healed before I reached out to Rose. My old wounds are difficult enough to take in when people first meet me. I didn't want my family's first impression to be one of shock and pity.

Family.

The word causes another nervous buzz through my body. While I have dear friends who I love, it's not the same. Rose is mine. From the moment I felt the first tickle in my womb to the moment I take my last breath, she is rooted in my soul.

It took me nearly a week after the cast came off to craft the email I finally worked up the nerve to send:

> Hello Nasrin (Rose),
>
> I do not know how to say this except to be direct. I am your birth mother, Davina Taheri (now Davina Lister). Thanks to a guardian angel, I have found you. You owe me nothing, but if you would like to meet, I would love nothing more. If you don't, I understand.
>
> You have lived in my heart every moment we were apart, and regardless of your choice, I am at peace knowing you turned out so beautiful and well.
>
> Forever yours,
> Mom

The response came nearly three hours after I hit send, one hundred and seventy-two of the most excruciating, longest moments of my life, the screen on my computer refreshed so many times I'm surprised it didn't seize up in protest.

Her reply read:

Dear Mom (it is such a strange word to write),

The tears will not stop flowing as I type this, so please forgive me if there are typos. I was told you were dead. For the past twenty-three years, that is what I believed. I do not know what emotion is stronger, my euphoria or my rage. YES! I want to meet you. And I want my daughters to meet you. I have two, Rosie and Davia, four and five. As you can see by their names, I never forgot you. You too have lived forever in my heart.

Please let me know when we can meet. This is so unreal, like my deepest wish has been granted.

Always your daughter,
Rose

That was a week ago, and I've been making myself crazy since. She and her daughters are coming for the day. We will have lunch and go for a ride in the boat. Both were her ideas. She remembered how I liked to cook, and she never forgot the time she spent with the colonel on the Merrimack.

I emailed several photos to prepare her and the girls for my scars. Rose assured me they are comfortable with wounds. Her daughters have accompanied her and her husband on their rounds since they were babies. She said they are determined to raise them with as much compassion and understanding as possible.

I can't believe she is a trauma surgeon. My second mother and the colonel would be so proud. They both believed Rose was brilliant and would someday go on to do great things. It turns out they were right.

I take a clipping from a honeysuckle bush and return inside, my heart skipping and my brain pinging this way and that.

Our first few emails were stiff and formal, a shy dance as we revealed ourselves slowly, putting on our best faces, terrified of the other's opinion. But quickly, her sharp wit revealed itself, and we fell into a rapport so familiar it was as if time reversed and then sped forward, all the time we'd lost erased. She was still so remarkably her, and I was still me, and the banter between us was exactly how I imagined it would have been had we not been separated at all.

She remembers a great deal of her childhood, both from her time in America and in Iran. I was relieved to hear she's had a good life. Her father doted on her, and two years after they moved, he remarried. I tried not to be hurt when she told me her stepmother was a good woman, kind and caring, and that she treated Rose as her own. But the sting lasted a full night and into the next day.

At the moment, Rose is not speaking to her father, so angry with what he did. I responded that anger is a wasted emotion, more detrimental to the bearer than the target. We had found each other, and that was all that mattered.

That only enraged her more. It turns out she never outgrew her fiery temper. So I stopped advising her on her dad and focused instead on the present and our reunion.

She asked how I found her, and I told her about the extraordinary summer—about the cabin and the Egides and about Banjo getting caught in a snare—all of it leading to the remarkable note Marie left in my mailbox.

Like it was meant to be, I wrote, our fortunes and destinies entwined.

She wrote back:

> Grandma always did believe in fate. Perhaps she
> had a hand in it.

I smiled when I read that, both that she remembered my second mother so well and at the notion, imagining my second mother, and perhaps the colonel, sitting on a cloud laughing as they chucked lightning bolts our way, blowing up our worlds as they watched with great anticipation to see what sort of electricity we formed.

Now, the day of the visit is here, and I'm so excited I can't sit still. I set the jar with the honeysuckle on the counter and wash my hands. One of the queens nuzzles my leg, and I bend down to scratch her ear.

The three girls have adapted well to their new home, though all of us miss Teddy. Every few days, I visit him and wander the woods. Though the cabin is gone, I still think of it as home. Teddy has made the shed his castle and seems quite content ruling over his domain.

My phone buzzes, and I pull it from my pocket to see a meme from Brendon of two white-bearded old men sitting on the bank of the river with fishing poles, the river parted where the second man's lure is dropped. The voice bubble over his head says, "Not funny, Moses!!"

I smile, then laugh. Almost every day, Brendon sends me something—a text, a meme, a word challenge, a puzzle. His way of checking in and staying in touch. I was right about him. He's a good kid, and he's going to grow into a good man.

I text him back:

How does Moses make his tea?

Almost instantly he replies:

HeBrews it.

My thumbs fly to seal the joke, knowing he would get the first part but not the second:

That Israeli how he does it.

He sends back a laughing face, and I tuck the phone back in my pocket and check my reflection in the mirror. I got my hair cut for the occasion, trimming it to shoulder length, something I haven't done in a decade, and I bought new clothes—a fresh pair of khakis and a red-and-white plaid shirt. Not that it helps. I'm still me, and my scars can't be disguised. But I want Rose and my granddaughters to know I'm doing well and don't need anything. I can take care of myself and will not be a burden.

I hear a car turn onto the drive and look out the window to see a white Volvo station wagon making its way closer. I leap out the door and shudder as an afternoon gust chills me, but I don't return inside for my sweater, too excited to delay our reunion even a second.

The car stops, and the driver's door opens.

I step from the stoop as Rose steps from the car, and time stops.

Faces change, but eyes remain the window to the soul. Her eyes, my first mother's eyes, the eyes I see when I look in the mirror, look back. Twenty-three years gone, yet it feels like less than a breath. She is here. In front of me. My Rose.

I lift my hand in a wave, and she smiles as her eyes run over my scars with a surgeon's appraising gaze. I open my mouth to say something when the back door of the car flies open and a girl pops out, string-bean skinny with two dark braids past her shoulders. She looks at me, tilts her head, and is about to say something when another small person leaps out behind her, this one younger, with a shock of black curls around a perfectly round face.

"My mom says you have a beehive," the little one says, not seeming to notice my scars at all, which catches me off guard. While Rose said her children have been around trauma patients, even the most hard-boiled soldiers find my face unsettling the first time they meet me. The older one is doing a heroic job holding back her reaction, but I see the slight wince as she tries not to stare.

"Rosie, you need to introduce yourself," Rose says.

"Hi, I'm Rosie," Rosie says impatiently. "Do you have a beehive?"

I hold in my giggle. "Do you like honey?"

She shakes her head categorically no, as if the question is preposterous and entirely off topic. "Can I see it? I want to see the bees."

I glance at Rose, who is smiling wide as she offers a shrug that says, *You wanted to meet us. Well, this is us.* And I realize Rosie walks to the beat of her own unique drum, one that pulses to a wonderful, curious rhythm all its own.

"Come with me," I say, holding out my hand.

She takes it, and I feel like my heart might explode. And I wonder if too much happiness can do that, literally blow up your heart. It feels possible, and if it is, I can't think of a better way to go. But as Rosie and I walk, our arms swinging between us, I know this is no ending, and I look up at the heavens and smile, unsure if I'm imagining it or whether I actually hear a distant revelry on the breeze, the sound of angels laughing as they congratulate themselves on their devilry.

AUTHOR'S NOTE

Dear reader:

This story started out about money and what is valuable in this world. As happened to so many when the pandemic struck, COVID did a number on my family. It was a roller coaster of ups and downs that rocked our world and made us take a step back and reassess our lives. There was a period where we thought we might lose everything—our restaurants, our home, our livelihood. We made it through, and each day, I'm incredibly grateful knowing how many weren't as fortunate.

A few months after the lockdown restrictions were lifted, I was at a city council meeting to advocate for an architecture project I was working on. There were a dozen items on the agenda, and mine was number eleven. So, for two hours, I listened to the small and big concerns of our city. I was impressed by the council members who were patient, thoughtful, and professional, and equally appalled by an older couple, a pair of lawyers, who bitterly objected to each and every motion. I knew about the pair. They had a reputation for doing this, using their legal skills to stick it to the city any way they could, a vitriolic long-held grudge for their own project's denial years before.

Watching them, after the world had been through so much, I found myself angry and wondered how they'd come to be the way they were. They were obviously wealthy. Their home was a sweeping mansion overlooking the ocean in one of the most beautiful places in the world. Yet they spent their time and energy being nasty and resentful and trying to make everyone around them as miserable as they were.

The next day, the couple who do our gardening arrived. Normally, I'm not around while they work, but that morning was particularly beautiful, so I was writing outside. As I sat jotting down ideas for my next story, I listened to them talking and laughing as they went about their business. I knew they'd been through some incredibly tough times because of the pandemic. They'd lost clients, and two of their children had moved back home because they'd been laid off from their jobs. Yet there they were, marching on without complaint and still finding reasons to be happy.

And that's how the idea for this story was born, the simple, age-old question *Does money make happiness?* It's not a novel concept. Prince-and-pauper tales have been told since . . . well, since *The Prince and the Pauper* by Mark Twain in 1881. But I wanted to explore it in a modern-day context and take a deeper dive into where true happiness and contentment are derived.

Of course, the story ended up different than I imagined, and the theme became secondary to the plot. But it's where the inspiration came from and provided an underlying current throughout.

Soon after I decided on this premise, I read a news article that gave the story its backbone: River Dave was an eighty-one-year-old veteran who had been peacefully living for twenty-seven years in a cabin that wasn't his on timberland beside the Merrimack River in New Hampshire. The new owner of the property, upon discovering River Dave was there, sought to have him evicted. River Dave refused to leave and was arrested. While he was incarcerated, his cabin burned down.

Sound familiar?

The story was perfect—a lovable, quirky character contentedly living off the grid without material wealth at odds with a less happy, wealthy landowner.

And the novel was born.

I hope you enjoyed traveling the pages with Davina, Marie, Leo, Hannah, Pen, and Brendon as much as I did.

Best,

Suzanne

P.S. Any remedies written about in this story are from research I did about folk medicine. They are not meant as recommendations, and I have no expertise in healing or medicine.

ACKNOWLEDGMENTS

No one does anything alone. Thank you to my daughter, Halle, my first reader, who generously read this story when it was ugly and offered invaluable feedback and unyielding encouragement even when it was truly at its worst. Huge thanks to my agent, Gordon Warnock, second victim of my unpolished, half-developed plots and characters, whose honesty and discerning eye made the story immeasurably stronger. Thank you, always, to my editor, Alicia Clancy, who has a gift for finding the exact spot where a story needs to be worked out, and whose perfect notes made the story sing.

Thank you to Gabriella Dumpit, Alex Levenberg, Danielle Marshall, Hannah Hughes, Kyra Wojdyla, Elyse Lyon, Jenna Justice, and the entire Lake Union team for shepherding my books into the world with such care. Thank you to Mary Ruth Govindavari, who read the story with a keen eye toward my treatment of PTSD, grief, and body-image issues and shed light on how to sensitively deal with each with understanding and compassion.

Special thanks to Kathleen Lynch for the beautiful cover.

Thank you to my husband, Cary, and son, Joe, who inspire me every day to write stories about devotion and family, and to Lisa Anderson and Jacquie Broadfoot for their friendship and for brainstorming titles with me. Thank you to fellow architect Lance Polster, who said "That would be a great idea for a story" when I offhandedly mentioned the city council meeting, which segued into a conversation about money and how it doesn't necessarily make happiness.

Thank you to the *Boston Globe* and the *Guardian* for their reporting on the River Dave story, which inspired this novel. Thank you to the friendly Laguna Beach firemen I ran into at Gu Ramen when I was picking up dinner, who generously talked to me about how they fight fires in remote locations without access to hydrants or roads. Thank you to the men and women who bravely serve in our armed forces. I read so many of your stories as I was writing this novel, and your heroism and sacrifice astound. Thank you to the Juliet Club and the legions of secretaries that thoughtfully respond to letters of the heart and inspired Hannah's storyline.

And finally . . . thank you to Starbucks. Without your coffee, Wi-Fi, and entertaining customers, some of whom made it into the story, this book might not exist.

DISCUSSION QUESTIONS

1. Pen believes her sister's spirit manifests itself in butterflies and birds and is therefore still with them. Do you believe spirits linger for a time . . . or possibly forever? Is Pen's sense of Bee's presence real or, as Pen alludes, simply her "wish" for it to be true?

2. How do you feel about Brendon not clarifying the truth about Bee's death and allowing everyone to believe she went back into the pool without him knowing? Do you think Leo might have purposely altered the truth to spare Brendon the blame? If a lie results in less suffering, is it justified?

3. Do you think Marie's decision to move in order to have a fresh start was the right one, or do you agree with Hannah that "the dents and scratches" go with you and it takes more than a change of scenery to heal deep wounds?

4. Banjo plays a minor but significant role in the story. Several times, the characters reflect on how he reacts to hardship—the loss of Bee, the cone on his head, losing a paw. Do you think there's a lesson to be learned in how animals cope compared to humans?

5. Davina is badly scarred. Have you ever known anyone with a physical deformity? What was your reaction when you first met them? Were you eventually able to see past it?

6. How do you feel about collecting things for someone you lost as a way of keeping them around? Do you ever talk to loved ones who have passed?

7. Do you think Marie was right telling Davina to leave, taking her to court, and calling the sheriff when Davina returned? How do you think Marie should have handled things? How do you think Davina should have handled things?

8. How do you feel about Leo going behind Marie's back and giving Hannah the migraine tincture? Do you think Marie was right to feel betrayed?

9. How do you feel about the Egides being vilified in the press? Do you think the news and social media have too much power to destroy people's reputations and lives?

10. Davina's scars go deeper than her skin. She says it took years for her to recover enough to be a mother, and by then, Rose was mostly grown, and she didn't want to disrupt her life. Do you understand her decision, or do you think she made a mistake?

11. How do you feel about Brendon and what he did? Do you agree with Davina that doing one thing bad doesn't make you a bad person and that you can redeem yourself by doing things that are good? Do you think a five-to-one ratio seems about right?

12. The butterfly effect is the idea that something small, like getting a coffee, can have much larger effects, like altering your career. It's the notion that the world is deeply interconnected and that a small occurrence can influence a much larger complex system. This entire story came from a pinprick hole in an arm floatie, that infinitesimal event influencing countless lives. Can you think of a time when your life was impacted by the butterfly effect?

13. In the story, fire destroyed so much. Have you ever been in a fire or known someone who has? How do you feel about Danny Canton being blamed for the fire?

14. How do you imagine the future unfolding for the characters?

15. Who was your favorite character? Why?

16. Movie time: Who would you like to see play each part?

ABOUT THE AUTHOR

Photo © 2015 April Brian

Suzanne Redfearn is the award-winning author of six novels: *Hush Little Baby, No Ordinary Life, In an Instant, Hadley and Grace, Moment in Time,* and *Where Butterflies Wander.* In addition to being an author, she's also an architect specializing in residential and commercial design. She lives in Laguna Beach, California, where she and her husband own two restaurants: Lumberyard and Slice Pizza and Beer. You can find her at her website, www.SuzanneRedfearn.com, or on Facebook at www.facebook.com/SuzanneRedFearnAuthor.